T0077700

PEARL

A Caribbean Story

Melanie R. Springer

PEARL
A CARIBBEAN STORY

iUniverse books may be ordered through booksellers or by contacting:

iUniverse
1663 Liberty Drive
Bloomington, IN 47403
www.iuniverse.com
844-349-9409

Cover Painting: Melanie R. Springer

ISBN: 978-1-4401-2271-2 (sc)
ISBN: 978-1-4401-2272-9 (e)

Print information available on the last page.

iUniverse rev. date: 07/06/2021

DEDICATION

For some very special people who mean the world to me, and who have made a positive difference in my life. Without you this book would never have been published:

To Giulia for believing - and for never tiring of hearing the latest exploits of Omar and friends at bedtime. To Paola for supporting – the girls miss you much "mini-market"

To my aunty Wendy for inspiring – for opening a world of art, reading and writing.

To Paul Medford for motivating – Meds your confidence in me has kept this little engine going.

To my sister Nicola for all her loving and protecting –don't stop. And to my mother Jeanette for being all of those things; in addition to lending her decades worth of literary wisdom to the editing of this book, making it by far a better book.

•

Also to all of my friends for being true friends, you know who you are.

* PEARL *

Pearl was dead. The unnaturally pale soles of her feet protruded from the blue bed sheet. She must surely be dead. That seemed the only logical explanation for her lack of action.

Omar stood frozen to the spot, his very shadow seeming to cringe with the crash of the lamp as it hit his sister's lifeless hand and fell to the floor. All he could think of was the startling contrast the pale grains of sand made against her dark skin. He looked down at his own feet sprinkled with more sand, and dotted with little pinpricks of blood which oozed from his flesh where shards of yellow porcelain had penetrated.

And still Pearl didn't budge. She'd slept in her clothes again; the blue cotton shorts with the white frilly flowers and that gawd-awful seersucker shirt with the moth-eaten holes near her nipples. Mummy would be mad. That was the one thing he'd never understood about adults; why they'd make such a big to-do over a little thing like that - sleeping in your clothes.

What he really wanted to do right now was to take a piss. But in order for that to happen, he'd have to unglue himself from the floorboards first. Jeffrey and Chicken would be wondering what could be taking him so long in getting back with the money, but for that he'd need his feet too. So convinced was he of Pearl's immortality that he expected her to rise at any moment and land him one wallop with what remained of the lamp. Maybe she'd even make him eat the money he'd stolen. It was at times like these that Omar became truly overwhelmed by how unlucky he appeared to be.

How exactly he got himself from the room, Omar would never remember. He just suddenly became aware of walking through the dark seemingly endless passageway that led to the living room. The house was empty. Where had his mother gone?

Of course! Omar remembered. Mummy had gone over to her friend Annie, where the two of them were making pudding and souse for the church picnic on Sunday. They would be preparing it from scratch, pig guts and all...*disgusting!* He'd still been in bed when his mother Loretta had come into his room that morning with a pile of fresh laundry. From there, she'd yelled at Pearl to pick up hers from the line when they were dry, that all the soup needed was to throw in the vegetables, and for the dumplings to be made, also not to forget to feed the pigs and then open the shop.

All this had to be done by ten o'clock that morning. Omar didn't envy girls one bit.

Through the open doorway Omar could see Jeffrey and Chicken, his two best friends, still sitting on the front steps where he had left them. The bright afternoon sun made their faces glisten. The two boys were a sight to behold arguing as they usually did over which marble belonged to whom. Jeffrey as usual was getting the better of Chicken. Those two were as different in personality as they were in appearance, and it was often said that had they been from a larger community, friends they would never have been.

Jeffrey, it was obvious was going to be a six-footer like his father. He was already bigger than the average twelve year old. Just before summer his mother had had to let down the hem of his school shorts and one could clearly see the white seams from over a year of good pressings. Chicken on the other hand was just about as skinny and as yellow as his name implied. This of course was his grandmother's fault entirely. "'Cause she was the one who just up and walked over the Mexican border one morning, into Belize and take grandfather away from the game of dominoes he was playing wid de boys."

Ausencia Delgado walked across the Mexican border wearing leather sandals that were skin thin by the time she set her first foot into Belize. Then, only a young woman of seventeen, Ausencia left her home and a world of forgettable memories with never a backward glance. She walked and walked across rocks and tumbling rivers, through villages and over savannahs, in the direction her nose pointed. The only indication she gave of her departure was a sudden intense look at the sky before she pointed her right index finger towards the sun and spat. Ausencia turned her body in the direction her spittle blew. Following a line straighter than any compass, she took only what was on her back – a satchel with ten dolls, given to her, one from each of her sisters.

More than once her journey cut a path directly though some startled villager's home. She would neither slow her pace nor veer her course, instead with a polite hello would continue on her way with a singular determination that lasted eleven hours and eighteen days. She arrived in Corozal ahead of the midday sun and stood boldly before her future husband with only a pocketful of English. Pointing at his chest before turning a delicate finger upon hers she said "Me husband – you wife." Not long after, she got married and bore three children, the youngest of them was Chicken's mother. How they ended up in Bim, and how Chicken became part of his group of friends, was another story altogether.

Omar, one could say had a bit of both boys in him. He ran from any trouble that could result in a beating, but he could do his share of hustling too. That was what had gotten him into this mess in the first place. Omar sat down on the steps next to Chicken and rested his head on the railing remembering what had brought him to this point.

On that fated Tuesday morning, Omar paused, perched on a supple tree branch surveying all that lay below. No rain had fallen for quite some time and so the grass was yellow. Above, the virtually cloudless sky was a dreamy blue.

As Omar climbed the tree, he watched out for his sister down below. If Pearl were ever to catch him, God only knew what would happen. He'd definitely lose face in front of the guys, simply because she would make him come down out of the tree before he could get a chance to fulfil the bet. This was to climb the massive mango tree, which stood in the very centre of Mr. Cumberbatch's yard; climb to the top and retrieve a minimum of three plump juicy fruit, beckoning under the midday sun.

Where was Pearl anyway? He had to keep a look out. He could see his dog Commando running wild circles around the neighbour's chickens. The dog barked excitedly, getting a real thrill out of scaring the birds half to death. Once again the foolish animals had found their way into his yard, but had yet to figure their way back out. Now they squawked and fluttered from one end of the yard to the next, butting their heads against the fence and leaving a trail of red and black feathers each time Commando got close enough to snap at them.

Omar chuckled, proud of his dog's hunting skills. He refocused his attention on the rusted blue pick-up parked outside. In the back was tied one of his mother's pigs ready to be taken to market. Pearl must still be in the back by the pens helping the driver Patterson bring out the other pig. He'd seized this opportunity to pick the mangoes, knowing that his sister would be too busy with the loading of the pigs to concern herself with his whereabouts. Just as the thought went through his mind, Pearl reappeared and Omar lost his balance, nearly falling from the tree. He slid down the branch grabbing at young leaves, trying to hang on for dear life - his feet dangling in mid air. Omar counted to three and then tried to swing himself back up without alerting Pearl. His partners in crime watched from behind the galvanised fence, horrified - they knew full well what would happen if either of them was caught. Mr. Cumberbatch was a man well known for getting violent when he found people in his yard...especially if those people were Omar, Chicken and Jeffrey.

Omar managed to scramble up just as Pearl looked over in his direction. He hugged the branch, hardly even breathing and tried to ignore the army of red ants climbing up his arm. He peeped through the leaves at his sister. She and Patterson were being dragged as they pulled the last pig, which was resisting noisily its one-way trip to market. The pig squealed and bucked. Patterson cursed loudly when he barely missed losing a few fingers to a cruel bite. The noise coming from his yard was ear-piercing, Omar thought. Between the squeals of pigs and the squawks of chickens the noise was enough to drive any sane person crazy. Pearl looked up at the sky for God, begging his assistance. Omar drew himself up smaller, sending up his own prayer that she would look for God elsewhere. For the moment his prayer was answered. Breathing a sigh of relief, Omar retuned to the job at hand, balancing carefully along the slender branches and filling his pockets with mangoes. He'd already collected the required three, now each additional mango would be worth a total of twenty-five cents. This was a great deal of money to any young man...enough to make him forget about the potential threat below.

"Oh Lord! Dem pigs heavy!" Pearl swore as she wiped her sweaty brow. "I can't understand why Mummy can't do like other people and raise only sheep or goat. Pigs smell stink, they nasty, mek nuff noise, give nuff trouble and can't even give you no milk!"

As if to confirm her statement, the pigs squealed and grunted moving around the truck agitatedly. Patterson laughed as he shut the back of the pickup and got behind the steering wheel. Omar could hear them clearly from his perch in the tree, their voices carried up by the wind. He kept quite still, realising that the end of the pig saga signified the beginning of Pearl's search for him...just in case he was doing something he shouldn't be doing. "When next you coming again?" enquired Pearl. "Mummy say to tell you dat she got two cows ready to slaughter. You could come next week?"

As he turned on the ignition Patterson responded. "I ain' sure yet. It depend on if I have other business out this side. I going let you know though"
"How?" asked Pearl
"Well call you nuh!"
Pearl laughed. "You forget that phones don't work out here?"
"Girl I been coming here so many years and I still can't get used to this place. Not one phone in this whole place don't work?"
"Not one. Well...not true. Don't mind it catching dust, Mummy still got hers plugged in. Sometimes at night, it does ring by itself you know, especially when the moon full." Pearl looked up at the distant moon made faint by daylight.
"You joking me right?"
"I look like I joking?"

A sly smile creased Pearl's face as she stared intently into Patterson's eyes. She liked to keep people wondering. Just like this place did. Dumbfounded, Patterson peered back at the young woman who had erupted into sudden inappropriate laughter.

Whit's End was a strange and unusual place. Some would say that it was an enchanted place. There were others however, who ventured to say what no one else dared to; that it was a wretched and cursed place. Whit's End had a history. A history of pain and betrayal; where good had not yet succeeded in her triumph over evil. In the world of the spirits, a battle had been fought. In truth, it was still being fought, and for nearly 300 years the opponents had been at an impasse.

At Whit's End, the canes grew of their own accord, and every year when they were at their sweetest and their fullest, those same canes combusted into flames. In that stretch of Barbados countryside, cane grew for miles, and as far as Omar's eyes could see, those canes reached out and embraced the village where he lived, like an avaricious lover. It was not unkind to those who lived within its fertile embrace. It was unkind only to those who tried to change the way things were and had always been. In this place where the spirits ruled, there was no room for modernity. The land would not allow it, as owner after each new owner would inevitably discover. In those fields nothing would grow, that had not always grown there. In that soil nothing could find a sure footing that had not been naturally made. Many had tried. The majority had failed. As much as the custodians of Whit's End desired it, they would not smoothly move into the 20th century, to a world of advanced telecommunications. Plainly put, phones did not work here. The interference caused by the battle that raged was as noisy as a swiftly-moving train. Advanced communications was the key to progress; neither good nor evil desired it that much.

Omar's mother Loretta did not believe in Whit's End superstition. In fact she had little time for it. There were too many responsibilities around the house, with the shop, her livestock and with her children growing up. Having moved to the area as an adult, her senses were dulled to the subtle changes of energy; how and why the wind direction suddenly shifted. Indeed she did not feel the cool breaths of her long dead ancestors. who with daily ritual caressed her neck, restoring equilibrium, when life seemed suddenly too great a burden to bear. Neither Pearl nor Omar was so immune however. Their moods shifted as the spirits fought. Peace in the house determined by current status of battle. As Omar looked out from his perch in the tree, he felt the winds shift against his favour.

"OMAR!" Pearl who had not long ago been laughing

suddenly started hollering. "OMAR! Get down from that tree now!" How had she spotted him? Omar watched as the pick- up drove off with the driver's last words going unheard, and knew that he was in for it. Pearl had already found herself a fat stick and was headed in his direction. "What you think you doing up there, how many times Mummy have to tell you not to trouble other people property? Wait till I catch you boy!"

That was exactly what Omar did not intend to do. He hurried down the tree sliding and bouncing, acquiring many bruises along the way, in a desperate attempt to reach the bottom before his sister did. By this time Jeffrey and Chicken were nowhere to be seen. Omar in an effort to catch sight of them snagged the pocket of his shorts on a protruding branch. Pearl not so encumbered was getting dangerously closer with each step, the stick menacing in her hands. He managed to hold on to the five mangoes he'd picked as he made that final leap to the ground. Unfortunately, Pearl as if possessing super human strength arrived just in time to catch him. All Omar saw was a blur of pink and red. She landed on him covering him with insults and blows. The stick broke with the first stroke. Pearl, without even missing a beat, continued with her bare hands. Truth be told, the blows didn't hurt, although she certainly tried. It was more the public humiliation that hurt. Public being Jeffrey and

Chicken who would tell everyone at school the first chance they got. This was not good.

"Man! How you could leh she tek dem 'way?"
"How you mean I leh she Jeffrey? Chicken you believe this man! How I leh she tek them 'way...as if I could stop she. I only ten years old! She nearly twice my age and twice my size. It bad enough she going tell my mudda. That mean I cyan watch Thunder Cats nor none uh my favourite cartoons for a whole week. Don't even mention the extra set of licks I going get."

The boys were crouched around the back steps of Jeffrey's house, where Omar had found them hiding. They looked sullenly at the sky, grieving over their loss. Although they'd never quite expected Omar to succeed, there had been for one brief moment such a real possibility. The possibility of having ripe, juicy mangoes sliding down their throats, dripping over their fingers, whetting their palates. This made the disappointment almost too much to bear. "Man you owe me twenty-five cents." declared Jeffrey.
"Me too" parroted Chicken pointing his finger in Omar's face.
"For what?" Omar, his eyes round, demanding an answer from Jeffrey.
"Well, we never get to eat de mangoes"

"But you see them!" Omar was incredulous."
"The bet was one mango each person or twenty five cents each no mango"
"Man you got to be joking! All my pants tear up and I got cuts all over me and you talking 'bout I owe wunnuh! I pick de mangoes and you see me pick dem, and since I pick five, each uh wunnuh owe me twenty five cents."
"Twenty-five cents!" Jeffrey shrieked. "Alright, deal Omar. Nobody don't owe nobody nothing 'cause we ain eat de mangoes but you pick them, so we even right Chicken?"
"Even? I still can't believe that he leh he sister do he so, I woulda never leh my sister do that to me."
"What you know Chicken? You ain got no sister, so you can't talk."
"Oh yes I can! Because even if she had do that to me, I woulda never let she get away wid it."
"I woulda do she something too, then she woulda never try dat again."
"Do she something like what Jeffrey?"
"Put frogs in she bed or something."
"My sister ain frighten for nothing so." A disgruntled Omar began dusting off dirt from the back of his shorts and legs.
"Well work obeah 'pun she then"
"Obeah!" Omar and Chicken cried out simultaneously.

"Man you crazy?" Omar was becoming quite disgusted with the entire conversation. "You really gone off now Jeffrey!"

"Yes Omar, my grandmother always telling me 'bout how she had a great aunt that used to tek something that belong to de body like piece ah hair or clothes, and it is work you know."

"And Jeffrey, when I get this piece of hair or piece of clothes, what I supposed to do with them?"

"I hear about that," exclaimed Chicken getting all excited. "Then you's say some magic words and..."

"NO, no, no, Chicken! Nothing like that, the most important ingredient is a chicken and some of it blood..."

"Boy! Now I know you really mad." Omar frustrated got up to walk away. "Where you expect me to get chicken blood from Jeffrey?"

"But you got chickens all 'bout you yard"

"Jeffrey! You can't see that I in enough trouble already. My mudda ain stupid you know. She know how much chickens she got."

"Dat is true. But she don't never kill none?"

"No. I cyan remember the last time I see she kill one. She's only really use them to sell eggs in the shop."

"So if we can't get chicken blood what else we could use?"

"Well, how 'bout meat blood, that wouldn't work?"

"What you mean by meat blood Jeffrey?"

"I mean if we use meat that your mother buy from the supermarket...when it defrost you is don't find blood?"

"Yeah, whenever I see meat defrosting it does bleed, and my mother have so much meat in the freezer that she wouldn't notice if I take one."

"Well then that is what we could do." Jeffrey stated. "And I going find out 'bout the rest of things that you have to mix wid the blood. I know you is got to get a doll and stick pins in it or something so, but I ain know what else, so I going have to ask somebody."

Omar paused for a minute. "But even if we have the blood from the meat, what we going do to replace the chicken?"

"Hey hey! We never think about that."

Chicken propped on one elbow studying this new development. The obeah thing seemed to be getting a bit too complicated for him, but since Jeffrey was so certain about it, he guessed he was game. Omar thought about it for a while biting his nails intensely. He was sure he would at least be able to grab one of the roosters by its tail feathers with only a modicum of difficulty. Surely using the feathers of a chicken would be as good as using the animal itself. If he couldn't get the pretty ones from the rooster's tail, there were still enough stray feathers flying about the place that he could pick up off the ground. Jeffrey agreed that this could work even though he had to admit he didn't like chickens that bad enough to risk being attacked by one, and maybe they could draw straws. To everyone's surprise Chicken volunteered himself for the task. Their surprise came not so much from the fact that Chicken guarded some secret fear of the fowl, but from the fact that he had volunteered at all. The boy was notorious for not wanting to commit himself to anything that could be used against him at a later date.

"Why you all looking at me so funny? I say I would do it. You all got a problem with that?"
"Well, no Chicken" said Omar still looking a little puzzled. "We just thought that you would have a problem doing it."
"Why would I have a problem doing something like that?" Chicken was becoming more confrontational by the second. "Look don't mek me change my mind hear! Wunnuh going get me vex jus' now wid this foolishness."
"Alright Chicken, it cool, it cool." Jeffrey figured it was time to jump in and save the moment. "We want you to do it, we ain got nuh problem wid that."
"So then we cool? Everybody cool..." sighed Omar. "Chicken ain got no problems, so we ain got no problems neither. Deal?"
"Deal." They responded in unison. With everything settled, it was back to their usual play, even if a little low key. The boys had decided that it would be a good idea to keep out of the sight of adults for a while. One of them getting into trouble was enough for the

day. Instead they lay under the sun, warming their bodies, each absorbed in his own thoughts.

Jeffrey was full of ideas for the obeah ceremony, the things they might need and how he could ask his family about it without raising their suspicions. After that his thoughts went to this girl at school whom he liked. Her name was Maria and she was quite pretty. She usually had her hair back in one with bangs falling over her forehead. Jeffrey smiled at the thought of her until he remembered where he was. If his friends saw him with the silly grin on his face... well neither of them were into girls yet...as a matter of fact, GIRL was still a bad word in Omar and Chicken's vocabulary. If Jeffrey so much as let on that he was changing his mind on the subject, he would never hear the end of it and he could only imagine the scornful looks Chicken, especially, would send his way. Jeffrey sighed with regret. One day they would understand. Until then it was probably a good idea to keep it to himself.

Chicken who loved food was already wondering what his grandmother Ausencia might have cooked for dinner. If he was lucky she'd be in a good mood, satisfied Chicken hadn't given too much trouble lately. Then, she would make him hallacas. He loved the hot spicy corn dish with meat on the inside. It had been a rare treat these days because Abuela - as she was often called – was getting on in years and hallacas were so time-consuming they made her very tired. Since Chicken had seen banana leaves on the kitchen counter as he left home that afternoon he figured it was going to be his lucky day...maybe he would go home and help her wrap them a little later.

A pensive Omar plucked a blade of grass and ran it between his teeth. He heard Jeffrey's sigh and studied his friend, wondering what it was that had made him smile and then frown so. Sometimes he didn't understand Jeffrey these days...ever since he'd started first form at secondary school his personality had changed. Sometimes he said really weird things... for example with the whole idea of the obeah. Omar didn't know if he really wanted to go through with it. He didn't even believe that sort of thing actually worked. He wasn't even sure about the whole Jesus Christ issue anymore and he still went to Sunday school every week. It was maybe two, three years now since he'd found out there wasn't a Santa Claus, but he still got presents at Christmas anyway, so he supposed it didn't really matter. Maybe there were some things you did just because, and maybe the obeah thing was like that, you did it just because, and it could be fun or maybe it would really work. He didn't know and he wasn't going to think about it right now. The sky was a nice blue and the clouds were white and fluffy, it was much more fun imagining the different shapes he could see moving inside them.

Omar, Chicken and Jeffrey all fell asleep under the afternoon sun, and there they remained until well after six in the evening. Chicken, all good intentions aside, never made it home in time to help Abuela, but sure enough he had hallacas for dinner. Since his two friends had accompanied him home, they each got a hallaca to take with them. Jeffrey had his for dessert after a hefty dinner of cou-cou and flying fish, while Omar ate his with a snack box of fried chicken and chips which his Uncle Junior brought back from town.

* PEARL *
2

The steps of the house were worn, smooth like a baby's bottom in some places and splintered in others. The entire house seemed to lean on its side, like an uncertain shrug or a tired sigh. Even the dark brown paint was so old that it seemed more like an epidermis than simply paint. The smooth parts were from twenty-eight years collectively of twelve year old Jeffrey and his sixteen year old sister Shelly trudging to and from school, and the numerous times in between when their friends came over to visit. Stella, the children's mother was something of a homebody weighing a total of two hundred and fifty pounds. She always chose the right hand rail to hold onto whenever she went outside. As a result it leaned very obviously to the right. The numerous rings on her fingers had caused splinters to kick up in the wood that were only aggravated by idle children picking at them and using them as tooth picks. The rail itself would shake at the slightest touch; it was only a matter of time before the entire structure collapsed.

Only once in Jeffrey's lifetime had the stairs ever been fixed...and that had only been the replacement of one plank on the third step. There was an ongoing joke that the reason the actual house leaned so much on one side was that Stella spent her entire day either in the kitchen, eating the majority of the stew that she cooked for her family, or in the front room in the two-seater, the only chair wide enough to fit her ample girth. All of these were on the right side of the house, including the bed she shared with husband Garry. Few knew that she actually slept on the left, but it probably wouldn't have mattered.

The true reason for the house's crooked appearance was an issue less worthy of gossip. It had happened in a time when a younger Garry was still new to his trade, (masonry), his own house being the first foundation he ever attempted to lay on his own. Although he'd correctly measured the depth, and the bricks were even, the mortar he mixed on the left side was thicker and stronger than the mix on the right. By the time Garry realised it the mortar had turned to cement, and he didn't have enough money to re-build it. His mother had said there was a lesson to be learnt in it for him somewhere. But obviously, he couldn't let too many people know, otherwise who would trust him to build their homes? So he compensated by not maintaining the house, and allowing the neighbours to continue to spread the tale of Stella's weight being to blame.

It was Thursday afternoon and Omar, Chicken, and Jeffrey sat on the front steps in their usual positions: Jeffery on top, Chicken on the left side of the second step and Omar on the right leaning against the bandy railing. They were discussing the upcoming calypso finals during the Crop Over Festival, and what they would do on Kadooment Day. "So who you say going win de Calypso finals then Chicken? Omar say De Mighty Thunder and I say Coco Boy"
"B...B...Brown Paper Bag?" Chicken stuttered.
"You asking me or you telling me Chicken? 'Cause once we bet 'pun it you cyan change yuh mind, hear." It was obvious that Chicken was unsure of his choice not so much because he lacked faith in Paper Bag but more, because he feared parting with five dollars that he didn't have. The stakes were getting higher every time. Jeffrey could afford to bet a whole five dollars because he'd just got presents of money from all the aunts and uncles for his twelfth birthday. Chicken on the other hand was going to have to clean out Mr. Beckles'-down-the-road's- pigsty and chicken coop to cover this one if he lost.

The truth was neither Omar nor Jeffrey were that sure of their bets either; they were just better at hiding their uncertainty. "So deal fellas?" Omar held his right hand out and hooked his index finger with Jeffrey's and then Chicken's to seal the bet.
"Deal" agreed Jeffrey, then suddenly whispered, "Shhhh...."

Two pairs of footsteps could be heard coming from inside the house. The three friends looked up at the sound of approaching male laughter and girlish giggles. "Tha' is my sister and she boyfriend Derek", whispered Jeffrey. "Come quick, follow me and don't say nothing." Jeffrey and the boys scrambled off the stairs and hid by the side of the veranda. Just then the door opened and a pair of long slender legs barely covered by a plaid mini skirt walked out first.

"Derek why you have to leave so soon?"
"Cause I got to go back to work babes. Come give me one more kiss to last de road"
From their vantage point the boys could practically see right up the couple's nostrils and were hard-put to hold back a snigger or two at the moaning sounds Shelly made. When Derek's hand found its way up her skirt, Chicken, who had been bravely trying to contain himself, finally burst out laughing.

"Chicken! Shut up!" Jeffrey clamped both hands over Chicken's mouth while Omar held him down. Unfortunately, it was too late. The entire commotion was enough to wake the dead. When the lovers broke apart the rest was inevitable.

"Who that is?" Shelly bounded over to the railing, nails biting into the soft wood. "Jeffrey Marshall you Badbehavemaliciousbrute!" she shouted "What you down there doing wid dem boys spying on me for?"

By this time the other two boys could also no longer contain their laughter and were falling all over each other in hysterics.
"It wasn't me Shelly, I tell these two idiots not to stand there."
"We was just pitching marbles and we loss one over here."
"You was pitching marbles and loss one over here! So where de rest uh marbles, Omar you eat them?" You could have heard a pin drop in the interminable seconds after Shelly screeched her question. "Wait till I ketch de three uh wunnuh!" Shelly stomped down the stairs intent on doing damage almost wringing her ankle on the last one. She broke the fall with her hands exposing her T-string covered backside in the process. This sent the boys into a renewed fit of giggles.

With what was left of her dignity Shelly hauled herself up using Derek as support, then pulled her brother by the ear and punched him between the shoulder blades. "Man Shells I sorry man, I sorry. I ain going do it no more man, Leh me go nuh!"
Derek shook his head, a smile in his words. "Shells check yuh later, I going back to work."
"Hold on there Derek I coming now." He jangled his keys distracting her from the scuffle with her brother. Omar and Chicken took advantage of the moment and dragged Jeffrey away. They ran out of the yard with her shaking her fist, still carrying on. "Jeffrey if

I ever catch you or any uh you foolish friends round me again boy, it going be me and you."

The three boys ended up panting and breathless at their usual spot - a grove of clammy cherry trees. Omar was still holding onto his stomach and laughing so hard that he almost choked. Chicken felt it necessary to give him a few good slaps on the back to cure him of the problem.
"So what we going do now?"
"Leh we play Cowboys and Indians, I going be de cowboy and de two of you is de Indians."
"No man Chicken! We was playing that since Infants B.
"So then what else to play?"

The boys paused, racking their brains, trying to come up with something exciting, but which would be at the same time mutually beneficial to all egos involved. This wasn't always so easy to do. Somebody always ended up with the boring role, usually Chicken. The one game he absolutely refused to play again was Hide and Seek. His first problem with this game was there being too many places to hide. This meant walking a lot and being tired a lot. The second problem was that he always ended up being the seeker. What made the situation worse is that Omar and Jeffrey were notorious for changing hiding places *mid-seek.*

It was during one of these exceedingly long games - Chicken had been looking for his two friends for several hours - that he suddenly realized what they were up to. It was the straw that finally broke the camel's back. Chicken became so angry, that he refused to speak to his friends for an entire week. Even then, relations continued to be strained until Jeffrey decided to bribe him with sweets. Omar even gave Chicken his coveted Tiger's Eye marble, which he'd been trying to win back ever since. His attempts to retrieve said marble became so obsessive that Chicken finally felt it necessary to inform him that "he wasn't as stupid as they thought, and he could see what Omar was up to. That he wouldn't be playing with the marble anymore." From that day the marble remained by his bedside (in an old ring box his mother had given him) "as a reminder of the sort of friends he had."

The boys, with all this in mind, thought long and hard about what game they might play next. Omar, who sat with his back propped against a boulder, finally gave up and rested his head on his knees with his arms folded. "I give up. I ain know what to play." Chicken sat next to him, his feet stretched out and shoulders slumped with the most forlorn expression on his face.

"I know!" Jeffrey jumped up. Suddenly everyone was alert, eyes focussed on him. "I know! We could play

Super Striker! I going be de Super Striker and Chicken going be de Metallic Hero Worshipper and Omar is de Notorious Villain."

"De who? De Notorious Villain, what I want to be a notorious villain for, and how you get to be de Super Striker, where you hear 'bout dis game from anyway?" Omar didn't want to admit it too soon, but the game sounded like a good one and he was extremely excited to hear what his character could do.

"Well you never see how in the comics dey got all these super heroes dat does shoot fire balls, or ride pon ice, or like Spiderman dat does swing from the buildings wid he web." Chicken nodded his head in agreement. "I like Spiderman, he real cool boy."

"Well de men at school decide to mek up we own super heroes, and so Super Striker, he does strike people with a laser that does come out uh he hand. But dey is don't dead unless he catch them and put them in a head lock and let the laser light pass through one ear and come out the next."

Omar was too excited to sit any longer. "Dat sound good boy, so what the Notorious Villain does do Jeffrey?"

"Well he always in Super Striker way and causing trouble all 'bout de place."

"I did know so you know." Chicken chimed in as he got up. "And ah bet yuh de two uh dem is brothers or something."

"How you know so good?" Jeffrey exclaimed, impressed with his friend's intelligence.
"So who is the metallic whoorshipper? Dat is who I supposed to be?" asked Chicken.
"The *Metallic Hero Worshipper,"* corrected Jeffrey. "He is this robot dat de Villain make, because during the day the Villain is a scientist. So anyway he make this robot that could do almost anything like a human but it got all kind uh weapons attach, and he's do anything that the villain tell him to do. You could even control it by remote...and he's walk funny like a robot."
"You mean like stiff stiff stiff?" Chicken demonstrated. With his knees and elbows straight he started to walk. "You mean like this? And he does say, Y.E.S.S.... M.A.S.T.E.R ... real slow" Chicken did a 360° turn, robot style, making Jeffrey and Omar giggle.
"Do that again Chicken."
"Yeah, that real funny." Omar agreed.

Everybody had a good laugh at Chicken walking around like a robot until eventually the game started in earnest. The Villain terrorised imaginary citizens, while Metallic Hero Worshipper went elsewhere accessing confidential government information using a pin in his index finger to load it onto a computer hard drive in his head. Responding promptly to an alarm set off by local police forces, Super Striker would come victoriously to their rescue.

In one of these moments of mortal combat. Omar caught hold of Jeffrey's shirt a little too roughly as he tried to escape. The shirt tore at the pocket when Jeffrey broke away.
"Aye! Man Omar, watch what you doing'."
"Sorry t'ing."
"And you grab hold a my chest so hard, I must be all bruise up." Jeffrey stopped and held up his shirt to investigate the damage. "Look my skin all bruise up and t'ing," he said, while rubbing the area to soothe the ache.
"I done say I sorry."
"You know that de last time we did play this game at school a boy get beat up real bad by a girl for the same t'ing."
Metallic Hero Worshipper stopped shooting fireballs for a minute to ask 'who boy it was that let a girl beat he up'.
"How you mean! You ever had a fight wid a girl yet? You, them is be vicious yuh! I would never like to fight wid a girl." Omar's voice was filled with respectful fear. He then proceeded to demonstrate the differences in the way boys and girls fought.

"Chicken you ever see a girl fight? When a boy cuff yuh, he does just cuff you BOOM so..." Omar made a swipe with his fist. Chicken ducked. "But when a girl going fuh yuh, boy she does jump 'pon yuh and scratch yuh up, all in yuh face and t'ing and bite you too."

"Uh huh," agreed Jeffrey taking over, "Just so! That is wha' dat girl Maria Williams do tuh de boy. He miss an' hold on to she bubby, and you know how it does hurt when you grab a woman breast. Well Maria holler for murder! And then turn round pun de man and put a karate chop in he suh hard that she really didn't need to hit he after dat."

Jeffrey did an imitation of Jet Lee for dramatic effect. "But it like she did shame too, 'cause when Kirk – that is de boy name - realise dat he did actually touch de girl bubby he start to laugh and that mek she more vex and my girl latch on pon the man and start scratching out he eyes and biting he..." Jeffrey continued to re-enact Maria's movements. He lunged at Chicken. "She even break de man glasses and t'ing." The two boys fell to the ground. Jeffrey who landed on top was really getting into his role as the evil Maria. "Then she start slapping he in he face and grinding he head in the dirt." Chicken finally managed to push Jeffrey off and got up with a helping hand from Omar. "Well! Leh me tell you. Man, when she did done wid he, well he school clothes didn't no good no more."
"He cry Jeffrey?" Chicken always seemed to be overly concerned about the manly image.
"How he could cry? Apart from the fact that he did so shock...everything happen so fast. You know de men woulda never leh he forget it if he hada cry."

"Well anyway de game done after that I imagine." said Omar.
"Yeah after dat it did done."
"Yeah, I t'ink dis game done too, 'cause it getting late and I going home before my mother or Pearl come looking for me."
"That is a good idea 'cause I getting hungry anyway."
"Alright fellahs so check wunnuh later then." Omar turned to leave.
"Oh yeah though Omar, wha' 'bout the obeah deal, we still going work it or what?"
"I don't know, I still thinking 'bout it Jeffrey. Chicken you wasn't supposed to find out from your grandmother what to put in the pot?"
"No Omar that didn't me! Is Jeffrey! Wha' my grandmother know 'bout obeah? She come from Mexico. Dem don't do obeah over there."
"But Chicken, you ain got two grandmothers, the other one don't come from Barbados? She coulda know."
"That is true, but I don't live wid she. Anyway it ain me, is Jeffrey family that does do that sort a thing, sticking pins in people and thing."
"I ain tell you that my family does still do that. I tell you that they say in the old time days; they know people who used to. These is the nineties, nobody don't do nothing like that no more. If somebody do you a wrong you does carry dem court or shoot them or something."

"So how come if nobody don't do that no more wunnuh so eager for me to do it?" Omar was indignant and slightly offended.
"Because yuh idiot, you is a child. You cyan neither tek nobody to court, cause you ain got nuh money and you ain got neither gun to shoot nobody with."
"Besides that..." Omar said thinking it over. "Pearl is my sister. I ain want to kill she nor send she jail, I only want to frighten her little bit, leh she see how it does feel."
"Now see? That is why we going do it."
"Yeah and it going be fun too." Omar laughed, now in a good mood.
"Yeah if we do it at night time, we could build a bonfire and everything, and wear sheets like duppies too."
"Yeah, and see how the moon out? If we do it tomorrow it going be full moon by then."
"Yeah dat cool." Agreed Chicken.
"But men, we can't let nobody know we doing this hear!" Omar's voice went down in a conspiratorial tone. "Leh we swear pun it."
"Yeah leh we swear."

Each boy spat in the other's palm rubbed their hands together and then laid them one on top the other. Jeffrey cleared his throat as he prepared to recite the 'pledge of secrecy'.
"We the members of the Lodge of Secret Brotherhood Club..."

"We the members of the Lodge of Secret Brotherhood Club..." Chicken and Omar repeated.
"Do solemnly swear...."
"Do solemnly swear...."

"That whatever goes on between us,
Remains secret and known only to us.

Whichever one of us does not keep this promise,

Will have broken the Brothers'
most solemn code of honour.

Let our mouths be filled with
flies and cockroaches,
And our tongues vanish into thin air.

This is a just and righteous punishment
For the breaking of our trust."

Omar and Chicken repeated these last lines with a reverence befitting a Sunday morning sermon.

By the time the boys finally finished their ritual with a solid handgrip and some chest thumping it was well after six, and surprisingly dark for a hot summer night. It was definitely time to go home and check the pot for dinner. They ran up the path leaving the grove of clammy cherry trees far behind. When they reached the main road, Jeffrey turned left towards his house, while Chicken accompanied Omar the rest of the way till they reached the Walcott home. There they said goodnight and Chicken broke into a run anxious to leave the empty road behind; the sudden plunge into darkness and Whit's End otherness causing the fine hairs on his back to rise.

When Omar got home, the self same Shelly who had threatened him and the boys earlier for being in her business was there watching TV with half the neighbourhood. She sat inside next to Pearl while various others stood outside or by the front and side doors. Wilson Davy, alias 'Big Davy' who was always trying to "chossle" his mother was the only one bold enough to occupy her coveted chair, which sat directly in front of the TV. Omar did notice that he Davy only ever perched on the edge of the seat as if he had just sat down that minute or were about to get up. He usually ended up staying there for the entire evening while Ms. Walcott sat watching from the dining table with the excuse that she was shelling peas or sorting rice. The result was that they had years of rice and peas stored up in the outside freezer that would probably never be eaten.

The object of all this attention was the nightly soap opera. The series was even older than Pearl. Yet, Barbados was still viewing the 1970's version. Omar could not comprehend the attraction to the series and usually tried to stay away until after seven o'clock when the Soap was over. But lately he noticed that both his mother and sister were becoming anxious about his whereabouts and the late hours he came home. It would definitely make life easier if he got back early on those days when there was nothing to do in particular.

Omar sat down to a dinner of rice and peas and lamb stew. His mother's voice pierced his thoughts. "Boy you wash your hands before you eat?" The fork froze midway to his mouth.
"No Mummy."
"Omar go and wash your hands." Loretta didn't even look up from her shelling.
"Yes Mummy" Omar got up, dragging his chair along the floorboards as he went.
"You see what I tell you Mummy?" Pearl was glad to have a witness to her brother's indiscipline. "If you wasn't here, you t'ink he woulda listen to me? He always rolling 'bout in de ground, an' digging up in de dirt an' never want to wash he hands. Nasty!"

The scowl on her face reflected Pearl's annoyance with her brother, he let out a long chupse saying, "Why you don't mind you own business though Pearl, and stop trying to frighten me wid dat ugly face!"

Every single one of the people who didn't belong in the house turned their eyes on the family, a silent message to be quiet conveyed. Big Davy flapped his hands agitatedly. "Shhh...nuh? Wunnuh mekking we miss de show."

"Wha happen jus' now Davy?" came a voice from the window."

"I ain know, I think Gloria just ask de man ta marry she." Davy said this very fast so that he wouldn't miss anything else.

Omar, hands washed but still dripping wet, went back to the table and proceeded to eat his rice and peas.

"Omar you say your grace before meals?" Once again Omar paused fork in mid air.

"No Mummy."

"Then say them Nuh!"

"SHHHH!" The whole house vibrated. "Ms. t'ing we jus' miss hearing if de man tell Gloria yes or no."

"Hush nuh leh we hear!"

The voice from the window started to cuss, "Man I cyan stand 'bout here, I jus' miss wha' he say again, every night is de same t'ing. Yuh is cyan hear wha' de people saying pun de TV."

"Omar why you don't behave though nuh boy, an' stop causing yuh mudda suh much trouble."

"Yuh see Mummy!" interjected Pearl. "Everbody done know how much trouble Omar does be giving. And I cyan never still get no satisfaction." She chupsed long and hard, her face in a pout, arms folded. "Come

Shelly man, leh we lef in here, I tired ah all these foolish people."
"Yeah, and yuh cyan even hear nutting pun de TV, leh we go out by me an' watch it over there Pearl."
Pearl and Shelly flounced out of the house. Ms. Walcott looked up from shelling her peas, her face serious, hands poised over the tray.
"Pearl, I want you back in this house before eleven o'clock, you hear me?"

Even though Pearl and Shelly were already out the gate, Loretta knew they had heard her. But as was typical of Pearl these days, she just chose to ignore her mother. The rest of the house was glad to have obtained silence at last, and happily watched the remainder of their soap opera in peace and quiet.

* PEARL *
3

A soft light glowed from a little bedroom at the back of the house which leaned to one side. In it a small transistor radio belted out the tunes of the latest dancehall music. The two girls flipped through magazines seeing by the light of a bare bulb in the ceiling above. In the privacy of the room they let their imaginations run wild. They imagined which of the movie stars they'd go out with if they lived in Hollywood and which of the designer clothing they'd look better in than the stars themselves.

"Look at this one Shells."

"Which one?"

"The one that Jennifer Lopez got on. Boy! She always look good though, nuh?"

"Yeah, she and Jada Pinket. I never see the two of them dress bad yet." Pearl pointed at the picture outlining the actress's contours in a slinky black dress.

"You feel we could make this one?"

"Yeah, but not for the fete tomorrow! I like what we making already."

"Yeah me too. You think that the black suit me though?"

"Of course the black suit you. You and I have almost the same shape so if you think that it look good on me, then I don't see why you should feel that it wouldn't look good on you too."

Shelly sighed. She was always worried that her boyfriend Derek wouldn't appreciate how she dressed. Looking good was important to her. That was one of the reasons she loved having Pearl as a friend. Pearl was a natural born seamstress, destined to greatness. She shared among other interests, Shelly's tastes in clothing. Not only clothes but other things as well. They shared the same ideas about having their own businesses someday and maybe fashion was the way to go. So many people seemed content to get up every morning and go to work for someone else, make that person rich, yet it seemed that the same amount of effort could be put into being self-employed with much more satisfaction at the end. Shelly flicked the pages absentmindedly while Pearl leaned over her shoulder and pointed out a design that caught her fancy every now and then.

The girls could easily spend hours fantasizing about their future, where they would be, what they would be doing. Now that they were out of school, they were thinking about it a lot more, and worrying whether or not they had what it took to make it in the world. Tonight though was filled with excitement. They had been looking forward to this fete on Saturday for weeks and now finally it was almost here. All they had to do was make a few minor adjustments to the dresses and they would be set for the next night.

Omar rocked back and forth on the old slop bucket, with Commando at his side. It was sometime after eight and having nothing better to do he'd spent the last hour and a half watching the rest of the soap opera and the news with the adults. Now Davy and three other men had migrated outdoors and were deeply engrossed in a game of dominoes. Omar understood the game a lot better when he was playing rather than just as a spectator. Sometimes he was lucky enough to win a game, but these men were pros and had track records longer that Omar's ten years. They were not about to let him play. Dominoes to them was as serious as cricket, and on hot summer nights the entire male population would assemble outside Ms. Walcott's shop front with their make-shift chairs and old rickety tables. Sometimes their chairs were nothing more than old milk crates and propped up cement blocks. Whenever the men arrived for a game, Loretta would complain, that they were 'uglying up' her place with garbage, and why they didn't go someplace else to play anyway. But everyone knew they wouldn't have been able to see to play on those moonless nights if she hadn't turned on her powerful 180-watt spot that shone over the shop's yard.

And of course dominoes were not dominoes without the ubiquitous bottles of rum. Before the game had barely begun, someone would invariably shout...
"Ms. Walcott, why you don't open up de shop and leh we get something to drink!" to which her reply would always be...
"My shop close at six o'clock. If you want something to drink, go home and drink it!"
"But why we should go home if the party here?"
"What party? I don't want no foolish drunks lying 'bout on my doorstep, setting a bad example for my children."
They would banter back and forth until eventually the little side window would open, and the Mount Gay and Cockspur would come out by the bottle.

Years of bottle caps and stoppers of all kinds lay embedded in the pavement around the shop. Bits of worn down, broken glass bottle glistened amidst the gravel path at the entrance like semi precious jewels. Omar studied the enlarged shadows the spotlight cast of the men as they slammed their dominoes. Giant sized hands came down with such force that the table rocked dangerously. Davy as usual was winning making the men chupse and question whether he wasn't tired of being king yet, and if his crown weren't too heavy, because if so they could help him out with it.

Omar got up from his bucket and walked around the group, intrigued by the way each was able to calculate what the other had in his hands. Their bodies swayed from side to side in anticipation of inevitable victory, or defeat. Omar peeped into the players' hands, trying to figure out what their next moves might be. He liked the idea of hanging around big men, especially since they always seemed to be laughing and joking and having a good time like Davy. He just wished they would let him play. When he grew up he wanted to be a master domino player and be able to throw back nuff liquor no matter how much and still never get drunk. He pulled the bucket under Davy's right arm hopeful to learn a few tricks from the master.

Omar could have sat there for ages stealing sips of rum and slamming down dominoes whenever Davy's turn came around. It would be Commando's completely erect ears that first alerted him to Jeffrey's presence. Until that moment the waist high mutt had been content to sprawl on the cool cement, head resting on large front paws. The fact that Commando showed little loyalty to his owner was well known in the neighbourhood. The lopey part-Labrador, part-Pitt Bull and God only knew what else was much more like the village dog than a personal pet. He loved anyone who gave him something to eat and always had to be in the middle of wherever the action was. The action until that moment had been the game of dominoes outside the Walcott house. Now he'd run off into a dark corner wagging his tail ferociously. Omar couldn't see anyone beyond the picket fence, but he imagined that the level of his dog's excitement – Jeffrey was one of his favourite people – and the little gravel rocks landing mysteriously at his feet were indication enough that his friend was nearby. Why all the secrecy? Omar was not sure. But he got up as naturally as he could, trying not to distract the others from their game.

"Jeffrey?" he whispered.
"Yeah, is me" Jeffrey whispered back. "Come with me Omar, I got something to show you."
"Yeah?"
Jeffrey nodded in agreement. "...and it way better than dominoes."
"What it is, something good on TV?"
"Yeah yeah, come with me quick before it finish." Jeffrey was already heading away from the house when Omar protested.
"But Jeffrey, where you going? We got TV right here."
"Not this one Omar another one." He winked at his friend hinting that he shouldn't argue.

They walked with quick steps away from the house and up the road with Commando for company. The dogs over long nails clicked in time on the cool asphalt. Whatever it was that Jeffrey had to show Omar was apparently very secret. He wouldn't tell him anything, only that they were going to his house and that they had to be very quiet. That Chicken wasn't in on it was even more peculiar. Fortunately the journey was a short one, because Omar spent every single minute of it trying to get Jeffrey to reveal the secret. They crept into the house quietly, leaving Commando whimpering outside.

The boys talked in whispers as they went towards Jeffrey's bedroom. All the house was dark except for a crack of light peeping out under a bedroom doorway. Even inside Omar persisted with his questions, until Jeffrey pulled him up and made him swear not to make any noise, or tell anyone about what he was about to see.

"But how I could promise you these things when I don't even know what it is? You could at least give me a hint."

Jeffrey sighed. "Alright. You ever see a girl naked before?"

"You mean besides my sister...actually I could only say I see my sister naked, if wearing a bath towel count as being naked...no why?" Omar was definitely puzzled. Jeffrey nodded knowingly.

"Well you going love this then. I want you to know it is only because you is my best friend that I ain

making you pay, because if it was anybody else I woulda done get five dollars for this."
"What you got Jeffrey, dirty magazines?"
"I got better than that, now Shhhh..."
Erratic snores could be heard coming from one bedroom, while from another room, came the sound of female laughter and music.

Jeffrey put his finger to his lips and led the way forward. He very quietly pulled his bedroom door closed, locking it with the key. Omar's eyebrows rose in question. Jeffrey then motioned for Omar's help in gently moving the large bureau closer to the bed and against the wall. As the two boys struggled under its substantial weight, Omar realised that the voices he'd heard were coming from the room next door.

"But wait..." he whispered. "That is my sister voice?"
Jeffrey only nodded.
"She in there with Shelly? What them doing?"
Jeffrey put his finger to his mouth to silence his friend again and gestured for Omar to follow as he climbed on the bed and from there to stand on the top of the bureau.
"You going see just now."

The wall dividing Jeffrey's room from his sister's was made from wood like the rest of the house, with the typical one-foot gap between wall and ceiling. Between Jeffrey's and Shelly's rooms this gap was filled with beautifully decorated latticed exes through which fresh air passed freely. Now Omar would discover they had a multi-purpose. Omar had no idea what to expect when he peeped over that wall. He most certainly had not expected to see anything that would dramatically affect the course of his life. His eyes nearly popped out of his head at the sight before him. It was a miracle he managed not to make a sound. Jeffrey watched his friend's reaction with glee.

They were looking down into Shelly's bedroom where the two girls lounged practically naked except for their almost non-existent panties. Pearl sat sprawled in a chair putting the final touches to a sequined party dress. Shelly lay on the bed, legs swaying in the air as she flipped through Hollywood magazines. One magazine was full of women in fancy evening dresses, inspiration for the dress to which Pearl was applying her final adjustments. Pearl bit the thread with her teeth after tying the last knot to a sequined strap of the black silk dress that bore tassels on the hem. However, all that was of little interest to Omar; he'd found something much more intriguing to watch.

He looked at Shelly's breasts with awe. He had nothing to compare them with, yet instinctively he knew that hers were perfect. His mouth watered in the same way it did when he saw ripe juicy mangoes and he wanted to pick these too. Until that moment Omar had never before thought of breasts as functional in any way other than as being a source of milk for babies, or as the things that brassieres were invented for. Of course they were always a useful point of attack...a vulnerable spot when fighting with girls... especially Pearl. Still, looking at Shelly now, her two perfectly round breasts erect, the nipples pointing straight out and piercing the air like arrows... he couldn't imagine why he had ever wanted to do that... they were beautiful.

As Shelly stepped into her dress, the two soft globes rocked gently against each other making Omar's grip on the wooden divider tighten. Shelly shimmied the black silk up her body pulling the thin straps over her shoulders. Omar broke into a sweat just imagining the luscious form barely hidden beneath. He had completely forgotten about the existence of Jeffrey, so totally mesmerised was he by the seductive dance seemingly performed for him. When Jeffrey grabbed hold of his shoulder Omar just squeezed his eyes shut trying to clear his vision. Even if he'd wanted to speak, he couldn't have, all coherent thought blown from his mind. Jeffrey grinned broadly, understanding what Omar was going through.

While Omar and Jeffrey watched from above, Shelly and Pearl continued to chatter away excitedly below oblivious to the two pairs of eyes watching them. Someone had turned up the music and the girls danced and sang as they made adjustments to their party dresses. Shelly was extremely pleased with her dress and was discussing with Pearl how the effect could be made more dramatic by simply deepening the V of her cleavage. What Omar saw was a beautifully manicured finger sliding between the sleek fabric and her luscious mounds. It travelled up and down, loud echoes of her previous movements. Omar felt as if he were being touched all over. In the beating of his heart and the pounding in his ears, his body throbbed. His stomach lurched. His head reeled from the excess of sensations...sensations too strange and too new for his young mind to handle.

He only noticed his friend's irregular breathing when the bureau on which they stood trembled. For one moment his eyes lost sight of their focus and in that moment Omar suddenly became aware of his sister's own nakedness. Pearl held only a deep red velvet dress in front of her, an exact replica of Shelly's. Her naked back reflected in the mirror, giving the boys full view of her figure. When she bent over to put the dress on, both boys closed their eyes. Omar wasn't sure he wanted to see so much of Pearl. Jeffrey, on the other hand, seemed to be in some sort of pain, because he was grabbing his crotch and saying aye aye...

"What happen to you Jeffrey?" he whispered.
"Ooh ...nothing, nothing, I cool... Sssss...aye"
He continued to look at his friend sceptically, until encouraged rather agitatedly to direct his gaze

elsewhere, at the girls preferably. When Omar looked back Pearl was fully dressed and blowing kisses at herself in the mirror. He watched the two of them dance around to the music experimenting with different poses, accentuating their womanly curves. There was no doubt in his mind that Shelly was a beautiful woman. What was scary, however, was the realisation that she and Pearl were almost identical in figure. Anyone not knowing them, seeing them together, would most certainly have taken them for sisters. If this were the case, then did it not mean that his sister was also good looking? The thought that someone might find Pearl attractive was too unsettling an idea for Omar to consider. He was more than relieved when Jeffrey finally motioned for them to get down from the bureau because the show was over.

Omar picked his way off the bureau helping Jeffrey put it back in place. He flopped himself on the bed and did nothing but stare at the ceiling. Jeffrey just sniggered and kicked his feet where they hung over the edge.
"So you like the surprise?"
Omar stretched and sat up, looking long and hard at his friend before answering. "Boy, you does do that everyday?"
"Fairly."
"But you's don't be shame looking at your sister so?"
"Sister? I does be looking at Pearl!"

"Pearl! You bring me here to see Pearl!"
"Shhhh...no you idiot! You watch my sister, I watch yours."
"Oh."

Omar stayed silent for a long time. He would never be able to look at women in the same way again. Suddenly he understood why his Uncle Junior spent so many hours in the bathroom getting ready and so many more cleaning his motorcycle till it shone. He'd never understood all this fuss about boyfriend, girlfriend, or someone wanting to kiss a miserable creature like Shelly...or Pearl and even taking two buses and waiting long hours just to visit either of them. But now he realised that neither she nor Pearl behaved the same way with him and his friends as they did when guys they liked were around. Shelly wasn't the same around Derek, nor was his sister, for that matter, around other guys. He realised that he'd never seen them cuss or carry on in the way they did around his friends. In fact he would say, they were sweeter than ice cream and cookies in the company of men. The world - Omar thought was beginning to get too complicated.

Pearl woke up scratching and itching. She pulled at the collar of her blue T-shirt inspecting her shoulder.

The wooden floor felt cool under her bare feet. She wriggled her toes and then walked out into the sitting room yawning and stretching to work out the kinks. "Mummy!" Still heavy with sleep, Pearl stumbled over the telephone cord irritated by its uselessness.

"Mummy!"
"Uh hmmn?" Loretta responded from the kitchen.
"Where you are?" Pearl asked, examining the soft inside of her wrist and elbow. "You cook something for breakfast? I hungry."
"No Pearl, I didn' have no time for that this morning. I think they still got some cornflakes in the cupboard, unless you want to eat some macaroni pie from yesterday."
Pearl dug in the fridge searching for the macaroni pie. She stretched again. "Jeeze! You could believe my head still hurting me from last night? Boy that perfume must be real strong boy!" She peeled off the saran wrap covering the Pyrex dish, then paused to rub her eyes. "And my eyes feel all swell up swell up. It look so to you?"
"Come here let me see." Pearl walked over to her mother to be inspected. "They look red enough fuh true. But like you got a rash on your face too. Come in the light and let me see." Loretta pulled Pearl closer to the window where the light was brighter. "...But Pearl, you know you got a rash in your face and on your arms and everything! Girl what you went doing, bathing in that perfume? I tell you already about

sharing other people things." Loretta looked at her daughter, noticing that she'd slept in her home clothes but deciding to say nothing.

"Mummy why you don't stop with them old fashioned ideas 'bout sharing people things? ...don't wear this body shirt, don't use this body brush or lipstick... Shelly is my friend, we's do everything together. If I get a rash is not because uh she, is just because my skin don't like the perfume, and maybe it is not the one, maybe is because we was mixing the lot of them at the same time."

Loretta harrumphed and went back to chopping her seasoning. Pearl observed her mother, noting the muscled hands which chopped the spring onions into small bits. The smell was strong. She also noted that her mother always smelled of onions, or manure or....

"Well I done tell you what I tell you. You are a big woman and does do what you want. Next time, just don't come running to me."

"I ain come running to you. I just ask you if my eyes was swell or not!"

"And what you call that? If you want to know if your eyes red, go and look in the mirror next time!"

"Yuh see, that is why I can't talk to you, you always got to turn everything into a big issue."

"Big issue! Listen girl don't bother me no more. Why you don't go and find something to do. Go and clean your room or something!"

"How you mean clean my room? My room always clean! You should tell that to Omar or Junior, them room ain see broom in days...got suh much dust yuh could plant potato in it. As for the cobwebs...neither of the two o' them don't do nothing in there!"
"How the room could still have cobwebs? Pearl I didn't ask you to take a broom to in there for me ever since?"
"And why I should do it? Them fingers brek?"
"You know that Omar too short to reach up there Pearl."
"So he should do like I used to do when I was little and stand up 'pon a chair nuh!" Pearl changed her mind about the macaroni pie and chucked it back in the fridge. "Where the milk is? We ain got no more milk!"

Loretta leaned over Pearl and pulled the carton of milk from the compartment in the door. She shoved it in her daughter's hands. "The milk right in front of you! Why you don't shut up and use them two red eyes of yours and try and see the things that right in front of you!"

Pearl slammed the fridge door shut stomping from there to the cupboard for the cornflakes and her bowl. "And stop trying to mash up my things. I tell you already, don't slam that door so hard!"

"How you mean you tell me already? You like you got your children confuse yuh, I ain Omar. Look I gone man, I ain got no reason to be listening to this." Pearl strode from the room still muttering to herself. "...slamming fridge door...she never tell me nothing so before... talking foolishness."
"Don't feel that I cyan hear you Pearl Walcott." Loretta called from the kitchen. "I could hear you good enough!"
Pearl chuckled as she straddled a chair. She leaned her arms on its back and proceeded to pour out her cornflakes.
"And sit down properly in my chairs too you hear girl." Loretta didn't have to look.
Pearl obeyed, righting the chair. "Mummy where you put them headache pills that I had on the table last night?"
"I put them back where they supposed to be."

Pearl got up and went to the bathroom cabinet. I can't be walking round with this headache all last night and today too. My head hurting me too bad. Mummy you sure these pills working cause I ain see no expiry date?" Pearl pulled out some calamine lotion and started rubbing down her face and arms as well. "Mummy!" She strolled back into the kitchen.
"Yes Pearl?"
"You could rub down my back for me? I can't reach." Loretta looked towards the sky and sighed. "Lord what to do with these children? They wun grow up an' lef

me 'lone though nuh...Pearl I deep to my elbows in seasoning!"
"But Mummy I can't reach, do it for me nuh."

Giving up Loretta washed her hands briskly under the sink and grabbed the bottle of calamine from Pearl. "I don't want to hear nothing 'bout how I got you smelling like onions."
"I ain say nothing Mummy."
"Feel I don't know you? Now tell me where you want this." Loretta slapped the calamine lotion on Pearl's shoulders rubbing the creamy liquid in vigorously. "Good. Now go long and leh me do what I have to do in peace."
"Thanks Mummy." Pearl went about her business leaving Loretta singing one of her favourite hymns, "*Blessed assurance Jesus is mine...*"

* PEARL *
4

It was the perfect night for a bonfire. The moon was full and large. There was not too much wind, but just enough to get things going. The boys huddled in a circle over the bits of wood and newspaper, excited. Jeffrey poured generous amounts of kerosene over the dry sticks, and then lit a piece of paper he had shaped neatly into a funnel. The fire burst forth, casting long shadows on the boulders beside them. Twigs popped and crackled as they expanded under the heat. Jeffrey fanned his fire proudly, delighted with how quickly he'd managed to build it up. Omar held the can of chicken blood steadily in both hands, making sure not to spill a single precious drop. It had been a stroke of good luck that he'd gotten the chicken blood.

That same morning, while his mother had been in the yard collecting eggs for breakfast, the old paling-cock had attacked her. *Again!* It was to this ruckus that Omar awoke so early on Friday morning. The paling-cock had gotten it into his head to take offence at his hens being disturbed. Jumping down from his usual galvanized perch by the breadfruit tree, he had charged at Loretta, spurs first.

Poised like a majestic eagle before attack, eyes fierce, beak apart, wings spread wide; he swooped down on the hand that fed him in a fiery, red haze. It would be the last foolish decision he ever made. In one equally majestic gesture Loretta reached out and grabbed him by the very spurs which threatened, and held him suspended in mid-air. No amount of flapping or squawking would loosen her grip. Without even sparing a thought for the eggs she'd just dropped Loretta held firm, determined to be the victor. So angry was she that beads of sweat gushed from her pores, in spite of the gentle morning sun. Loretta grumbled to herself. She was fed up with hearing that disgusting bird crowing at all hours of the morning...a quarter past four, twenty past five, ten to...whenever he decided to come down from the paling he'd be fighting with the hens and the other roosters. The idea of him even thinking about attacking her was so unthinkable... *No!* There'd be no scrubbing down of surfaces first! Angry woman marched indignant fowl straight over to the chopping block and with one swift movement of the axe, took his head off. Now, there was one less force resisting her. Loretta blew a breath of cool air onto her nose and tried to calm herself.

Omar saw all this happening from his bedroom window and his thoughts went immediately to a plan of action. Who knew when next his mother would kill a fowl since she mainly kept them to sell eggs. He ran into the kitchen where the pot with lunch was already bubbling and turned up the heat to all. Uncle Junior was the first to notice the smell and stuck his head out the bathroom window hollering for his sister. "Loretta, yuh pot burning!" There was nothing Loretta hated more than having to throw out a good pot of food. She tilted her head at an angle catching a whiff of the burning fumes. All thoughts of vengeance forgotten, Loretta hurried in to save her burning pot. She dropped the fowl right there, its body still twitching, its head hopping about. While his mother ran in through the back, Omar ran around the front with an old mackerel can and a grin splitting his face from ear to ear. All he had to do was place it at the edge of the chopping block and let the blood flow. In truth, it seemed like quite an undignified end to such a proud and valiant bird. But it was not to be helped. In any case Omar was way too pleased with his sudden good fortune to ponder over the cock's demise for very long. Sneaking through the back gate, he cut across the pasture behind Mr. Cumberbatch's house. He would take the blood over to Chicken's.

When you are ten years old and subject to communal interrogations and public embarrassment, it is always best to take the safest route and be on the lookout for potential threats, especially if you were up to mischief, as Omar well knew he was. To ensure that he avoided any possible witnesses Omar skirted a few more houses and took the long way around the pasture - just to be on the safe side. His goal in sight, Omar tiptoed over the gravel path leading to Chicken's side door. He squatted on all fours when he saw a shadow pass by and virtually crawled along the side of the house until he reached his friend's bedroom window. Since Chicken was an only child, his house was Omar's obvious choice at which to hide the evidence. In Jeffrey's house there was busy body Shelly who was just a little too friendly with Pearl for comfort.

"Chicken!" Omar peeped over the windowsill and rapped lightly on the pane. "Chicken, wake up." Omar rapped again, pressing his face against the glass, only to jump back in surprise when Chicken suddenly appeared and pushed the windows open. Omar barely missed a nasty blow to the head.
"Omar! What you doing out here?"
"Shhh...Chicken, wha' you open de window suh hard for?"
"What time it is? It ain even six o'clock, wha' you doing up so early, and why you whispering for?" Chicken said all this in a fairly loud voice which had Omar running for cover and promising himself to look for new friends when he went back to school the next term.
"Shhh..." he said again. "Comma quick."
"Alright I coming." Chicken turned to go outside and bumped into his bed with a bang. "Aye!" he cried out in pain.

"Antonio!"
"Yes Abuela?"
"Everyth*ee*ng all right in there?"
"Yes ma! I good."
"Oh, because I thought I heard a noise." Chicken's grandmother shuffled to his bedroom and peeped by the door. Omar ducked, his heart beating so hard the cloth of his shirt vibrated.
"How come you have the window open Antonio? I hope you d*ee*dn't sleep with it that way, if not you'll catch a chill."
"Alright Abuela." Chicken had his back to the window, hopefully blocking Omar. "I going close it just now."
"*Ees* not during the day you supposed to keep it closed you know Antonio, *ees* at night." Abuela spoke slowly, pronouncing her I's more like hees. She walked away mumbling to herself. "I don't know what to do with these young people, they feel they know everyth*ee*ng."

"Omar, you still there?" Chicken leaned out the window looking for his friend.
"Yes. Listen Chicken," he whispered. "don't bother to come outside, just hide this someplace safe for me." Omar handed Chicken the mackerel can.
"Wha' is this?" Chicken asked, putting it to his nose. "This smell like blood."
"Yes is blood. I get de chicken blood."
"You get de chicken blood!"

"Shhhh..."

"Cool..." Chicken stared at the can in awe, and then paused, his expression perplexed. "But wait, Omar you kill one uh you mudda chickens?"

"No yuh *idiate,* she kill it."

"You mean she kill de chicken for you? You mean you tell she wha' we was planning to do?" Chicken's voice rose by decibels.

"No listen, she ain know I got de blood, she just kill de chicken because..." Chicken looked as if he were about to ask another barrage of questions. Omar decided to cut him short.

"Look I going explain later. Put this way for me, and don't leh nobody see you got it. Hear?"

"Alright Omar, I hear."

"Good then, I gone! I going come back a lil' later dis afternoon, when my mother busy wid de shop and ain going be looking for me. Omar made to leave and then turned back. Chicken, who was still gazing at the can of blood in his hands, jumped when he saw Omar again.

"And Chicken..."

"Yes?"

"Remember to bring one of your grandmother's dolls like Jeffrey was saying."

"And the pins to stick it with?"

"Yeah, don't forget the pins."

"Ok." Chicken nodded, ready to move away from the window.

"Oh! and common pins Chicken, not safety pins."
"Any sort a doll would do, as long as it soft I guess?"
"Yeah. But don't bring nothing that you feel you grandmother going miss."
"Alright Omar I got yuh."
"Good then, I gone."
When the boys parted, Chicken ran to the kitchen for a plastic bag. He put the can of blood in it, tied a knot, then placed it on the floor of his cupboard behind his shoes. Meanwhile Omar was headed over to Jeffrey's with the good news.

Back at home Loretta was too busy trying to salvage her ruined pot to even remember the dead fowl, or notice her son's absence. When Omar came out of his bedroom half an hour later, she assumed he had just awoken. Loretta looked over her shoulder and greeted her son. "Morning. You up very early this morning."
"'Morning Mummy." Omar said, faking a stretch.
"Come and give me a kiss." Omar walked over to his mother and got his good morning hug and kiss.
"I don't know wha' happen, but one minute I was sleeping good and then some noise must be wake me up. I don't know what it was."
"Oh, that must be the fowl I kill this morning."
"Mummy you kill a chicken? I thought we used to keep them for eggs."
"Not a chicken Omar...." Loretta turned back to scrubbing her pot. There was still burnt rice in the bottom. "...the paling-cock. That stupid bird had me

so vex. He feel to fly at me this morning when I going to collect some eggs for breakfast."
Loretta had worked up a sweat from all her efforts and stopped to wipe her brow on her sleeve.
"Anyway, he start to look real good to me in a pot of chicken soup. How you fancy some soup today?"

Omar did not have to feign surprise about that particular subject. He loved his mother's chicken soup. "Yeah! With split peas and dumplings too Mummy?"
"Yes love. Now go and wash yourself so we can eat breakfast…and call Pearl for me too please. Is about time she got up."
"Ok Mum."

Omar headed down the passageway shouting his sister's name as he went. "Pearl! Mummy say to get up." He banged on the door and pushed it open.
"Pearl."
"Umm..mn.." she mumbled.
"Mummy say to get up or she going beat you."
Pearl raised her head from under her pillow, ready to throw it at her little brother. She was apparently wide- awake now.
"My mother don't beat me, I am a woman. I don't know why you don't stop telling so much lie you know Omar."
"I wasn't lying, Mummy say for you to get up."

"Yeah, but she ain say nothing 'bout hitting me, so hush and lef my room before I pelt this pillow at yuh."

Omar felt it would be safer to retreat even though he was ninety percent sure Pearl wasn't really serious. As he walked out into the passageway Uncle Junior tackled him. He was coming out of the bathroom having already taken his shower, and smelled sweet with perfume.

"Hey star boy! How yuh doing, sleep good last night?"

"Yeah, I sleep ok. You now coming home?"

"No, but I got in real late last night. I didn't wake you up?"

"No."

"That good, that good. Leh we go and get some of that breakfast your Mummy making."

Everyone sat down to a breakfast of bacon and eggs, Kellogg's cornflakes, and Milo for Omar, while the women and Junior drank bay leaf tea. It was one of those rare occasions when the entire family actually managed to be at the table together. Loretta sometimes wondered if she could have done things differently to have her family like this always. However, not being one to cry over spilt milk, she acknowledged that it was difficult for most parents to raise their children successfully these days, and here she had to be both mother and father, not only to them but to her brother Junior as well. Of the two, she was admittedly worried about Pearl. Loretta had already confided to her best friend Annie that she didn't know what to do with the girl. She never knew whether the child was coming or going. Since Annie didn't actually have any children, her guess was as good as Loretta's. Take this morning for example Pearl had been the epitome of helpfulness. She'd gotten up as soon as Loretta had sent for her, and even volunteered to finish breakfast while her mother prepared the chicken soup. Though she would never expect Pearl to offer to do anything as demeaning as plucking a fowl, she was still touched by her daughter's offer to prepare the water and clean up the mess afterwards.

Pearl obviously was angry about something. Loretta didn't know if this was simply normal adolescent behaviour, since she had never had a teenage daughter before. Whatever her problems, they were exhibited by constant insolence. Pearl had just completed fifth form, but her grades had not been good enough to guarantee her an A-Level school placement. Loretta's disappointment was strong and after a week of suffering in silence she had outright asked her daughter what *were* her plans for the immediate future and the rest of her life for that matter. Of course they'd argued over it, ultimatums were not a thing Pearl took to kindly. Still, her mother giving her a choice between continuing her education at Community College, the Polytechnic or getting a job was far more palatable than the idea of working in the shop full time. Several weeks had passed since their "discussion" and mother still did not know what decision daughter had made. What she did know however, was that no adults lived in her house without contributing something to its upkeep, and since Pearl had made it very clear she was no longer a child... *"Well,"* Loretta muttered to herself, *"she could just wait and see what happen!"*

After breakfast, Loretta and Pearl set about opening the shop, while Omar had disappeared to God only knew where. From as early as six in the morning, the Walcotts left the shop's side window open so that people could purchase odd items such as a soft drinks or sugar. The rest of the shop remained closed until seven-thirty. The shop was just a little galvanized shed, which Loretta had paved in, its only public entrance, a double door. Loretta and Pearl served their customers from behind a long L shaped counter. On the left was a Coca cola machine, the only one in the village. On the right was the Pine Hill machine with juices and milk beverages. These two machines significantly reduced trips from freezer to counter for mother and daughter, as the hot summer days sent increasing numbers of thirsty patrons their way. Everything else was behind the counter, especially the liquor, so Loretta could keep a watchful eye over. Daily purchases of bread, cheese, biscuits, sardines, corned beef, flour, meal and toiletries kept the Walcott family in business.

Between Loretta and Pearl, they usually prepared a few fish cakes, cheese cutters, ham cutters and fried chicken to serve around lunchtime. Big Davy, who was a regular, always collected a corned beef sandwich loaded with pepper sauce for breakfast on mornings. Since he was usually late for the bus, Davy hardly ever had time to sit with them in the mornings; this day was one of the exceptions. It seemed for once he was on time and so kept Pearl and her mother company while they did their morning preparations.

"So Pearl muh girl, how yuh doing dis morning?"
"I good Davy."
"You got a paper there? Leh me see wha' going on in the world today."
"You want the Nation or the Advocate?"
"You done know I is a Nation man. So don't be showing me that other piece of foolishness. Ms. Walcott wha' wrong wid dis chile, that she trying to start wid me suh early in the morning?"
Pearl chuckled. She knew full well that Davy was a staunch 'Nation' supporter, and that the easiest way to set him off was to suggest that he read the other newspaper... otherwise he was easy to get along with even if he refused to stay at home and watch his own television. At least he wasn't stupid like some of the others, believing everything they saw on the foolish

soap operas and talking back to the TV as if the actors were real...and he was funny too. Pearl shook her head to clear it of her musings and went back to wiping down the counter tops.

* PEARL *
5

It was shortly after five-thirty in the evening when Omar wandered home after a long day's play. Jeffrey had abandoned him for a dinner of pizza in town with his father. Chicken, on the other hand, had decided to play it safe by going home before dark for a change. Recently his grandmother had started complaining about his late night wanderings, and had threatened to tie him to a chair if he kept them up much longer. He figured that the night of their big escapade was not the time to test the truth of her words. So with nothing to do and no one to play with, Omar headed home. He went over in his mind everything they had organised that day. Jeffrey had already managed to gather together a pile of dry twigs and Omar, his sister's hair. The can of precious chicken blood would remain safely hidden away until later that evening.

The sun had already begun its descent, and the neighbour's hens clucked their way over to a nearby pear tree to roost for the evening. The light turned everything a beautiful golden brown and as Omar walked into the sunset, the fine hairs on his arms caught fire, his tawny brown eyes witness to the sun's descent. Omar climbed the steps to his house like an old man, lifting one foot at a time, one slowly behind the other. He ran a hand absentmindedly along the banister, drawing invisible patterns with his fingers. Cradled gently in the other hand was his most recently acquired marble. The little scratching sounds his nails made alerted Pearl to his presence. Having already tidied the rest of the house, she was busily sweeping the living room. The windows were clean, the furniture polished, and all the little ornaments dusted and in place.

Omar trailed into the house and continued to run his hands over the back of the sofa and over the little glass and porcelain ornaments as he moved towards the television. He passed a little too closely to his sister's pile of dust and received a quick slap round the head for it. "Aye man! Wha' you do that for?"
"Watch where you going! You cyan see I sweeping. Look you just kick 'way my dust."
Omar rubbed the back of his neck to soothe it. "But you didn't have to hit me so hard." He whined, then stomped over to the television turned it on and plopped himself in his mother's chair. He had been feeling very peaceful and happy till then, but Pearl always seemed to have a way of spoiling that. Omar cocked his foot up on the chair arm and quickly became engrossed in a cartoon. While his sister once again swept her dust into a neat pile, he picked at loose scab on his knee, every now and then dropping

the pieces onto the newly-swept carpet. Pearl looked at him menacingly.
"Omar what you think you doing?"
"Huh?"

When his hand strayed to one of the many little ornaments on the table nearby, Pearl looked up again. The blue and green crystal bird he picked up clinked as it bounced another ornament. "Omar, what I tell you about playing with them t'ings already?"
"I wasn't playing with it, my hand just happen to brush it."
"Your hand just happen to brush it? So what the bird doing all the way over there then? I ain put it there, I put it all the way over here!" Pearl let go of her broom, marched over to the table and sternly placed the ornament back in its rightful position.
"And don't touch it again, yuh hear!"

No sooner had Pearl turned her back than Omar nudged the bird forward with his index finger. His sister froze mid stride, turning slowly with a look of such venom, that had Omar been a different sort of child he would have been afraid. Omar pushed the bird again, only this time it collided with another ornament. Pearl extended her hand in virtual slow motion, the last rays of the sun filtering through her uncombed hair making her look wild. When she grabbed hold of his hand, Omar felt his stomach lurch, but was determined not to give in to this weakness.

They fought silently, each trying to push the ornament the other way. Pearl's hold on Omar's wrist grew tighter with each movement. They stared into each other's eyes, looking for some sign of weakening or surrender. Omar tried to peal her fingers away but her long nails bit into his soft skin as she wrestled the bird from him, increasing her hold, squeezing and pinching so tightly that finally he had to let go. Omar's sudden lack of resistance so surprised Pearl that the bird slipped from her grasp and was in three pieces on the floor before she could even try to catch it. Omar didn't even see the blow coming. His only warning was a buzzing in his ears. The blow hit so hard, that he couldn't see straight. Instead he sat there stunned, with tears pouring down his face uncontrollably. When he finally caught himself, Omar jumped at his sister, intent on doing damage. They exchanged headlocks, kicks, cuffs and bites. He managed to grab hold of a breast and squeezed with all his might till the girl hollered for murder.

She yanked both his ears in retaliation. Omar didn't let go until Pearl picked him up bodily and slammed him into the sofa. Omar bounced back up like a boxer ready for the next round, barely missing a kick below the belt as he danced to the back of the couch using it as protection. Brother and sister feinted and parried, each trying to anticipate the other's move. Omar stuck his tongue out at Pearl and made funny faces sticking his hands in his ears. "Nani nani boo boo! Yuh cyan catch me though." He sang."That's why yuh ugly and yuh foolish and I going put frogs in yuh bed!"

"If you ever put frogs in my bed Omar Walcott, I would hurt you so bad, you would wish you was never born!"

Omar bent down still dancing from left to right and picked up a handful of the dust in the heap beside him and threw it at his sister.

"Boy! You could only be stupid. You feel that you could dirty up the house that I just clean and get way wid it? Wait till I catch you!" Pearl chased her brother in circles, jumping over furniture and toppling chairs. When he ran to scatter more of her dust again, she went at him with the broom, knocking him hard on the ankles. He retaliated with a can of Baygon, spraying at the air in front of her. To Omar it was all just a game and it seemed not to matter that he was making his sister angrier by the minute. That is, until he saw her pick up the big rock that held the kitchen door open. Then he figured it was time to run.

Omar tore down the passage-way with Pearl hot on his heels. He just barely managed to slam the bathroom door shut as the rock collided with it and, thankfully, not his head. The dent the rock made was big enough to push the wood out on the other side. One wouldn't have to look hard to see what was going on inside that bathroom anymore. The door bulged and shifted as Pearl tried to force her way in. She had somehow managed to hold the handle down before he could get a chance to lock it with the key.

"Omar Walcott open this door now!" She banged hard with her fist.

Omar pressed his entire weight against the door in a vain attempt to keep it shut as Pearl practically screamed it down on the other side. He swore silently. His sister was almost as strong as she was determined. He was certain that were she to compete in the Olympics, be it a marathon or heptathlon she could beat anybody... Jackie Joyner, Flo Jo... "Aye girl stop pushing me!" The door bucked beneath his shoulder. "Why you don't lef me 'lone. You feel you bigger than me? Just wait! I going grow up you know." Omar switched to his back trying to apply his entire body weight but his feet slid across the tiles, his toes gripping at nothing. "You feel you badder than me?" In truth the girl could run, jump, pelt and cuss better than anybody he knew and she never seemed to get tired doing any of it. He, on the other hand, was quickly losing strength. With Jeffrey and Chicken he'd never played this rough yet!

Omar jammed his feet against the toilet bowl and pressed his back against the door, but every blow that Pearl gave reverberated through his body. The seat cover, not having been designed for exactly that type of use quickly succumbed to the pressure. Omar slipped, the door flew open and Pearl, not expecting so sudden a retreat, catapulted into the room. She crashed into the cabinet headfirst cracking the mirror. Momentarily stunned, she gazed at a dozen jagged reflections of herself and at Omar who sat on the broken toilet behind her panting for breath.

Trembling with anger Pearl pointed a finger at her recalcitrant brother. "Omar Walcott let me tell you something. I spend the whole afternoon cleaning this house and when Mummy come home, she expect it to be clean. I am not doing it again. So before I pelt some more cuffs in you, you better get up and go out there and clean up that mess that you make. And you better pick up that bird that you break. And when Mummy come home you is the one that going explain to her how it get so, not me." She stomped off into her bedroom and slammed the door shut. Omar sat on the toilet counting to ten, waiting for Pearl's inevitable encore. She opened the door at seven.
"And if I even step on so much as one of them pieces of glass, boy you going wish you did never born!"

Still short of breath, Omar eventually pulled himself up from his perch on the seat figuring he might as well do what his sister said and start cleaning. It was not as if he had anything else to do...in any case he supposed sweeping could be fun just as long as you didn't have to do it every day. He had just started picking up the pieces of the broken bird when his mother walked through the door.

The first thought Loretta had was that a thief had broken into her home, but since the television and stereo were still there, she began to worry about her children instead. She was following a trail of strange marks on the floor when she noticed Omar, his back to her, kneeling over something on the carpet.

"Omar what happen here, what you doing down there on the floor?" Omar turned to look back at his mother, exposing the piece of broken ornament in his hand.
"Who break that?"
"Pearl break it Mummy."
"How she break it?"
"She grab it from me."
"So if she broke it why are you cleaning it up?"
"Because she tell me to."

Loretta didn't wait to hear the rest. She was just so incensed at the sight of her home in such a state. The last thing she needed to do after a hard day's work was deal with difficult children. All she wanted to do was take a good shower and get rid of the stink of animal.... but instead her expensive ornaments were on the floor and her furniture scattered about the place '*like they buy with money from a money tree.*' She marched down the corridor, arms swinging. Her rubber boots squeaked leaving dusty footprints, adding further to the mess.

"PEARL!!!... Pearl come out here now!"

Pearl rested in her bedroom with the radio on, oblivious to the storm about to break. When Loretta first passed the bathroom she simply glanced in its direction. It wasn't until she'd travelled a few paces past the small room, that it finally hit her. The door was hanging on one hinge. Omar, who had been right behind her and not about to miss any of the action, collided with his mother when she suddenly stopped.

Loretta hands akimbo, cocked her head to one side, mouth open incredulous. "What happen to that door?" she asked too softly. Omar instinctively took a step back, no longer so certain he'd made the right decision to follow. He hesitated, afraid of his mother's reaction.
"I say what happen to my bathroom door!" she pointed for emphasis. "It got a hole in it."
"Pearl pelt a rock at it Mummy."
"Pearl what?..PEARL!!!"
Loretta was back down the corridor at full speed with Omar running behind to keep up with her long strides. If asked why he was still following, he wouldn't have been able to answer, except to say that sometimes his

mother's presence was so compelling even in anger, that he was drawn to her against his very will. His sister was definitely in trouble now and he was extremely glad he wasn't Pearl.

Omar hovered just outside the bedroom door while his mother blasted his sister. Pearl, who hadn't been expecting the situation to unfold quite as it did, was at a loss for words. How could she explain the damage done in the two hours that her mother had been away?

"...but Mummy, is not like it happen so! You see, I don't even know why I bothering to explain when you done take Omar's side already." Pearl crossed her arms and pouted.

"I don't take sides! I'm dealing with facts. I want to hear you explain to me how you manage to put that hole in my door and why every time I come home I have to be dealing with this foolishness. Loretta strode back over to the bathroom and vainly tried to right the door as it swung on one hinge. "And my mirror! Look at my mirror!"

"That is Omar doing, he let go the door on me."

"That is not true Mummy, don't believe her."

"What you was trying to do girl, kill your brother?"

As the argument travelled from bedroom to passageway, Omar retreated to the living room. Several of the soap opera regulars had already assembled for the evening's programme and were listening intently to the real life drama in progress. "Omar boy," a voice whispered from the window. "what is that you mudda and sista fighting 'bout?"

Omar perched nervously on the arm of a chair and tried to ignore them. He was beginning to feel a little guilty now, but only because in this instance he knew he had provoked Pearl. However he never understood why she took everything he did so personally. He figured even if it hadn't really been her fault this time, it would teach her to leave him alone and make up for all the other times she'd bullied him in the past.

The argument, now in full gear, had progressed into the living room. Omar's eyes followed his family worriedly. Loretta stood over Pearl gesticulating, making sure she righted every chair and cleaned every molecule of dust.

"...But Mummy...you see, none uh this ain fair, because all I was trying to do is what you tell me to do."

"I tell you to break my things and try to kill your brother?"

"You see! That is why I ain talking to you any more. You always on his side. You don't even want to know why it happen. Omar don't do nothing round this house...he don't even have to clean his bedroom, 'cause Junior or you always doing that."

"Well he's a little boy, how much you expect him to do?"

"He ain so little no more! He got a dog and he don't even feed it. If it weren't for me, Commando woulda starve by now."

"What dog got to do with a hole in my door? Answer me that, I want to know."

"How you get so old fashioned? Everybody else I know... at all the other houses I go to, the boy children got responsibilities...even Omar good friend Jeffrey... you mean just because he's a boy he cyan wash dishes!" Pearl's voice rose as her frustration increased.

"Listen, stop trying to find excuses, because I don't want to hear anymore. My show about to start and I don't want to hear any noise. I want silence." Loretta positioned herself in her favourite chair, which Davy had sensibly vacated. Pointedly ignoring her daughter, she hummed some unknown hymn to lighten her spirit. Omar counted to ten, certain there was more to come.

"All you got to do for me is fix back that bird and buy me back a bathroom door...and if I so much as step on one piece of glass, it going be me and you."

"Fix back? I ain fixing back nothing!" Pearl's chest heaved with loud objection, her nostrils flaring, her breathing erratic. Omar watched entranced as she became increasingly hysterical, clearly on the verge of tears. "Is not my fault that it break. Is that stupid little boy sitting down there, playing like he all innocent...I would like to know what you would do in this house without me. You feel I don't do nothing? Well I should dead tomorrow, *then* you would see!"

Loretta continued to ignore her daughter, intent on watching television. Pearl was so angry she began to cry uncontrollably as she pointed at Omar.

"...but no! All I got to do is wait, 'cause when this little son of a bitch grow up..." She twisted one of Omar's ears for emphasis, making him squeal.

"Aye Mummy! You see what she just do to me?"

Loretta stood up, all pretence of watching television forgotten. "What you just call me?" Heads, which had turned with interest minutes before, now turned even further and the volume on the television was shamelessly lowered.

"I say that when he grow up, that because of you he ain going have any respect for women. If you would put some good licks in he now..."

"You just call me a bitch?"

I never call you a bitch Mummy... I..."

"So if he's a son of a bitch, what that make me, not the bitch?" Loretta clasped her hands over her head and looked up at the ceiling in exaggerated prayer. "It was too good to be true. I should have known better than to expect that we could get through a whole day without something going wrong in this house!"

"Mummy, I never..."

"Listen Pearl Walcott, let me tell you something. Get out of my sight before I do something to you that I would regret."

"Mummy I didn't..." Pearl took a step forward grabbing hold of her mother's arms, eyes imploring.
"Go away, in your bedroom or someplace else where I can't see you..."
"No Mummy..."
"...but you see that fete tomorrow that you been planning all week with your friend Shelly? Well you could forget about it. You ain going nowhere now."
"How you mean I can't go, I have to go..."
"Take your hands off me girl!"
"...and I too big for you to tell me where I can't go!"
"Let go of me girl!" Mother and daughter grappled with each other, applying almost equal amounts of pressure as they staggered around the room.

Pearl's hands gripped her mother's arms tightly while Loretta pulled at her daughter's fingers with all her might. She shoved Pearl one final time, sending her stumbling into the back of the sofa. "That is where you wrong Pearl, because as long as you living in this house, you got to do what I say. And you could take the time that you home to think about how to respect me, instead of feeling that you are so much woman... and you could spend the time trying to figure out how you going pay me back for the things that you damage, because if you so big, then big people does got to pay when they break other people property in the real world."

A voice from the window said 'Amen.' Man or woman Omar couldn't tell, but he suddenly remembered that he had a mission to accomplish and if he didn't hurry his friends might give up on him. He looked out the window. It was not completely dark outside but the night was falling quickly and the moon had already risen above the trees. He could tell it was going to be a good night.

Omar escaped to his bedroom where he began collecting the items he'd hidden for the obeah ceremony. He could hear Pearl, still crying and carrying on to herself in the bathroom while she rummaged through the medicine cabinet. She made sure she spoke loud enough for everyone to hear, saying that they all made her sick, so sick that she needed to take something to ease the pain. Omar chuckled to himself. His sister could be so overly dramatic sometimes. One by one he gently lowered his collection of talismans to the ground and quietly slipped out the bedroom window after them.

* PEARL *
6

Omar squatted for a few minutes outside the window, allowing his eyes to become accustomed to the relative darkness. He was to meet Chicken by the big dunks tree where the road came to a dead end. From there they would head over to their usual spot together, where eventually Jeffrey would join them. They didn't want to give anyone reason to suspect that they were out together, or up to any mischief. Omar breathed a sigh of relief when he saw his friend already there before him.

"What keep you so long man? I been out here for musse near half hour already with the mosquitoes biting me up and thing. You tell me we supposed to lef our house when 'Days of Our Lives' done start and tha' was ever since. You know out here scary enough when you out here by yuhself. I hear werewolves howling and all kind a thing."

"Man my mother and my sister were quarrelling and thing. I couldn't lef till I mek sure she was watching TV and wouldn't miss me."

"Oh...wha' 'bout Jeffrey, he still meeting us there?"

"Yeah."

The boys made their way to the clammy cherry trees in virtual silence, each absorbed in his own thoughts, wondering whether they would get caught, or whether the obeah would work at all. They walked through the grove pushing aside the broad leaves and nimble branches which grazed their skin before snapping back into place. In the darkness of the trees it was impossible to see the little berries hiding in clusters around them. Each time they grabbed hold of a branch, the berries would invariably burst leaving gooey stains on their hands and clothing. Their slippers slapped and crunched against rocks and dried twigs adding to the eerie atmosphere. When an angry cattle egret protested with a loud scream at their disturbance of his sleep, the friends' doubts increased. The bird flew away to a higher branch on another tree, its white feathers glowing in the pale moonlight. A hundred other feathers ruffled and fluttered echoing the egret's displeasure. The boys stood still for a moment, unsure of how or whether to move on.

When they finally broke through the oppressive embrace of the trees, Omar and Chicken inhaled large gulps of air, exhilarated by their newfound freedom and conquest over imagined evils. The two large coral boulders shone like beacons in the night, religious relics from some early age. The boys talked loudly filling the night's silence with their voices. Chicken unpacked the items he'd collected in his makeshift bundle, using one of his mother's old sheets. Each of the boys was to bring an old sheet as part of the ceremony and wrap it around them toga style. Now Omar rested his on top of one of the boulders and concentrated on organising the can of blood, his mother's cou cou stick, and a carefully selected array of talismans all in a neat line.

"You remember to bring the doll Chicken?"
"Yeah."
"Leh me see it."
The doll was one of Abuela's from her extensive collection of Mexican souvenirs. Omar turned it over in his hands examining the intricate weaving of its shawl. He could just make out the red, white, and green threads. He squeezed the doll till his fingers met through the soft cotton of its stomach. Omar smiled, it bounced back when he let go. The doll was perfect.
"Cool, you bring the pins too?"
"Yeah...you think we should stick them in right now?"
"No. Wait till Jeffrey come. That is part of the ceremony... but where he is though? He taking very long."
"You know."
"...but maybe we could stick on the hair. We could stick on Pearl hair to the doll now."
"Yeah, what you going stick it with, you got glue?"
"I got glue *and* a needle and thread. Which one you feel would work better?"
"It depend. The glue should be faster."

"But wait Chicken, you got to take back this doll or we could keep it?"
"Nah dread, my grandmother got so many of them she ain going notice. I find this one in the cupboard."
"So I could take off the hair then to put on Pearl one?"
"Well of course."

Omar worked on pulling off the doll's hair; it was nicely braided into two fat black plaits which had been sewn on quite securely. He had to yank quite hard before it would give way. Chicken picked up the clump of Pearl's hair which Omar had collected from one of her combs. He balanced it on top of the doll's head trying to imagine how it would look when stuck.
"So where the glue?"
"The clammy cherries."
"You going pick clammy cherries now!"
"No foolish. I picked them before. How you expect me to find them things in the dark?"
"But Omar, you sure that going stick?" Is one thing to stick kite paper, but is another thing to stick Pearl hair to a piece uh cloth."
"Well if it don't work we could always sew it."
Chicken was sceptical, but Omar went ahead and burst the little berries he'd gathered anyway. They were the nice dark orangey-brown ones. Not too old or too young, but just ripe. The goo that oozed out was rich and thick. He squeezed it from the berries onto the doll's head, spread it around a little, and then placed

Pearl's hair on top, a few strands at a time. Chicken marvelled at his precision.
"Boy you getting very technical"
"Well how else you expect it to stick?"

When the job was done, Omar licked his fingers to rid them of the sticky substance. It was sweet to taste and Omar smacked his lips in satisfaction. Chicken grimaced.
"It ain look bad at all nuh?" Omar held the doll up to the moonlight and the boys examined his handiwork.
"Fellahs!"
"AAH ahh!" Omar and Chicken clutched each other in fright, completely unprepared for Jeffrey's sudden arrival.
"Jeffrey! You near give we a heart attack! How you could sneak up on a man so?"
"But wunnuh ain hear me? I was hollering for you ever since. If it wasn't for your dog, I musse woulda never find my way through them trees."
"My dog? Commando out here?"
Jeffrey looked around. "Well he somewhere 'bout, must be chasing rats or something."
"Boy wha' tek you so long? We out here waiting 'pon you ever since!"
"Yeah, it tek you suh long to eat lil dinner?"
"You! I had to play I sick yuh. When we get there they had so much people, since is Friday night everybody want to eat out and it take forever for we to get food. And then my father see one uh he friends and

play he talking 'bout cricket and all bundle a things. Man I had to hold me belly and play I sick to get back here in time yuh. All like now he feel I in my bed sleeping. I had to puff it up with some pillows and ting, so I can't stay bout here too long, in case he miss me."

"Well like tonight ain a good night for none a we, so leh we get started quick then."

"Yeah I ready men."

Jeffrey took charge like a drill sergeant, making sure that they had all the ingredients.

"We got the chicken blood Omar?"

"Check."

"Where it is?"

"There in the can."

"We got the pins and needles?"

"Check."

"What about the doll?"

Omar held it up, pointing to Pearl's hair already glued to its head.

"Very good. It look real. What about the newspaper"

"Got that too."

"Good, so we got everything and I got the kerosene oil to light the fire and the mixing bowl to work the obeah potion in.

The boys draped their sheets over themselves, first wrapping them around their waists then dropping the corner over one shoulder, toga style. Jeffrey, who

was supposed to be the obeah priest/witchdoctor of sorts, draped his sheet over his head and shoulders. He argued that the look was much more distinguished, befitting someone of his stature. He held three long feathers in each hand - from the rooster's tail no less. These he would use to help gain the favour of the obeah spirits. Omar and Chicken were his subjects and would do everything as he commanded. The bonfire sizzled, its flames dancing happily over the dry twigs. Jeffrey pulled a long stick from the fire and drew a large circle around them in the dirt. Then he stretched out his arms and began chanting.
"Abra cadabra doom bo loo boo !...repeat after me."
"Abra cadabra?" Chicken snorted. "Wha' sort ah obeah language tha' is boah?"
"The only one I know foolish! You going repeat after me or not?"
"How we supposed to repeat after you, when you ain even know what you saying?"
"Shut up Chicken" Omar smacked his friend on the head with the doll and then nodded for Jeffrey to continue the ceremony.

The boys began their tuneless humming, accompanied by the steady beat of Chicken's drum, fashioned from an old Bico ice cream container. He squatted by the fire nodding his head to the rhythm. One by one Omar added the ingredients to the mixing bowl, while Jeffrey swayed from side to side, waving his chicken feathers in the air. First to go in was the blood, followed by more of Pearl's hair, then some water, dirt and a handful of clammy cherries thrown in for good measure. These were supposed to gather strength from the four elements: water, earth, wind and fire. The boys reasoned that if obeah spirits truly existed, then they would surely come when these were all together.

As each ingredient was added, Jeffrey would suddenly lean forward and chant, palms lifted skywards.... *"Uhh hang guh hang guh, uhh hang guh hang guh, Pearl will learn, Pearl will learn."* Then Omar would let out a shrill *"ieeeh! Aye aye aye ieee!"* He'd roll his eyes into the back of his head and pretend to have difficulty staying upright. Chicken was similarly afflicted, becoming so possessed by spirits that he would convulse on the ground unable to beat his drum. Unfortunately he kept spoiling the effect by bursting into fits of giggles, especially when Commando showed up chasing a frog around the fire. The poor frog could barely hop and was bleeding out of one eye. The dog brought his catch over to Omar, proud of himself. Omar patted him on the head. "Good boy Commando, good dog." Each time the frog tried to limp away Commando chased after it barking and turning it onto its back.
"But c'dear he really doing that frog bad enough though. Omar why you don't tek it 'way."
"And do what with it Chicken? The frog almost dead, he ain' going live too long."

"Well I don't know, but how you would feel if somebody do you so?" The boys momentarily suspended their ritual to consider the animal's fate.
"The best thing to do is kill it quick. Pass me one uh them rocks there Jeff."

No sooner had Jeffrey tossed the rock to Omar, than the frog was dead and mixed up in the obeah concoction without another thought. Their chanting resumed, Omar recommenced stirring the mixture with the new addition rolling around inside. Jeffrey chuckled to himself thinking of his mother. If she only knew what her son was up to. To her, kitchen utensils were sacred; in fact anything to do with the kitchen was sacred. Seeing these children with her good mixing bowl full of chicken blood and a dead frog rolling around inside would have been enough to give her the heart attack she was always threatening to have.

They chanted until their voices became hoarse. Commando ran around them in excited circles as they danced and called out to the spirits. Abuela's doll had been stuck in its hands, feet, stomach, and head before they finally ran out of pins. Each boy sprinkled it with a few drops of the potion mumbling gibberish. They took turns singeing its hands and feet with the fire. By the time they figured it was time to go home, the doll was beyond recognition.

They transferred the potion - frog and all, into a rusted enamel pot, which Omar had found in his mother's back- yard. Pearl's effigy was placed in the very centre. Then they doused the fire with water, kicking dust over the remaining embers at their feet. It was time to go home. The rest would be up to Omar. He had to find the right moment to slip it under Pearl's bed. The three friends gathered their paraphernalia together and walked forward feeling a sense of accomplishment. They had little doubt, after a ritual as complete as theirs, that Pearl could ever be the same again.

* PEARL *
7

"You get de money Omar?" The boys stopped arguing as Omar sat down on the porch step next to them.
"What Jeffrey?"
"I ask you if you got de money."
"Oh, yeah." Omar was quite obviously distracted.
"I bet you tief that from Pearlie nuh."
"And so what!" He became instantly annoyed. "That ain got nothing to do with you."
"So what tek you so long then?" Chicken challenged.
"I wasn't gone so long."
"Oh yes, you was in there a good, ten minutes. What happen, Pearlie catch you again?"
"She tell you dat she going to tell you mudda 'pon you?" "She hit you again Omar?"
"She couldn't ah hit he, we woulda hear he hollering all de way to Bridgetown if she hada hit he."
"Wha' happen Omar?"

Questions were being fired left, right, and centre. Omar couldn't help feeling it was like having two annoying mosquitoes buzzing around his ears. He raised his hands to cover them in a desperate attempt

to block out their noise. His friends almost missed his mumbled reply: "No I break de lamp."
"You break de lamp?"
"What lamp, Pearl lamp?" The buzzing in Omar's ears grew even louder. He looked up sorrowfully. "Yes, Pearl lamp."

This unwelcome news had Chicken jumping to his feet, looking furtively over his shoulder. "You mean de de de lamp, in P...P.PPearl room?" the stutter he normally managed to conceal was suddenly out of control. "Cheeze on! Where she is? I ..I..I...going home now before de licks start sharing, c.cc...ca 'cause I ain want nobody to think I had anything to do w..w... wid it."

Jeffrey practically bent himself double with laughter. This was typical Chicken, one hundred percent gone and quicker than a house could burn down. "Man, nobody could clear out faster than you boy"

"Pearl ain know yet; she still sleeping." Omar mumbled again. He dragged himself up the banister and stood. "All the sand that was inside the lamp spill on the floor. Wunnuh could come and help me clean it up?"
"Help you do what!" both boys shrieked.
"If the three of us clean it up together, we could be out of there before Pearl wake up."
"Before Pearl wake up? You mean she in de room?"

Jeffrey started collecting his marbles and putting them into his pants pocket. Meanwhile Chicken had already found his slippers and was putting them on his feet.

"So what wunnuh doing, wunnuh going just lef me?"

"But Omar *you* brek de lamp, not we!"

"You can't be for real! What if she wake up? All ah we going be in trouble..."

"But that is only *if* she wake up."

"How you mean *if*? Pearl just like my sister and my sister don't miss nutting. If I even pass by she bedroom door, she know it."

"But Jeffrey, what you feel going happen if she ketch me in there? She going tell Mummy and everybody going find out we were betting again."

"What you trying to say Omar, that if you get catch you going tell on us and make all uh we get in trouble? You know what my mother would do to me if she hear that I was out here betting fuh money?"

"All I trying to say Jeffrey is that if the three uh we go in there and clean up, we would finish faster. We could be real quiet and be out of there in two minutes. If I go inside and pass the things to you from the door, she wouldn't hear me walking 'bout in the room."

Jeffrey and Chicken harrumphed, still unconvinced by Omar's reasoning.

"I can't believe that wunnuh don't want to help me. When I think 'bout all the times I get *you* Jeffrey and *you* Chicken out uh trouble...and all wunnuh got to do is help me clean up lil' sand and cyan even do that. *Boy! you's really know who you friends is when you need them."*

Omar turned away from Chicken and Jeffrey and headed towards the house dejectedly. His head hung sorrowfully, his movements deliberately slow. He was a real pro at making his friends feel guilty. The two traitors watched him climb up each step by painful step, their doubts reflected in their solemn gazes. When Omar turned back for one last look, his eyes watered over and his bottom lip quivered dangerously. By the time he'd turned the door handle, Jeffrey and Chicken had caved in. They walked grudgingly up the stairs behind him, the resentment pouring from their eyes enough to burn holes in his back. Omar on the other hand underwent a truly miraculous recovery and was suddenly all smiles. He held the door open for his friends and let them pass through. Jeffrey held up a menacing fist. "You going pay for this boy."

Omar, Jeffrey and Chicken tiptoed stealthily into the house, only to freeze in perfect synchrony whenever a loose floorboard gave under their collective weight. Omar led the way, still afraid to voice his concern that Pearl could be more than just sleeping. The boys entered the dim room, its blue walls adding a surreal quality to the entire episode. With a feeling of dread they watched Omar bend down to pick up the fallen lamp. Their eyes narrowed, bodies prepared to run, should one hair on Pearl's body even appear to move. They passed along the bits of broken glass as in an assembly line at a factory - Omar to Jeffrey - Jeffrey to Chicken. Chicken, nearest the door was dropping them into a bag lined with newspaper. This was closely followed by a dustpan filled with sand, then Jeffrey whispering in a silence so profound as to be deafening; "She still sleeping?"

Omar who had just started picking up little fragments of glass off the floor jumped at the sound, spun around and bumped into Pearl's hand where it hung over the bed. There was a collective gasp as the friends watched her perfume bottle fall and roll along the wooden night table, the rumble seeming more like the engine of a 747, than that of a four-inch bauble which dropped to the floor with a tinkling crash. Yet unbelievably, Pearl didn't budge. It was at this moment that Jeffrey's curiosity got the better of him. Fascinated by Pearl's lack of movement, he began to lightly prod and poke her. Chicken and Omar watched in horror, completely riveted to the spot. Jeffrey blew on her face and tugged at a loose strand of hair. "Omar you sister like she knock out or something, 'cause I never see nobody sleep so hard yet."

Chicken, inched closer to the door, trembling as he begged Jeffrey to stop troubling her. "Omar, you think she sick?"
"I don't know Jeffrey. Check and see if she breathing."
They all held their breaths as Jeffrey pressed his weight on the bed and leaned over Pearl, resting his head on her chest.
"I don't hear she heart beating. And I cyan feel no breath coming out uh she nose neither."

The boys stared wide-eyed at Pearl, then at each other.
"You think she dead?" asked Omar in barely a whisper.
"I don't know."
"What we going do?"
"We got to tell somebody."
"We ain't got to do nothing! I ain't going to do nothing argued Chicken. This ain't got nothing to do wid me and I going home." Chicken who had actually found himself hovering over the body gripping Omar's hand, suddenly let go and spun around to escape the room. In his effort to do so, he tripped over Omar's foot and crashed into the bed, stubbing his toe on something in the corner. A white enamel pan went skittering across the floor leaving a trail of blood and feathers in its wake.
"Wha' tha' is?" Chicken's voice rose higher as he held his hurt toe.
"Oh shoot! de obeah pot."
"Omar, we forget about de obeah!"

"Oh Lord Jeffrey! You think it work?" The three boys were almost hysterical with fear. Omar grabbed hold of Jeffrey by the shoulders, his nails biting into the older boy's worn blue T-shirt.

"You think we kill Pearlie wid de obeah Jeffrey?"

"Oh Lord bless Moses." whimpered Chicken. "We in real trouble now."

For the first time in their lives the three friends were at a complete loss for words. And not even their over-active imaginations could figure a way out of the mess they'd gotten themselves into this time.

Somehow, they managed to clean up the mess of blood and chicken feathers. And somehow, they managed to flush the mangled frog down the toilet. But no one knew what to do with the doll. No one knew what the doll could do to them. Jeffrey fingered the knotted plastic bag hidden in his back pocket. Had he really volunteered to dispose of it? What if the curse still lingered and could somehow be transferred to him?

Beside him Omar drew in a deep breath. He wished fervently that his life could be as simple as a rented movie, where with the push of a button he could rewind into yesterday and undo all that he had done. Chicken, not quite so inclined to such flights of fancy, frankly wished he wasn't there. Instead they found themselves standing a stone's throw away from Omar's Uncle Junior, working up the courage to tell him about their unfortunate discovery. But how did one go about confessing a crime without actually being punished for it?

Omar stared out ahead. Less than ten yards separated him from his past and his future; the path to inevitable change, an open side-door and a cold cement step caressing the soles of his feet. He shivered in spite of the warmth generated from the two bodies huddled so closely beside him. As they stood there poised on the threshold of indecision, Omar pulled into him energy and strength from all the forces around. To his nostrils came the scent of hot earth and limestone gravel baked in the sun. It mingled with the scent of grass, farm animals and the unmistakable odour of fear and man. It was the sweat of his uncle's hard labour glistening on his brow as he worked on his motorcycle...the sweat of his own fear dripping from his armpits like a tap with a washer gone bad. Just a few yards and they'd be able to touch him. Yet it seemed like such a task. Omar projected his thoughts across the distance, willing his uncle to look up. As if on cue, Junior raised his head, smiled and waved.

Junior was about twenty-eight. This Omar knew from a birthday dedication some woman named Sandy had made over the radio several months ago. What he actually did for a living was a question that had never crossed Omar's mind however. He was just simply his Uncle Junior with the motorcycle. The Honda CBR 1100XX Super Blackbird. Of slim build and average height for a man, Junior possessed one of those ageless black people faces that didn't do you much good when you went looking for a job. Prospective employers automatically seemed to lump him into the category of young and inexperienced. It was a constant source of irritation for him. Hence the goatee beard which he presently sported, hoping to add a touch of maturity to his unlined features.

As usual he was fiddling around with that precious motorcycle of his. He was always adding another feature, always washing, always polishing. The Blackbird, which incidentally was red, had never spent a night alone outside. It slept in Omar's and Junior's small bedroom with a special cover to prevent the paint work getting scratched...and Omar absolutely was not allowed to touch. He still remembered the one time Junior had given him a ride when it first came home. They'd cruised all round the countryside, testing hills and curves. Whenever they found a piece of straight road Junior would show him just how fast his racer could go. *Up to 300 Km an hour! Four cylinder! 143 horse power!* Omar didn't know what any of it meant, but he'd sure had an unforgettable time. They'd both felt like kings. Omar because he was the very first passenger Junior had allowed to sit on his Blackbird and Junior because he'd gotten a great deal trading in his Kawasaki Ninja ZX-6R for an unbelievable price. The Blackbird's arrival brought to the house a week full of excited tension. "It was not that he hadn't liked his Ninja", Junior said. It was just that the Blackbird was faster, sleeker and best of all had more room than the Ninja, which translated, meant he'd be able to take the girls for a ride. Of all of the motorcycle's attributes that final feature seemed to have been the deciding factor.

Omar guessed his uncle must have at least been ok looking since he was always talking about "*his girls*" or "*a hot date wid de outside woman.*" On the other hand, if Pearl and Shelly were to be believed, the three women to one man ratio in Barbados had a lot more to do with his uncle's success rate in the female department than with any particular charm or good looks he might possess. Whatever the reason, Junior's number two pastime was the "*women*" followed closely by personal grooming, and then somewhere after that was let Omar hang around and learn a trick or two. So having taken care of the personal grooming and just having finished polishing his Blackbird he was in really good spirits when Omar and the boys showed up.

Jeffrey pushed his friend forward.
"Aye." whispered Omar irritably. "Don't push me."

It felt as if everything around him had come to a virtual standstill, as if he were moving in slow motion. A non-existent wind rushed past his ears and Omar felt as if he would faint. Jeffrey shoved him again.
"Guh long man, we right behind you."
With a resolute sigh, Omar shrugged his shoulders and took a tentative step forward.
"You boys behaving wunnuh selves out there?" The boys did not respond.
However, Jeffrey's hand rested heavily in the small of Omar's back, silently urging his friend forward.
"Eh? I can't hear you." Junior said without turning around.
"You all very quiet." He blew on the Blackbird's side mirror and rubbed off an imaginary spot. When the silence continued, he finally stopped paying tribute to his machine and turned around shaking the excess water out of his shammy.

"What you all doing over there in that corner whispering so?"
Jeffrey with a nod from Chicken gave Omar a big shove. It sent him hurtling forward several feet in Junior's direction.
"You got something to tell me boy? I hope you ain getting into no trouble. "Where Pearl?" Omar fidgeted with his hands and clothing, looking everywhere but at his uncle.

"Junior, we think something happen to Pearl." That Omar was able to get so many words out of his mouth was a miracle, which could only be attributed to the great trust he had in the man before him. He was so much more like his own big brother than his mother's younger brother. Junior had been living with the Walcotts for as long as Omar could remember. The fact that they shared the same room made Omar feel even closer to him, although these days Junior spent more time away than at home. Omar still felt his uncle was the one person in the house to whom he could relate most. Junior always seemed to make time for him. Even when he caught Omar doing something wrong he never made a fuss about it like Pearl did by telling his mother. He had his own nice way of dealing with the situation.

"You *think* something happen to Pearl? She crying or something?"

"No..."

"She send you out here for me?"

"No..."

"So what make you think something happen to her then?" Junior stood with his feet apart, arms folded across his chest and looked down at Omar, a grin spreading across his face. "Listen Omar, I tell you already that your tricks can't work on me. I'm a big man!"

Chicken and Jeffrey fidgeted restlessly from side to side. "Tell de man Omar..."

"Oh Lord and he got the two friends in on it too! Alright Omar, leh me hear this one now."
"But Junior, I already tell you!"
"Tell me what?"
"That something wrong wid Pearl!" Omar stomped his foot in frustration, he knew it was his fault his uncle didn't believe him.
"Something like what Omar?"
"I don't know you got to come and see."

Junior raised his chin laughing. "So this is the part where I supposed to follow you..." All three boys nodded in agreement. "...and then a bucket a water going drop on my head when I walk through the door right?"
"No Junior, honest she in the bed and won't move."
Junior gave his nephew three hearty slaps on the back and went back to his motorbike. "Forget it my boy, I ain falling for that one. Come with something lil' newer next time."
"But Junior I serious!"
"Forget it Omar, he don't believe us." said Jeffrey leading his friend away.
"Yuh right I don't believe you." Junior said still chuckling.
"But Junior, I swear. Pearl laying down in the bed and she ain moving." continued Omar, still trying to reason with his uncle. "Look, you see Pearl for the day yet?"
"Yeh I see Pearl this morning."

"Where she was?"
"In bed nuh."
"Well she still in bed all like now so. She's don't normally be in the shop? The shop ain even open yet." Junior looked across at the house, noticing that what Omar said was true. His brows furrowed wondering if the boys could indeed be telling the truth, or if they would really go to such lengths to play a silly prank. He scratched his goatee thoughtfully. "Listen Omar, I don't have time for you and your tricks this morning. I got people to see in town, but I going tell you what, if when I come back Pearl still in bed, we going call the docta. Ok?" Junior slapped the rag he was polishing the bike with over the fence and prepared to leave. Already pumping gas into the engine he smiled at his nephew. Omar ran after him. "Junior, where you going? When you coming back? Wha' we supposed to do?" After the dust had finally settled, he still didn't have an answer.

For what seemed like an eternity the three friends stood there speechless, staring at nothing, until the rain started falling. Whatever the length of time, the rain seemed to bring with it an ominous sign of untold troubles to come. It began with absolutely no fanfare. No warning drizzles or grey skies, no loss of leaves from briskly swaying trees.

Up until that moment the sun had been blistering hot - the entire day, week, month, year. Now in less than a heartbeat, all that had changed. Suddenly people were forced to scamper for cover like wild animals attempting to outrun a forest fire. The clouds simply rolled in and water let loose. Big, fat, pregnant drops which fell like rocks and pelted everyone and everything in their path. Young plants bent under the weight, ill constructed drain pipes clogged up and spilled over. And the rain just kept moving forward intent on covering the entire island. Coconut trees tossed their fronds every which way, unable to withstand the strong winds. And Omar, Chicken and Jeffrey stood in the middle of it all, incapable of movement - As taken aback by the sudden change in weather, as they were by the realisation that Pearl was dead.

Omar stood in the rain looking down at his mud splattered feet and soaking wet clothing. The sky was a roiling mass of clouds and water. He held out his hands watching the water droplets fall in big fat globs. His eyes played tricks on him turning simple raindrops into blood trickling ominously down instead. If there was a God then he must surely be angry. All three boys shivered and hugged themselves, inconsolable. They parted ways with few words, each to his own home and his own bed, absorbed in his thoughts, tormented by guilt and fear of retribution.

* PEARL *
8

Junior had hardly been roaring down the road for more than three or four minutes when the rain started falling. The once brilliant sun was suddenly cloaked in a blanket of cloud so thick it seemed night would never again see day. It came from the direction of home and with each roll of thunder crept over Junior a greater sense of foreboding. As Junior looked over his shoulder, his thoughts returned to his last encounter with Omar. Had he been right to leave his little nephew and friends alone? Should he have believed their fantastic story? Was it at all possible that something had truly happened to Pearl?

"Nah man." Junior spoke out loud, looking over his shoulder one last time. He could feel the rain behind him almost racing to catch up and all the hairs on his body prickled with anticipation of the hard pellets soon to hit. Raindrops as loud as a hundred footsteps closed in on him, rushing him like an angry mob, making one liquid sculpture out of man and bike. Water seemed to pour from every available crevice in Junior's body. He squinted in an attempt to see through the blinding showers. Should he go forward or turn back? Suddenly before he could come to a decision, Junior's entire world turned on its axis, a sharp explosive jolt the only warning of impending danger. He struggled to hold on for dear life as the motorcycle bumped and twisted crazily across the road. Tufts of dirt and grass spewed out from beneath as he lost control of the bike running into a wall of khus khus. With thin blades snagging his clothing and tearing his flesh, Junior fought wildly to stop the bike's descent over a steep ditch, pressing brakes, using his feet to dig into whatever rock, shrub, or anything that still seemed securely imbedded in the earth. When he finally came to a halt, his bike several feet away, Junior got up panting for breath, legs shaking uncontrollably. All he could do was stare at the metres long skid marks he'd left behind.

Omar walked like an old man towards home. Bent in two he hugged himself, crying. His tears mingled with the rainwater. He didn't want to go inside, be in there with the dead body, but he couldn't imagine where else to go. How could he tell his mother that her daughter was dead and that he had killed her? He walked through the house soundlessly, feeling miserable.

For the first time in his life, Omar had a headache. He had a stomach-ache too, but not from over eating.

As he walked along the dark passageway that led to the bedrooms, he started pulling at his rain soaked T-shirt and shorts. They landed in a pile by the bed, causing a large puddle to quickly form. Then he rolled into bed and lay on his side pulling the covers with him. Omar dared not look in the direction of Pearl's room but he could still feel the light filtering through to his in the shifting shadows of rain clouds floating by. The only reason he hadn't closed his door was because it would make his mother more suspicious to see it so in the middle of the day.

When Chicken reached home his grandmother was looking worriedly out the window. She waited for him with blanket in hand. She hauled him in and slapped him on the back of the head, as she cussed him in Spanish for getting caught in the rain and making her worry so. "Ay *mi madré! ay mi madré, no sé qué hacer con este niño":* What to do with this child. Abuela stripped him right there in the middle of the floor. She bundled him up in the blanket, even forcing hot tea down his throat before she sent him to bed so he wouldn't catch cold.

Jeffrey fortunately was spared that humiliation. However, because he was unusually quiet he instantly became a source of entertainment for his sister Shelly who began teasing him about being lovesick over some girl at school. '*...the minute he found out who had gone about spreading his business he'd fix them.*' Jeffrey mused vexedly to himself. '...*all he needed to do was show them what had happened to Pearl, tell them it was his obeah, and then they'd all be scared. Hell he was scared!*' Jeffrey sat in front of the TV with remote control in hand, raising the volume louder and louder hoping to drown out his sister's taunts. But all he could think about was that harrowing trip to and from their playing field by the clammy cherry trees, where he'd hidden the bedraggled doll in a quickly excavated grave. After which he'd spent the next half hour trying to get the incriminating mud and gravel from under his nails.

Omar knew the law very well from watching so much TV, especially the silly soap operas which you couldn't help but hear all over the house...'cause with every Tom, Dick and Harry talking loud giving you ongoing commentary, Mummy would always be turning up the volume. Those people were always killing one another and getting into all kinds of trouble with the law. So Omar knew without a doubt that you couldn't put a ten-year-old minor into jail for accidentally killing his sister. But he'd heard about Dodds and other places for boys who had gotten into trouble and were too young for a real jail. He also most certainly didn't want to end up in any insane asylum like the one down Black Rock.

He'd seen the vacant look in those people's eyes holding onto the gates, calling out to anyone who would listen and he hadn't forgotten about the four who had escaped by burning down an entire wing of the hospital just so that they could get out and party with all the other Kadooment revellers. '*Them was real mad people.*' He, most of all, could not imagine having his hands tied behind his back in one of those white coat things. He remembered that from a movie where even the walls of the room were padded so the guy couldn't hurt his head whenever he started running about like a monkey. God only knew what they would do with him! Omar stared at the wall thinking these terrible thoughts, certain that if necessary God would create a special place in hell for him.

Eventually Omar fell into a fitful sleep. He lay across his bed, wrapped in sheets damp from his wet body, having dreams of hellfire and damnation. Spirits in white sheets taunted him. The rain, which was pouring down in violent torrents, entered his sleep to the rhythm of drums and howling winds. Had Omar not already been wet he would have been soaked anyway with the sweat of his own fear. He trembled in his sleep, the words Pearl, Pearl chanting ominously in his dreams.

While everyone else was either indoors or wrapped up, a frustrated Junior attempted to shelter from the rain under a nearby bus stand. The explosion was apparently the result of a punctured front tyre. The cause, a beer bottle, which some individual had carelessly discarded in the road. Whether from a passing car or someone awaiting the bus, the bottle was there and now Junior was forced to stop. He ran a reverent hand over his wounded bird, calculating the cost of repairs. The left side-mirror was completely shattered. He knew he should consider himself lucky since he'd forgotten to wear his helmet, but how was he supposed to feel when his thousand-dollar paint job was all scratched up! He was not in a good mood at all.

Junior pulled his shirt collar up over his head and folded his arms. The old country bus shelter under which he stood was of simple construction. With a pillar on either side and a slab on top, it stopped none of the rain from coming in. "I cyan barely see in front of me. Damn country cyan even mek a bus shelter that does keep off de rain. I getting wet from de back, front and de top too." Junior chupsed, then chupsed again. "If I ever catch de man dat drop dis bottle here, it going be me and he! Rain wetting my face, in my mout' and all."

Junior remained huddled under the inadequate shelter of the bus stand for more than fifteen minutes before the skies finally offered small reprieve. He looked over his baby checking to see if she was any worse for wear

from having been exposed to the rain. The Blackbird had never slept anywhere other than in his bedroom, and was only ridden in the rain when he had no other alternative. He was known for taking the bus if the rain fell for more than two days straight. Now he stood over her crooning.
"You ok baby?"
"I so sorry you get wet"
"I ain even got nothing to wipe you off wid." Look at how your tyre tear up though nuh". Junior looked up the road with hope and apprehension in his eyes, but all he could see was endless khus khus grass and sugarcane.

Junior spent what felt like an eternity just staring into space. The rain had let up some more and was now just a faint drizzle; already patches of blue had begun to reappear in the sky. Gradually he became aware of the distant drone of an engine accompanied by the low *Boom..Boom..Boom* of dub music. Junior instinctively adjusted his clothing. Whoever they were, they were coming fast.

A bright red L200 suddenly appeared around the bend playing a popular old dub tune by Beanie Man. As the pickup zoomed past, the driver's gaze met Junior's. Both heads turned, eyes locked in recognition. It was Michael, from work. He'd know those pale grey eyes set in a face too deeply tanned to be a tourist anywhere.

The truck came to a screeching halt some twenty-five metres up the road.
Michael stuck his head out and hollered. "Wait! Junior dat is you?"
"Michael?"
"Junior! What you doing out here in the middle uh de road?"
Junior held up his hands in helpless surrender then pointed at his broken bike. Michael put the L200 in reverse and backed up till he was alongside Junior. His arm hung out the window like a ZR driver's.
"My man wha' happen to you?"

A large blue tarpaulin covered the open back of the pick-up. Now it shifted. Until that moment Junior had assumed Michael was carrying a load of marl. Five pairs of curious eyes peered out at Junior, each wanting to understand the reason for the truck's sudden halt.
"Michael man, I just frig up my tyre man!"
Michael looked at the Blackbird, following the skid marks in the road. He knew how much Junior loved his motorcycle. "Jesus, but you like you skid far enough. The bike still working?"
"It seem so." Junior said revving up the motor.
"What direction you heading?"
"I was looking to go to town, I don't suppose you'll be able to give me a drop someplace, 'cause I can't leave my bike out here so."

"Man we going Cattlewash, to a party my cousin got down there. If you want, you could come down wid we first, I would drop de fellas off then carry you back. At most I might got to stay half hour to help them with a few things, but after that we could go."
"Yeah man! Thanks Michael, that could work. That sound cool."
"You want some help with that nuh?" Michael nodded in the direction of the motorbike. He opened the door and jumped out of the truck. Junior was beyond grateful. Both he and Michael worked in the sales department at the Toyota dealership in town. Michael was cool, even the way he spoke was easy going.
"Look at dem idiots back there do nuh, check Steven and Sean done drunk a'ready."
"I see them man, they ain even checking fuh me."
Steven raised a beer bottle in an unsteady salute to Junior, and laughed. "Yeah man Junior we checking you man." Steven and Sean also worked at the dealers. "Pass up de bike and we going mek room fuh the Blackbird, 'right fellahs!"
"Right!" everyone chorused. They hauled the Honda 1100 XX Super Blackbird up into the back of the pickup with the others. It was heavy and took up lots of room. Everyone had to move to the other side to accommodate the bike. Junior dripped his way over to the back corner next to it and held it firm. Rivulets of water trickled down his neck and his clothes stuck to

him, he felt uncomfortable. Michael got back behind the wheel and they drove off for the East Coast.

"Hey Junior you want a beer man?"
"Thanks Sean."
"Steven pass Junior a Banks man!"
Both Steven and Sean were white boys, friendly enough when they were at work, but Junior had never gotten too close to them knowing that they were in some way related to the owners of the company. Michael was much easier to get on with, maybe because he was mulatto, he was able to relate to both races...who knew? There were other pretty boys at the office whom Junior didn't like at all. He really hoped Michael meant what he said about just dropping the guys off, because if there was a whole load of Steven's and Sean's at the party, he didn't want to be there.

"Somebody change that damn music, man." Someone Junior didn't know started to complain about Michael's choice of music. He knocked on the glass by Junior's head. "This is Crop Over we shouldn't be listening to no dub music, we should be listening to calypso." Steven stood, kicking off the tarpaulin and started doing a little jig. "We should be chipping to some 'Paper Bag' or 'Mighty Thunder' man." Michael stopped the tape and tuned into one of the more popular stations. A slow Soca beat came on and everyone in the truck groaned. Junior held his head as if in pain. The same person who'd complained before raised his voice again. "I don't want to hear another Coco Tee song, he too foolish, Michael change the station!"

They finally settled on 99.9 FM, which was playing all of the more up-tempo party tunes. Junior sighed with relief and let go of his head. He took a long swig of beer and rested his head on the truck's back window. "That's much better." Actually he was surprised that Michael even had a dub tape. At work he and his friends were always listening to some sort of heavy metal music...not Junior's style... but then again they didn't have that much in common. He didn't have a white mother from the States or a father who was an offshore lawyer. Michael was into surfing and boogie boarding and all those little rich boy things. He was at least three years younger than Junior and could already afford his own ride. Junior would be paying for his Blackbird in monthly instalments for the next two years! No his life was very different. He took another swig of his beer and wondered for a moment what the others were doing back at home.

* PEARL *

9

Loretta Walcott was tired as a dog. It was years since she had made pudding and souse from scratch. Tomorrow was the church picnic and she and Annie had promised to bring a dish. They were going to spend the day up at Farley Hill praying for all the wicked souls who would be wukking up and down Spring Garden on Kadooment Day. She would have to pray for her brother Junior too. The hands she held out in front of her were shrivelled from washing pig intestine and chopping up hot peppers. *It was serious work!* While she had been grating sweet potato, seasoning sweet potato and boiling sweet potato, Annie had been grating cucumber and squeezing lime and chopping pigtail, pig ears, pig foot, and all the other parts of the pig that people were always complaining there was never enough of. Well there was no doubt in her mind that they'd made more than enough to feed an army - a spiritual army. She just needed to get out of her smelly clothes and take a bath. There was just one thing she couldn't figure out, Loretta thought, as she approached her house... why her children had to have her house shut down like when old lady Marshall down the road had died and nobody noticed till nearly a week had gone by and the body started to smell? Not even the shop's side window was open! She didn't want to believe that Pearl could still be in bed.

"PEARL...PEARL!" Loretta went to the front door shouting her daughter's name at the top of her lungs. "OMAR...PEARL!" It had stopped pouring buckets a drop but there was still a slight drizzle and she was getting wet. It was almost three in the afternoon, why was the house still locked up and the shop still unopened? Loretta ran around the back shouting for her children. She hadn't thought it necessary to take her keys with her when she'd left early that morning, after all Pearl was soon to get up. What she found at the back was her kitchen door gaping open and banging against the side of the house in the wind.

"PEARL...PEARL!" Loretta shouted again. She stared aghast at the cows still in their pens mooing like there was no tomorrow. All they knew was that daylight had come and they hadn't yet been let out to pasture. The lone remaining pig was not much happier either. He grunted and butted his head against his prison in frustration. To make matters worse, all the sheets, which she had spent so much time washing, had been left on the line and so were once again soaking wet.

Next to a wasted pot of food, there was nothing Loretta Walcott hated more than rain-soaked laundry. The smell of mildew, so hard to get out, meant washing them all over again. Since there was no longer hope for her being dry, she braved the weather and retrieved her sheets, all the time asking the Lord why He had given her the children that He had. There were still some clothes hanging there too. "Damn chile." Loretta chupsed.

"PEARL!" she shouted as she walked up the makeshift brick steps. "I thought I told you to take these clothes off de line!" Basket in hand she angrily collected the rest of the wet clothes. "Lord what to do wid that chile?" Loretta asked, eyes raised to the heavens. The sky looking so grey did nothing to convince the tired woman that the Lord above was even listening to her. "I would be more convinced 'bout you if you would send the rain when I actually want it. Lord sometimes you ain't fair you know, and don't feel to strike me down now because I say so." She shook up an angry fist. "'Cause who going look after them blasted children if I gone? Certainly not Junior, all he know 'bout is motorcycle and girls! Omar still need he mother and that girl Pearl, well Lord help she, I going kill she fuh mekking me have to wuk suh hard."

"Pearl!" Basket filled with clothes in hand and a few items slung over each shoulder Loretta stormed back into the house and headed for her daughter's room.

"Pearl Walcott! Answer me when I call you." Loretta Walcott, an impressive sight on a good day, was even more formidable with hands akimbo and a frown on her face on a bad day. She pushed open her daughter's door and stood at the entrance. Seeing the bane of her existence still sleeping so peacefully, totally oblivious to everything around her, did nothing to diffuse this anger.

"Damn chile still sleeping. Loretta spun around on her heels and went back to the living room where she'd left the laundry basket. She sorted out Pearl's clothing from Omar's, storming back to her daughter's room with the one pile. The door, which had closed back on its own, slammed against a cupboard wall as she entered. Loretta threw the wet laundry on top of Pearl, quarrelling with her unresponsive child. "Pearl Walcott, wake up! When I tell you to do something I expect you to do it, so stop pretending to be sleeping so hard or I going beat you wid de clothes." Loretta left her daughter's room for the second time then stormed back into the living room, the whole house shuddering in her wake. Broad hips and ample thighs moved in rhythmic symmetry with ample breasts and an even more ample backside. Her long denim skirt swished from side to side emphasizing each movement.

Loretta put herself to the task of pressing a pile of Omar's shorts, which she had long put off doing.

She'd better fold them too since the boy couldn't get anything domestic done to save his life. The child was growing up fast though, one minute he couldn't walk and was chewing on all her curtains and the next minute he was ready to take the Eleven Plus. "Good thing though 'cause I ain know how much longer this ole soul could raise children for." Loretta sighed and pulled out the ironing board. It felt heavier than usual today.

Junior had managed to doze off with the still half-full beer bottle in his hands. He hadn't even noticed when they'd folded away the Tarpaulin, but the gentle scent of green hills and wide-open spaces had woken him up. He breathed in the Atlantic Ocean the same time he opened his eyes to look upon it. Though he'd never been one to get caught up in nostalgia, Junior hoped that his children, if he ever had any, would one day also be able to experience Bathsheba and Cattlewash, to experience the exhilarating feeling that was the East Coast in their lifetime. Despite the erratic summer weather, the ocean looked calm, like an endless carpet of reflecting mirrors, glimmering silver-greys and dark blues. It was nothing like the bright aquamarine of the south and west coasts. It was much more. It was Barbados' back door to the rest of the world...beautiful and unspoilt.

The sun had come back out with a vengeance. The sky was a brilliant shade of blue and virtually cloudless. Junior could already feel his hair starting to curl into tight little knots from the heat. Not the most pleasant of sensations, and he knew it would be hell to comb later. In no time at all, beads of sweat began trickling down his face and under his arm. He realised for the first time that it was way past his lunch hour and he was thirsty and hungry as ever. His musings were interrupted by the sound of Sean calling his name.

"Hey Junior. Junior! I talking to you man."

"He can't hear you Sean, he day dreaming. Look he ain even finish the beer we give him yet."

Junior took another swig of the now very hot beer and made a face.

"Throw that 'way man. Ain't nothing worse than a hot beer, taste like cat piss." Steven made a disgusted face.

"You ever taste cat piss Steven?" Junior asked as he poured the contents of the bottle over the side of the truck.

"No but I figure it got to be at least as bad as that"

The truck came to an abrupt halt and everyone jerked forward. Junior rubbed his head where he hit it on the window. They'd obviously reached the party. Michael jumped down from the truck. "Alright fellahs we here!"

Junior hadn't even realized when they'd arrived. He'd been so caught up in his daydream that he hadn't noticed when they'd passed the smattering of blue and white, pale pink and green beach houses that dotted the shoreline. It seemed as if a lot of families had had the same idea this weekend...to get away from the craziness of town and Crop Over. It always amazed Junior that no matter how hot it got, it would still always be cooler on the East Coast, the air fresher. Maybe the tall swaying mile trees had something to do with it. No matter where he was, whenever he saw one, he always felt the sensation of being at the beach.

"Somebody give me a hand off-loading fellahs. These drinks here." Michael unhooked the back of the truck. "Junior you want to leave your bike out here in the truck since we coming back soon, or you feel safer bringing it in?"
"Yeah, I feel safer bringing it in."
"Things cool out here though you know Junior. Nobody ain going tief nothing from you out here; too far to run wid de goods!" Michael joked.
"That ain no problem. I going try an' see if I can't patch it up or something."
The others walked up the gravel path with Michael to his cousin's beach house, while one of the other guys helped Junior with the bike.

Though not situated on the beach itself, the house rested on an attractive spot opposite, at the base of a hill. It was set back a good fifty yards from the road, and looked out onto the coast. Painted a soft lemon yellow, the house blended well with its environs. The long green veranda closed in by a beautiful criss-crossing of wooden rails, afforded them an unrestricted view of the sea. Three jalousie doors opened out onto a long veranda and let the breeze into the rest of the house. From those same doors came party music. The truck's occupants glided towards the sounds, not even missing a beat when the music in the vehicle was switched off.

More calypso. It was impossible not to be caught up in the festivities, Junior thought to himself. It was just his luck to have no transportation on Kadooment weekend of all weekends. He entered the house in search of a phone, leaving the Black Bird to rest just inside the kitchen door. Michael was immediately swept up by his friends and only very hasty introductions were made to those who didn't already know each other. A dancing tourist lady, One of Michael's relatives "*obviously from abroad*" thought Junior, came dancing towards him with a rhythm all her own and shoved a straight vodka into his hands. She waltz-hopped her way from person to person offering drinks. Her back and chest, bright red from too much sun, were exposed in a stylish off-the-shoulder turquoise one-piece swimsuit. A floral sarong, tied at the waist, completed her ensemble.

Junior watched Michael being twirled around by a younger version of the first woman. '*...must be the daughter.*' He figured now would be a good opportunity to make a phone call. "Hey Michael! You could show me where de phone is? I going try an' see if I could make a phone call."

Michael did a twirl of his own before answering, forced to shout over the music: "Sorry man Junior, we don't have a phone here. None of the houses around here have phones; you would have to walk all the way to Barklay's Park or something if you want to use a phone."
"Shoot! I got to make a phone call real urgent. I got to call my friend Richard"
"Why wha' happen?"
"Nah, nothing much. He was going hook me up, tha's all. We just had plans."
Michael was twirled again.
Junior ran a hand across his brow. Someone had turned up the volume on the music again, making it hard to concentrate.
"What you say Junior, I ain hear you?"
As Junior opened his mouth to respond someone else shouted for Michael.
"I said..."
"Michael...Michael!" Both men looked up in the frustration towards the direction of the voice.
"YEESSss!" He screamed back.

"Come here!" The voice sang. "I need help with the barbecue." Michael's girlfriend Lisa, the female attached to the voice, hurried over and grabbed hold of his hand. "Come here a minute, I need help." She didn't even notice Junior, but he figured that was because she had already stocked up on a few drinks, so it was probably a major feat that she could walk at all.
"Wait a minute, Junior don't move, I coming back just now. As soon as I help Lisa we could go anyway."

Junior stood there his mouth slightly open, staring after Michael as he was dragged away by Lisa, marvelling at the sight before him. He figured he was better off trying to fix the Blackbird's tyre himself and clear out, because by the looks of this party, the people were going down pretty fast and he couldn't see Michael getting away from Lisa's clutches in any hurry.

It was a little quieter in the kitchen. From there he could see Michael through a window that looked out onto the back yard. He was valiantly trying to out a fire that was quickly spiralling up Lisa's wrap. She was hopping all over the place, making the job all the more difficult. Junior spoke to his bike shaking his head in resignation. "Now see, that is why I don't wear polyester. Look to me like Michael got he hands tied wid that one. He ain going nowhere for a good while. Alright baby, leh we see wha' we could do 'bout dis tyre." Junior rested his still-full glass of vodka on the ground and laid the bike flat. With a damp kitchen towel he set about cleaning the tire's surface to get a better look at the puncture. It was enormous, and on the back tyre there were smaller punctures as well.

The sight was enough to give anyone an instant headache. Junior spent precious moments contemplating his predicament, mourning over the state of his bike. There was no way he had enough rubber to patch that up, worse yet he'd more likely have to consider the cost of two new tires now. Junior felt in his jeans pocket for the keys. When he opened the little compartment, it was only to discover that his repair kit was missing. Junior chupsed and cursed loudly. He could envision exactly where he had left the kit, on top of a barrel by the almond tree, where he had been cleaning the motorcycle. Just as he had been about to put it away, Omar had come up to him with his ridiculous story.

In Junior's opinion, things couldn't get much worse. He got up. It was time to find Michael and get out of there. Junior went outside in search of his friend and noticed upon closer inspection that all the hamburgers on the grill were charred to a crisp. As he went back inside he was immediately caught up in a wuk-up session with Miss Rhythm herself. It was amazing that she hadn't fallen, so precarious was her balance. "You see Michael anywhere?" He asked.

"He's outside with Lisa" she responded with an American accent.
"Not any more. Where you think he could be?"
"Well he can't be too far, because his truck is still outside." She said pointing to the window. "But why don't you ask my daughter, she might know."
From the daughter, Junior found out that Michael had gone down to the beach with Lisa to collect some driftwood since they had managed to burn all the coals in the barbecue to cinders. He had even left specific instructions for Junior to 'Hang tight' because he would be back real soon. Junior's head throbbed. Obviously he was wrong about his prediction that things couldn't get any worse. He sighed and threw back the new drink that had miraculously appeared in his hand. He figured he might as well try to enjoy himself, as Miss Rhythm's daughter said, while he waited for Michael.

It was actually quite a good party now that he thought about it. The music was great, they even had a D.J., *and* the guy had an assistant. The two fellahs were playing all the latest releases and the mix was good. Junior felt his empty glass taken away and replaced with a full one. This time it was straight whiskey. Normally at fetes he was a staunch Guinness supporter, but he figured whatever was going to dull the headache would do. Before Junior knew it, he was swinging to the tunes and dancing up a storm with the daughter, the antics of his co-workers making him laugh every now and then. The drinks were being passed around like water and it wasn't long before Junior forgot his headache, Michael, Omar, and the hot date he might end up missing. Everybody was having a good time. Kadooment was less than two days away and spirits were high.

These were definitely trying times for Omar. He had remained in the same horizontal position for the past three hours. He'd apparently fallen asleep for a while, but now something had awakened him...it was the indefinable smell of his mother, and newly pressed clothes.

Loretta gave a small smile, shaking her head. Now in a much better mood for having vented her frustrations, she headed towards Omar's room with his folded clothes. Her spirits always lifted when she busied herself with the washing of dishes, pressing of clothes or the combing of Pearl's hair, (not that she did the latter anymore), but it was a memory she would treasure. She hummed 'His Eye is on the Sparrow' while carefully putting away her son's clothes. Then noticing that the room was almost as dark as Pearl's had been, she leaned over to pull back the curtains.

The rain had stopped falling, and Omar could no longer hear its heavy drumming nor even its slight metallic pitter-patter on the galvanised roof. Still he didn't find it the least bit reassuring that the usually dry sky was suddenly letting loose buckets a drop. The memory of Pearl's discovery rushed back at him. God was angry – this was a certainty. After all he had killed his own sister. He was a murderer! Omar inhaled sharply, and shifted under the covers.

Loretta jumped at the unexpected rustle of sheets and long sigh coming from the bed beside her.

"Oh God!" She exclaimed hand at breast. "Omar? That you? What you doing in bed at this hour boy? How come you see me in here and don't speak to your mother boy?"

What could he really say to her? Your daughter - my sister - is dead and it's my fault. I killed her.

Loretta gasped, eyes opened wide. For a second Omar thought he'd spoken aloud. His mother made a move towards the bed and rested her hand on his forehead.

"Omar, you have a fever? Child you have a fever and you soaking wet!"

Omar honestly couldn't respond. It was a relief to know that she couldn't read his mind.

"I don't feel so good Mummy." He said in a very weak voice. It was true. He had a stomach ache out of this world! And he really wanted to throw up or maybe go to the bathroom and if possible attend to both needs at the same time.

Loretta was very concerned and wanted to know how long Omar had felt this way and why he hadn't gone to look for her. "What about Pearl, you tell your sister?"
"No Mummy." He coughed and whimpered when his stomach constricted in knots. His mother stood before him, so loving and caring, and right then Omar didn't feel deserving of all that love and attention. Would everything change when she finally discovered what he and his friends had done? God only knew. He had long figured out that it was way better to confess his sins before they were discovered by his mother, *or Pearl!* The punishment was usually worse when they were made to find out themselves or via the neighbours...but this time he *couldn't* say anything. They had sworn to it under the clammy cherry trees. The punishment for revealing the truth would be far worse.

Omar groaned and held onto his stomach. It was the second time he'd done it unconsciously and his mother's concern increased. "Omar you feel sick? We going have to take you to the doctor. I don't know who would be open this late on a Saturday though. leh me ask Pearl to look up in the..."
"NO Mummy No!!! Omar cried desperately. "I just eat something that don't agree with me that is all. I don't need to go to the doctor, all I need is a lil' coconut water. I going feel better soon, ok?" Having said this Omar jumped up from his bed and ran to

the bathroom like his tail was on fire. It was a mess. He vomited on his way to the bathroom and then sat on the toilet for a good ten minutes recovering from a bout of diarrhoea. Throughout it all Loretta stood over him and watched. When it looked as if he'd finally regained control of his bodily functions she set about the task of cleaning up the mess, any thoughts of waking up Pearl temporarily forgotten in all the drama.

Omar tried again to dissuade his mother from finding the doctor, making his voice as chipper as he possibly could. "Honestly Mummy I feel much better now. I definitely think it was something I ate and now that I throw it up, I going feel better."
Loretta spoke from the linen cupboard in the passageway. She pulled out new sheets to change Omar's wet bed. "Ok, for now you don't have to go Omar, but if I see you looking any worse, that is it."

Omar went and stood beside his mother, arms resting limply at his sides. He watched her make the bed and fluff the pillows. He didn't resist when she pulled one of Junior's long vests over his head, tucked him into bed and kissed him on his forehead. If he'd been in the frame of mind to think about such things, Omar would have realized that he hadn't spent a whole day in bed like this, since he'd fallen sick with measles at six years of age.

"You want some tea? Let me make you some tea. Stay here, I going bring it to you." Loretta went to the kitchen and put the kettle on for tea then went outside to collect some bay leaves - good for calming the stomach. After that she set about the task of feeding the animals. The chickens she had taken care of first thing that morning, so only the cows and lone pig were left for her to worry about.

As Loretta made to turn on the stove, the faint scent of burning reached her nostrils. She looked around to see the green vegetables still where she'd left them, chopped on the counter. Dropping back the lid of the pot she'd just opened, Loretta turned away disgusted - her soup had completely boiled away. "What a waste!" She guessed she should consider herself lucky her house hadn't burnt down. Now she was really annoyed. Loretta slammed her fist against the edge of the stove with a real force and went after Pearl. The entire house resonated with her anger. Omar rolled over in his bed and covered his head, unready to face the inevitable.

"Pearl Walcott, get up *now,* and explain to me what the hell going on with you and this house!" Loretta pushed open the door with such a vengeance that it banged against the wall and splintered. She took one of the pants so recently thrown on Pearl's bed and began to pound her daughter's legs with it. The lack of response only incensed her further and she

dragged the bed spread completely off Pearl causing the clean clothes to fall to the ground. Loretta was beyond caring.
"Get up when I speaking to you girl!" she shouted.
Like a moth to a flame, Omar was drawn from his room. As much as he would have preferred hiding under the sheets, some stronger force compelled him to his sister's bedside. The scene he met was terrifying. His mother stood, bent over Pearl shaking her by her shoulders demanding a response, the realisation slowly dawning that something was not quite right with her daughter. In fact, something was very wrong. Mother and son gasped in one breath. Loretta moved her face closer to inspect Pearl. Omar leaned forward, an involuntary response to his mother's movement, his hands mangling his shirt. Somehow Loretta sensed his presence and looked around at him, eyes wild. She half knelt on the bed, still holding her daughter by the shoulders, alarm evident in her next words.

"Omar! Something wrong with your sister! Omar, what wrong with Pearl?"
Omar took a step forward, slowly shaking his head, but he couldn't bring himself to say more. Loretta turned back to Pearl, this time slapping her hard in the face, insistent.
"Pearl, Pearl wake up!" Still no response.

Neither of them heard Big Davy and Annie calling outside for Ms. Walcott. Nor did they hear when the two let themselves in. Davy had come to buy some soft drinks for the fellahs who would arrive at his house shortly for a game of dominoes. Annie had come over to see what was taking Loretta so long with the Pyrex dishes and silver foil she had promised for the souse.
"Ms. Walcott!" Davy shouted.
"Hello, inside? Loretta is Annie, where you?"

Annie, with Davy following closely behind, walked down the narrow passageway towards the sound of voices. Her progress was abruptly halted by the sudden collision with a solid form. It was Loretta.
Ms. Walcott wha' happen to you?" questioned Davy, alarmed.

Loretta, having finally realised that something was terribly wrong with Pearl, was on her way to call for help. Annie and Davy's sudden presence blocking her path only agitated her further.
"Oh God! Something wrong with Pearl! I got to call an ambulance!" Loretta ran to the phone and started dialling. She tried several times but could get no dial tone. Annie grabbed her friend by the elbow, noticing that she trembled uncontrollably, her hands gripping the receiver tightly.

"Loretta calm down and tell me what happen. You can't call from here. You know the phone lines don't work. They dead, remember?"

Davy stepped cautiously into Pearl's room. He found Omar standing in the doorway staring, eyes riveted to the bed. After a moment's pause he walked close to the bedside, brushing his fingers over Pearl's shoulder. "Omar, what happen, she faint?"
Omar shrugged and looked at his feet. He didn't have a clue what to do, and now there were people here too. The situation was becoming even more complicated.

Out in the living room Annie tried vainly to calm a hyperventilating Loretta down. With disjointed sentences Loretta was barely able to explain how she'd come home to find her house still locked up – all except for the back door which had been left wide open - the pot burning – food wasted - Omar sick inside with a fever - then Pearl.
"I have to go and find help." She wailed becoming hysterical again.
"Alright, alright." Annie patted her friend on the back and shoulders. "We will send Davy and you will stay here with me...but Loretta, if Omar sick too, you think is something that they ate?"
"I don't know. I didn't ask him." Loretta sobbed as the two women ended up on the couch with Annie hugging her friend, streams of tears down their faces.

"So why we don't ask Omar what happen then? Omar! Omar, come here a minute please!" called Annie.

Davy, just having given up finding a pulse, looked up and spoke quietly to Omar. "Omar, it sound like your mother or Annie calling you." The boy stood riveted to the spot like a statue. Davy shook his head and moved off the bed. It was a sorry situation he had before him. The girl wasn't breathing. As the bed shifted with his weight, a little brown bottle of pills previously unnoticed, rattled as it moved in Pearl's loose grasp.

"Oh shite! Oh Jesus Christ! Ms. Walcott, Ms. Walcott come here quick!"

Loretta and Annie bounded off the sofa, hearts racing and rushed to Pearl's bedroom. Omar who was still standing in the doorway was knocked out of the way.

"Look Ms. Walcott! What is that in Pearl hand?"

Annie leaned forward first. "Look like a bottle of pills..." Omar watched the expression on Annie's face change from curiosity, to one of horror as the realisation of what lay in Pearl's hand slowly dawned. The silence in the room resounded. It seemed that everyone had reached the same conclusion at the same time. They stared at each other for an immeasurable moment, dumbfounded. It was Annie who first broke the silence.

"Oh no Loretta! You think she try to...?"

Unable to continue, Annie left the question hanging and watched Loretta approach the bed and take the bottle out of her daughter's loose grasp. It was hers. Confusion clouded Loretta's features. The once full bottle was now almost empty. Annie turned towards Omar, certain that the little boy must know something.

"Omar. What you and Pearl was doing in here? Omar, you know what happen to Pearl?"

"We wasn't doing nuffing Annie, I come in here and find she so..." Omar didn't know what had made him say that, but it was too late, the cat was out of the bag.

"How you mean you find she so? Omar how long ago you find Pearl so, how come you ain tell nobody?" Loretta turned in slow motion to face her son. Her eyes, narrow with suspicion demanded an answer.

Omar stuttered. "I.. I.. I. we ..we weee..."

"We who, Omar?" Omar took a step back.

"Me me...Jeffrey and Ch...Ch...Chicken, c..come in here and find her sooo...and we tell Junior."

"You tell Junior?" said Loretta stepping forward. "So how come Junior didn't tell me? Where is Junior?"

"Junior gone out." The situation was not going well at all. Omar realised he'd better start thinking really fast if he wanted to escape the web he was rapidly becoming tangled within. Pure fear made him find his voice. He felt his mother's grip around the medicine bottle tighten like a vice around his neck.

"I don't know what happen to Pearl Mummy. All I know was that me and Jeffrey and Chicken was playing and I come in here for something and I see her so." He spread out his hand in Pearl's direction. "...so Jeffrey say to tell Junior but he didn't believe we so he went along." It was with the intention to redirect blame that Omar uttered his next words. "But Mummy, what you think happen to Pearl. You feel that Pearl take the medicine on purpose like how Annie say?"
"I never say so hear!" protested Annie, appalled at the suggestion.
"But why Pearl would do something like that Ms. Walcott?" Davy turned to his friend looking for answers.
"Mummy." said Omar feebly. "Remember when you and Pearl was quarrelling last night? what she say she was going to do?"
Annie's mouth dropped open and she raised her hands to hold her head. "Pearl say something 'bout 'if she was to die' last night!"
Davy shook his head with regret. "Well I hear her say so too but I didn't believe she was serious."

With crippling celerity Loretta's visage transformed before them. Her eyes turned hard, her body rigid. Her voice, when she finally spoke was as cold as ice. "Well it seem that my child wouldn't stop at nothing to get back at me. I can't believe what I seeing..." She dropped the bottle and walked out of the room, leaving Davy and Annie to deal with the situation the only way they knew how.

"Omar, what time you say Junior left here?"
"About twelve o'clock, I not sure."
"But is already after four...where he say he had to go?"
"Something must be happen to he..."
"But what you tell him that he didn't believe you so? If he don't come back somebody else would have to go!"
"Oh laaws, yuh shoulda neva sell de van Davy!" With both Jeffrey's father and Mr. Cumberbatch off to town, Junior's motorcycle remained the only other form of reliable transportation out of the district. If the buses were infrequent during the week, they were nonexistent on Kadooment weekends.

Annie went to find her friend in the living room while Davy carefully placed the bottle back in Pearl's hand. He figured the police might be needing it as evidence. Snippets of Loretta and Annie's conversation floated back to him from the living room.
"But Loretta, if Junior lef so long ago, something must be wrong, maybe we should go and get help too."
"For what?" said Loretta angrily "Junior living his life, the girl done dead. Whenever Junior decide to come back is soon enough for me." Loretta blew her nose and dried away the last of her tears and set about salvaging what was left of her soup.

Annie pursued the issue, not understanding where her friend was coming from. "But Loretta who say that she dead? Maybe she just unconscious."
"If she was unconscious she would still be breathing and she wouldn't be so cold." Loretta changed her mind about the soup, completely turned off it. She threw the pot's entire contents into the garbage and started rummaging around in cupboards for something else to cook. Her movements were rigid. She responded to Annie, voice rough with emotion. "You feel I don't know my own child? I know Pearl. I know that she spiteful good enough. I can't imagine that anybody would want to get back at me so bad that they would do that to themselves, but looka she there lying down in the bed stiff enough, ain moving."
Annie persisted. "Well Loretta I know she mention something 'bout dying, but you really believe that?"
"Annie, what you asking me for? You see the bottle same as me huh? That girl went to bed last night and decide she was going to fix me. This is not the first time that Pearl do something spiteful so..."
"But de child dead Loretta!" Annie stretched out her hands to Loretta, appealing to her friend's sense of reason. Davy walked in.
"Oh yeah! She dead?" Loretta shouted. "Well let she stop right there, see who going bury she!" Loretta slammed a jar of flour down on the counter. She had assembled an assortment of ingredients before her, none of which, if combined, would make a palatable meal.

In a calmer voice she continued. "When Junior come, he come. I got other things to do. I ain got no time for people who ain got no time for me."

After that it was clear there was nothing else the friends could say. Omar felt the guilt twisting his gut like a knife. He took the opportunity to retreat to his room. While it appeared he was safe from blame, he didn't think he really wanted to risk being in his mother's line of sight. If he continued to let them believe Pearl had committed suicide they would never have to find out about the obeah. There was just one thing that bothered him...the pills he'd seen under the bed. Omar rolled over to face the window noticing for the first time that the sun was back out. Sometime during all the drama, it had reasserted its position in the sky with a brilliance that in no way reflected his present mood. It was hard to imagine that all over Barbados, people were happy and enjoying life.

The canes were burning. The entire north east fields - owned by no one and tended by no one, were up in flames. First the rain, and now the canes. Loretta's phone was ringing, but there was no one at the end of the line. Everyone in Whit's End knew that, so no one bothered to answer.

* PEARL *
10

Life as she knew it in Barbados was dying thought Loretta. The corner shop, as Barbados knew it was dying. No one bothered to work off the land...they worked in town, ate in town, partied in town and shopped in town. Everywhere you turned there was a supermarket selling something better, tastier, prettier than her corned-beef and biscuits. Few people bothered to come to her shop anymore, and most certainly not the young ones who thought it smelled of stale pork and salt-fish. Yet on rare days such as today it seemed everyone needed something from the Walcott shop: First Davy, and now Belinda Murphy and her busybody sister, Sandra. There was no reason to be ungrateful, Loretta reasoned with herself; everything was for a season.

The two came at the side-door closest to the shop entrance knocking and shouting: "Yoo *hoo! yoo hoo!* Ms. Walcott you in dey?" Inside, everyone went silent. "Sandra look through de windah an' see if you see anybody."
Loretta leaned over the counter resting her head on her arms and whispered, "Don't answer."

Annie tiptoed over to her and whispered back. "If you don't answer, they ain going go 'way, cause she see me pass down this side and ain see me come back yet, so she know I in here."
Loretta was adamant "I ain selling nothing today. I ain got no time for this!" She resumed banging her pots and went about preparing her meal.
"SHhhhh." warned Annie. "You want them to hear you?"
"I *don't care if them hear me or not, I in my house!* Davy go and see what they want, but don't let them in."
"Alright." Davy opened the side-door where the sisters were standing. Sandra who had been trying to see through the frosted glass almost fell in. She had to grab hold of Davy's legs to save herself from landing in a heap at his feet. That section of the house was about two feet higher off the ground than the rest of the foundation. It gave Davy a commanding position and forced the two women to look up at him as they spoke.
"Davy! Wha' you doing hey?"

Davy cringed when Sandra's shrill voice rang in his ears. That entire family spoke the most common Bajan in the loudest voices he had ever heard. He dug a finger in his ear trying to clear the ringing. "What do you want Sandra?"
"Ms. Walcott in dey?"
"Yes."

"I did jus' cum ta buy sum shugga, we run out." Sandra, who could not speak unless it involved her entire body, was a sight to behold, her rude nose flaring as she spoke. The woman wore a too-small tank top and a-too-tight pair of leggings. Fat hung from everywhere and the flesh under her arm jiggled with each movement.
"The shop isn't open today."
"But wha' happen dat de shop shut if Ms. Walcott in dey? We pass by earlier an' did knocking knocking knocking an' nuhbody wun ansa."
"The shop isn't open today." Davy said again calmly.
"So wha' you'n Annie doing in dey den?"
"Annie?"
"Feel we ent see she in dey?" Annie, who had been hiding behind the divider eavesdropping, chupsed and walked off at the accusation.

The two sister's behaviour often triggered in others the unusual response of speaking the 'Queen's English'. Davy, feeling completely and utterly assaulted by their influx of 'green verbs', coupled with their unruly manner, instinctively pulled himself up a whole two inches taller. And compelled by a force far greater than himself, straightened his back, flexed his shoulders and enunciated carefully:
"I said the shop is not open today, Sandra. That means Ms. Walcott will not be selling you any sugar. Is that clear?"

Both Sandra and Belinda swung back their necks like turkeys in combat. Those were fighting words! Hands akimbo, they took on a more aggressive stance.
"So who you is, she bodyguard?" Her D cups pointing upwards defiantly, Sandra brandished an elaborately manicured index finger like a sword. "I did always know you did like she an' t'ing, but upwards ta now I woulda never tawt dat she woulda had dealings wid de likes uh you!"
"If de two uh wunnuh in samting how cum Annie in dey?" Belinda demanded.

Oh lord! Thought Davy to himself. When that dynamic duo got started, there was no stopping them. There would be nothing worse than having the two of them spread a rumour about his supposed relationship with Ms. Walcott, especially at a time like this. Sandra tried to push Davy aside to see what was going on indoors. When Davy blocked her path it only incensed her further, and if possible her voice went up another decibel.
"I smell ah fish in hey! Something going on, an' I waan know wha' it is. Ms. Walcott!"

It was as incredible to believe as it was to see, Sandra Murphy and Wilson "Big Davy" Chadderton engaging in a mini scuffle. The tallest, darkest, most-respected man in the neighbourhood, trying to get a grip on the squattest, surliest, most-vexatious woman God ever put on earth this side of the Atlantic to test the strength of angels. With the majority of her weight concentrated below Davy's waist, Sandra clearly had the advantage, and the struggle for supremacy leaned frighteningly in her favour.

"Look you feel you's de only body dat ever went inside dis house? I bin in hey before yuh know!"

Davy really hadn't wanted the situation to deteriorate to this level, yet his options for dealing with the woman appeared to be few. Deciding to give Sandra and her sister the information they so desperately sought seemed the most peaceful solution.

"Listen" he said in a conspiratorial whisper, grabbing hold of her hands. Ms. Walcott daughter Pearl like she just dead. That is why the shop shut."

"SHE WHA'...PEARL WHA'?!"

The shout from the two women was a near equivalent to standing in the middle of an explosion. Not only did it deafen, it knocked you back, which is exactly what Sandra and Belinda did when they heard the news. They stampeded past Davy with the force of a herd of wild buffalo and gained entrance into the Walcott household.

"Ms. Walcott, Ms. Walcott! Whey she is Davy?" All Davy could do was hold onto his stomach and try to recover from the assault.

"Ms. Walcott! Da is true wha' he saying 'bout Pearlie?"

"How she dead Ms. Walcott?" No one answered.

"How Pearlie dead Ms. Walcott, whey she is, she still hey?" The two women were on their way to Pearl's room before anyone could stop them. At the sight of the dead girl, their screams of '*Oh Jesus Christ*' and '*Oh Murder*' resonated through the house, past the shutters, over the trees, shattering the peace of Whit's End, causing the ancestors pause. Their quick eyes took in everything at once. They didn't miss the wet clothes on the bed and they most certainly didn't miss the little pill bottle which Davy had so carefully replaced in Pearl's outstretched hand.
"Wha' dat is Belinda? Them is pills?"
"Oh shite Belinda, look like de girl gone an' kill sheself."

The Walcott party followed the sisters back into Pearl's room at a more sedate pace. Even Omar roused himself to investigate the commotion. With the two women taking up most of the bedroom, everyone else was left to crowd by the door.
"*Ms. Walcott, that is what we think it is!*"
Davy swore to himself. It was the most perfect English he had ever heard come out of a Murphy mouth.
"*Belinda!* You remember how last night Foxy come by and tell we how Pearlie say she was going kill sheself?"
"*Yeah!* dat is true, but I woulda never believe dat she woulda do dat though, *hey hey!*"
Sandra and Belinda looked at everyone with wonder. Everyone stared back. It was amazing to see two

people so excited over the death of another human being. All that was going through their minds was written in the sparkle of their eyes. This had to be the best piece of news they'd ever have the privilege of spreading. It was obvious to them that apart from Annie and Davy, no one else in the neighbourhood knew...Yet. The sisters wondered who they could tell first, and just how much they could embellish the tale.

Belinda moved forward, investigating Pearl's clothing, and touching some grains of sand almost invisible on the table. Omar, who didn't miss the gesture shivered in spite of the heat. When Belinda's voice rang out, it was the epitome of concern; "But Ms.Walcott, how Pearl cud do you so though? Wha' it is dat she tek?" Sandra answered. "Well she obviously tek a lot a wha' eva it was in da bottle."
Belinda bent down to inspect the label. "wha' it say Belinda?"
"It say I.B.U.P.R.O.F.I.N." She read slowly, having difficulty pronouncing the name.
"But that ain fuh headaches? Dat shouldn't kill nuhbody."
"Well Sandra, if yuh tek enough ah anyting it wud kill yuh nuh."
The two sisters argued between themselves over the logistics of Pearl's passing while everyone continued to observe them from the doorway in mute fascination.

"But Ms. Walcott, you chile didn' nice *atall* if she do you so. Dat real spiteful though." Managing to inject a sympathetic tone, Belinda walked towards Loretta and placed a commiserating arm around her shoulder. "Wha' wunnuh going do, wunnuh call de ambulance a'ready?"

"Junior gone to get help." Annie pivoted sharply, surprised at her friend's response. These were the first words Loretta had uttered since the sisters' untimely arrival. Loretta swallowed; the lie left an unpleasant, metallic taste in her mouth. She didn't know why she had said it, but she wasn't about to take it back. Instead she stared down Annie defiantly, daring her to refute her words. "Till then, I'm not going to do anything. I have other children to look after. And if Pearl could be so selfish to do what she did, well, I don't have anymore time for her." Loretta headed back to the living room to fix her food. The others followed single file, all with the exception of Omar, who went back to bed and this time shut the door.

"But fuh real, yuh right though Ms. Walcott, If I hada had a chile dat did so spiteful so, I woulda lef she so de same way too. Dat ain nice wha' Pearlie do *atall*!"

"Hey *hey!* She don't deserve nuh sort a simpaty. Well I never see nuhting so yet *hey hey!*"

"Come leh we go home Sandra, give these people some time tuh demselves. Ms. Walcott, we going see

you later, but you like you got t'ings under control. I could see why you got de shop shut now though."
"Ms. Walcott, you want me to spread de word that de shop ain open tuhday?"
What Sandra really meant was - would Loretta mind if they spread the word of Pearl's demise? News like that was just too good to keep.
"The two of you could do whatever you want. Just shut the door when you leave. I have a lot of things to tend to."

Sandra and Belinda had great difficulty concealing their excitement as they made to leave. "Alright Ms. Walcott whatever you want. We gone, but tek care hear?"

Not even the common cold could spread in a room full of children as fast as a news flash from Sandra and Belinda Murphy on a mission. By seven o'clock that same night, every single individual in every single household in Whit's End St. Thomas, knew about Loretta Walcott's 'selfish chile Pearlie dat kill sheself, and how de girl suh spiteful dat she cud guh long an' lef she mudda and she little brudda home to cry.' And every house had at least one official representative who made it his duty to pass by the Walcott house and offer their condolences, because such a colourful rumour coming from even the most notorious of gossipers this side of Barbados was just too incredible not to be investigated.

For the next five hours the Walcott house was like a minibus stand, with people coming and going, going and coming back, putting in their piece and offering unwanted opinions. Some honestly wanted to help and share in Loretta's grief, but the majority were there because they were so affected by the two sisters' oratory skills that they needed to see the body for themselves - the body of the girl who could kill herself just out of spite for her mother. In less than three hours Pearl had taken on an infamy of mythical proportions.

Omar lay on his bed staring at the ceiling, a pastime to which he had quickly become accustomed. His eyes flicked back and forth from the tree-shadowed ceiling, to the light filtering under the door caused by the numerous people moving in and out of Pearl's room. He shivered at the memory of the fly he'd seen hovering over her body since late afternoon. Its constant buzzing seeming to taunt him 'Murderer, Murderer.' Omar squeezed his eyes shut trying to block out the gruesome images of hellfire and damnation.

More than three hours went by before Junior remembered Michael and that he was supposed to have returned long before. He guessed he could try to look for a pay phone and get someone to collect him, but the idea of walking so far didn't appeal to him - not to mention the possibility that even if he did find one - there would be no phone book in the booth. He figured his time would be better spent looking for Michael. He was feeling more than a little relaxed right now. Truth be told, he'd actually been having fun. Had it not been for the accident, he'd be getting ready to party by now. This summer there were so many good fetes to choose from: There was the house fete in St. George, some guy named Corey had invited him to, then there was the Shelter later on in the night - both Natalie and Raquel would be there – they were always fun. The following night would be Cohoblopot, with several bands that he wanted to hear performing. He'd meant to buy his tickets that afternoon so as to avoid paying ten dollars extra at the gate...then tonight he'd been hoping to put in a few hours sleep, have a bath, fix himself up and be in form for his almost date with Vanessa.

What a woman! Junior sighed. He'd been seeing her around for months now, but last week was the first time he'd been able to muster up enough courage to walk over to her and say 'Hi'. Though they'd only exchanged a few sentences he'd felt buoyed by her sweet smile, and the last thing she'd said before leaving the fete; that she'd be there the next week and would he be too? *Vanessa!* Oooh, sexy like Vivica, with spunk like Jada and a butt like J-Lo...*ooh my, ooh my!* How was he ever going to survive missing this chance of a lifetime?

Damn! He really had to get his motorcycle fixed. This was not how he'd planned on spending his weekend... he needed to get this thing sorted and fast, because there was no way she was going to take him seriously if he didn't show.

Junior took the steps down the veranda two at a time and trotted in the direction of the beach. It was the only place Michael could be. He stumbled over some rocks as he went up a little incline realising that he wasn't as sure-footed as he'd normally be. He looked at his watch. Where had the time gone? It was almost six o'clock. It seemed he'd only been waiting on Michael an hour or so. Junior stood on the beach and looked left, then right trying to decide which direction he should head in since he couldn't see anyone at either end of the beach, its shoreline extending further than his eye could see. Following a hunch he turned left and walked for about ten minutes before he finally conceded that his hunch had been wrong. It was ten minutes back in the other direction before he reached his point of departure and another fifteen added to that before he finally made out a few shapes in the distance beneath the fading light. The only other life forms he encountered along the way were a herd of cows happily grazing on bits of sea-weed by the water's edge. Their young rested several yards away, safely nestled beneath the protection of sea-grapes and shallow dunes. By the time Junior caught sight of Michael, the sun was about to set.

First it was a flicker of light in the distance that caught his attention. Later he was able to make shapes out of the dark shadows against the sand. As he walked closer, the group of people having a mini party on the beach before a bonfire became clearer. Everyone had a beer. Michael sat with a sleeping Lisa's head resting on his lap. Others sprawled around the campfire in similar positions. One person even held a bag of marshmallows, while he contentedly roasted a couple over the open flames. Nearly half an hour had gone by since Junior started his trek and he was tired.

Michael waved at Junior then spoke although he was still a distance away. "Junior man where you been? Come and sit, we watching the sun go down."
With deceptive calm Junior walked forward, the sand in his shoes and the resentment at having had to walk for the better part of an hour making it difficult to appreciate the friendly camaraderie of the group before him. The only reason he hadn't already caught a bus and left -Junior thought to himself - was because

there was no frigging way he was going to leave his precious motorcycle out here when Michael had a truck that he could use.

"Wha' going on Michael man? I thought you say we were leaving hours ago. What happen to de plan? You was supposed to drop off the fellahs and then give me a lift into town."

"Oh shite Junior, I didn't know you still wanted to go. I thought you decided to hang wid we."

"Michael I ain got nuh problem hanging wid wunnuh, but I got to take my motorcycle and get it fixed, I was supposed to be going someplace at eight o'clock tonight, now I don't even know how I going get there 'cause de bike ain working and I all de way in frigging Cattlewash. Junior figured it wouldn't hurt to exaggerate the time a little if it would help to make his case more urgent.

Michael was incredulous. "You say you had someplace to go at eight o'clock."

"YES!" Junior yelled back in frustration.

"But Junior you never tell me that!"

"How yuh mean I ain tell you? I tell you ever since we come here!" Junior sighed waving his hands dismissively. "Anyway is not as if we ain still got time. So if you ready, I ready. If we leave now, I could still get everything organise." The strange look on Michael's face prompted Junior to ask, "What?"

"But we cyan leave now Junior."

"Why not?"

"Well because my cousin just gone off wid de truck. He lef 'bout half an hour ago and I don't even know when he coming back. As a matter of fact, I told him to look for you and ask you if you still wanted a drop into town. So when I see you coming jus' now, I thought you had changed your mind and decided to stay. I sorry Junior man. I ain even know when he coming back."

Junior, who had been shoving the sand around with the tip of his shoe, now took a swallow of the beer someone had offered him. He thought about Vanessa again, and how much he'd been looking forward to seeing her all week long. He'd even organised it so that a friend of a friend could put in a good word for him through her brother...hell! He'd been rehearsing some hard lines and dropping them on the girls at work just to make sure he'd impress her... and now that the day had finally come, his plans to get home by eight, jazz himself up and show off his cool ride were all just wishful thinking. In his heart of hearts Junior knew this woman was not going to give him a second chance. He looked out onto the horizon, noting all of the subtle pastel highlights in the clouds. The sea was no way near as rough as it could sometimes be; still the waves tumbled over each other in a frenzied hurry to reach the shore. Junior cried silently. To him, it was a quickly darkening mass of endlessness. He felt he heard his wail in each crashing wave. His prolonged silence made Michael and the others uncomfortable.

"For real Junior, if I hada understood you, I woulda never do you so. We coulda lef ever since."
"So that mean I stran' out here...?"
Michael played with the grains of sand beside him. "I would like to take you, but to tell you de truth, even if somebody else would lend me their car, or if my cousin come back now, I ain in no state to drive nobody anywhere. We put down so many drinks out here. The only reason we still sitting here is because we cyan move. Only thing I could tell you is that ..."
"Tell me what Michael man, you don't know how you mess me up. I was supposed to meet some people, I was supposed to...man, I had a date!"
"You had a date?"
"Don't say it like you don't t'ink it could happen man..."
"I don't mean so, is just that I thought that you were going out with what's her name in accounts."
"Nah dread, that never nutting, that thing done long time. This girl different. This girl..." Junior clutched at the air in exasperation, searching for words to describe his incredible loss. "...man! She ain going never give me another chance."

A dreadlocked brutherin, who had found his way into the group via the loan of a lighter just minutes before interrupted Junior's tirade to offer a few words

of wisdom. “Nah worry ‘bout it ‘tall Junior man. Da is de name right?” He squatted in the sand with his long arms between his knees, pausing briefly to drag on a smoke. “Nah worry yuh head ‘bout it man. If de gyal a fe you, no matter if ye nah go home tonight or tamarrow night...a virtuous woman will wait on ‘er man. If she nah cyan wait, an’ get vex so quick, then yuh betta off widout ‘er.” The pseudo Jamaican accent did little to calm Junior’s nerves, but he forced himself to accept the unasked for advice “So sit ‘ere wid we yah. De fyah ‘ave yah man feel sweet and de sun setting pretty pretty...a man shud halways enjoy where he are, an’ nat where ‘e cannot be. So ‘old a seat ‘ere next tuh Iyah and res’ yuh foot. Tamarrow ah com’ soon enough.”
The others paused silent, wondering what Junior’s reaction would be. When he did nothing but continue to stare out at the horizon, someone passed a spliff to him. “Come Junior sit, don’t think ‘bout it no more, t’ings cool, t’ings cool.”

Junior conceded that there was little else he could do to change the outcome and so decided to sit down and make the best of a bad situation. He took what was offered and waited for the sky to darken and thc stars to take over the night.

* PEARL *

11

The movie had ended. The station had already signed out. Nothing was left on the screen but the static and sound of the television. Annie and Davy, the only two visitors remaining, cleaned up the mess of plates and plastic cups that littered the Walcott home. Omar stared at a half-empty glass of his favourite ginger beer. His eyes fixated on a lone fly that wandered along its rim. The house looked as if it had been burgled. One end of the sitting room carpet lay cocked up, a chair leg hooked into it. Nothing was where it should have been. It was not the way his mother kept house. The sweet smell of rum from an uncapped bottle was strong in the room. The familiar smell, which in the past had brought him comfort, now suffocated him.

Omar sighed. The shrill chirp of a well-camouflaged cricket did nothing to help matters either. His eyes surveyed the shadowy corners of the room, searching for its hiding place. The pale blue glow from the TV screen was the only source of light where he sat. Loretta half-slouched, asleep in her chair with the television watching her. Omar watched his mother too. He sat to one side of the large sofa listening to the low tones of Annie and Davy in the kitchen. He'd sat there for ages in the semi-darkness unwilling to move. The sharp pain in his stomach had since passed, but now in its place was a dull ache. He felt heavy all over. Omar didn't know which was worse. He looked at his mother again and sighed. It was his fault that she was still lying there at this time of night, exhausted. Omar sighed again, his grip on the sofa arm tightening as he fought the impulse to go over to her and confess everything. He knew he couldn't...he'd made an oath; he'd sworn never to tell. Omar battled with himself silently, the only evidence of his torment, the little hand that clenched and unclenched the rough fabric of the chair arm. As Annie walked out of the kitchen all she could see was the dark silhouette of his rounded head and the two long shadows that were Loretta's legs crossed at the ankles, the rest of her melding into the tall back of the chair.

Loretta's only child got up and walked over to the window. He parted the curtains, letting the moonlight filter in. He stood there a while looking out into the street and at the sleeping houses. When he turned back around and walked over to his mother, not even he expected it. When he knelt by her chair and whispered in her ear, no one could have been more surprised than he by the words that spilled from his mouth.

He whispered simply "I sorry Mummy, is my fault. I kill Pearl."

Omar looked up when the clinking of two glasses alerted him to Annie's return. She had almost finished clearing the table.

"Omar, that so sweet! You kissing your Mummy before you go to bed?" Omar bit his lip and tried to swallow the uncontrollable emotions rising out of him. Loretta shifted in her sleep, momentarily disturbed by their voices. He looked down at her one last time before responding.

"Uhhuh...I going to bed now." He pulled himself up and headed for the bedroom. "...nite Annie."

"...nite Omar."

He dreaded walking down the dark passageway that led to his room, to Pearl's room. The last thing he expected was to fall asleep. Who could achieve such a feat with a dead body just a room away? Omar felt his sister's presence now more than ever. It seemed that in death, Pearl had finally managed to accomplish what she hadn't in life: made herself acknowledged by her brother.

Thoughts of guilt and retribution tormented him all the way to his room, the sight of the broken bathroom door a constant reminder, as jarring as the cricket's high-pitched call in the deep of night. Somehow the insect had found its way to his room. Omar didn't think it fair that he had to put up with the annoying sounds of a cricket too... one thing was certain, he was not going to listen to that constant chirping in his head all night. Omar fumbled agitatedly between the two beds in the semi-darkness, pulling out one of his uncle's slippers, determined to silence the creature.

The chirping stopped immediately. Omar remained still on all fours waiting for the cricket to regain confidence and resume its loud call. He followed the sound stealthily to where it seemed loudest, between the open door and wall. Hand over foot, slipper poised in the air, he pushed the door away swiftly with his left hand while the other swooped down with determined force, smashing the bug into an unrecognisable pulp. Omar practically roared with the force of his efforts. "Tha' fuh lick yuh! Next time you would think hard before you come into my room and mek noise in my head!" He punctuated his words by tossing the slipper to the ground as he stood up, still hissing at his dead nemesis. Omar then flung himself onto bed, expecting to spend the rest of the night staring at nothing but the cracks in the ceiling.

"Omar!" came a voice from the window, nearly giving him a heart attack.

When Jeffrey and Chicken rapped on his bedroom window, he could have peed himself with fright. Omar sat up straight in bed turning only his head in the direction of the window. When he recognised his friends, he pushed up the shutter and climbed out. No questions were asked; none were necessary. From the looks on their faces it was obvious that the two had also spent the better part of the day worrying about the possible repercussions of their actions. Without a doubt it would also be the longest night of their lives. None of them would sleep easily for days to come.

The boys ran all the way to the only place they felt safe and unwatched. Hiding behind one of the big boulders, they discussed the events of the day, their minds completely boggled by what they had started. They talked in low tones till well past mid-night. The moon was even brighter than it had been the evening before and a cool breeze blew from the northeast. All three boys were wearing their pyjamas, the wind blowing at their thin cotton clothing in gentle ripples.
"Omar, you tell your mother about the obeah?"
"Of course not Jeffrey!"
"You see!" snapped an irate Chicken, jabbing Jeffrey in the ribs. "I told you he wouldn't tell."
Omar sat quietly by. He was ashamed of himself, of his girlish behaviour. If he didn't even trust himself how could he expect his friends to trust him? He would have to make sure that the incident with his mother was not repeated. Omar gathered his knees up under his chin and pasted a smile on his face, grateful for Chicken's confidence in him.

"I never said he would tell." defended Jeffrey. "I was just suggesting that it might be difficult to keep quiet about something like that if big people put pressure on you."
"I ain let nobody put pressure on me. I was in my bedroom the whole time."
"Well, just remember we make an oath...and you know what does happen when you break an oath?"
"I ain forget Jeffrey."
"Of course he ain forget that we make an oath Jeffrey!"
Omar tuned his friends out for a brief moment as he recalled the words he'd thrown about so carelessly. '... *let our mouths be filled with flies and cockroaches and our tongues vanish into thin air...'* The words rang with a hollow echo in his ears making him nervous each time he saw a fly or any other insect.

"I ain doubt nuhbody." Jeffrey raised his hands in defence. "I just saying..."
"Just saying what?"
"Well remember what happen to the Lodge Man."
"Wha' lodge man?" Both Chicken and Omar leaned forward, terrified and intrigued at the same time.
"The lodge man that break the oath."
"And, wha' happen to him?"
"Well....one day...he jus' walk out into the sea and he family never see he again."
"But how he break the oath?" This was more than just a minor detail to Omar.

Jeffrey leaned forward, answering in hushed tones. His friends leaned closer too. "Some say that he tell a bird. Some say he tell it to a tree. Others say that he write it in pee on a wall. The people never sure how he tell, or who he tell...but it was enough to know that he tell."

"So what's the situation at your house now Omar?"

The abrupt change in Jeffrey's tone jumped Omar. His heart pounded rapidly. Had he heard this news too late? Maybe it *was* already too late for him.
"Sound like Annie and Davy were still there when we pass by."
Omar tried to gather his wits. He couldn't let them see how worried he was by the story. "Annie and Davy still there. They cleaning up."
"Cleaning up?" cried out Chicken surprised. "You mean they had so many people over at your house?" He'd heard the rumours going around the neighbourhood about how Ms. Walcott was sharing out drinks like it was a Sunday picnic, but he hadn't realised it was so true.

Omar told his friends about the constant train of people who had been through his house to view Pearl's body. He would do anything to steer the conversation away from the reality of his having told his mother about the obeah.

Instead, he then told them about nosey Sandra and her sister Belinda who had eagerly spread the rumour of Pearl's suicide.
"Good." interjected Jeffrey "We better off letting them believe that is suicide, before they figure we had anything to do with it. Only thing is we know it ain suicide because all the pills that they feel she tek, Omar say he see pun de ground under the bed."
"If they find them, they going know is we?" asked Chicken a little perplexed by the growing complexity of their conspiracy.
"How they going know is we if none uh we ain tell nobody wha' we was doing?"
"Because the police going have to investigate..."
Jeffrey continued to explain the logistics to his once willing co-conspirators. It was crucial that they go over all the measures they had taken to ensure no one ever discovered what they'd done. With the contents of the enamel pot flushed down the toilet and Jeffrey's burial of the doll, they were satisfied that their secret would be safe so long as Omar got rid of that last remaining bit of evidence.

Omar re-entered his house the same way he had exited - through the window. Annie and Davy were still there, talking with his mother in low tones. He walked into Pearl's room for the umpteenth time that day, feeling as guilty as ever. The lone fly he'd seen earlier had been joined by several others. It was not a comforting observation. When Omar knelt down to gather up the stray pills, he felt certain he'd caught a whiff of a scent. But with the smell of food still so strong in the house it was difficult to be sure. His mother had cooked up a storm for all and sundry, saying that she couldn't very well not feed people who were kind enough to pay their last respects to a daughter that didn't deserve it.

Omar had not looked directly at his sister's body since the first time that morning. Now his eyes were drawn to her lips thanks to a fly that meandered there. He couldn't resist the urge to brush it away and got too close, accidentally knocking her face. The body moved. Omar's heart stopped. He dropped the pills. The entire room seemed to close in on him, though the body had since stilled. Rigor mortis had already begun to set in. The hand hanging over the bed was stiff, her fingers remained curled over the bottle. Omar scrambled to pick up what he could of the fallen pills off Pearl and the bed. He kept his gaze averted from her face the balance of the time.

When it was done, Omar let out a breath he hadn't even known he'd been holding. Back in his room, the ten year old folded the pills between a small handkerchief, and crushed them with a shoe heel. Satisfied there was nothing left but powder, he took the kerchief to the bathroom and flushed its contents down the toilet. Feeling a great sense of relief Omar ran back to his bedroom window, where the others waited anxiously outside for his OK signal. Then as suddenly as they had come, they were gone and Omar was alone again.

Fear manifests itself in innumerable guises; a gazelle, drinking peacefully by a waterhole sees nothing, but feels a quiet unease in the restrained stillness of her surroundings. Perfectly camouflaged, a lioness lean and serene, stealthily moves in on her prey, step by calculated step. Fear pounces in a golden haze with a rushing of wind past the gazelle's ears...and then, it's too late. Other times, fear is a happy fish dancing just beneath the surface of a placid lake. Oblivious, he flashes silver reflections on the water, until a sharp eyed eagle soaring high above suddenly makes a swooping dive, and fear grabs hold of him with sharp talons and even sharper beak. Then, fear is no more.

Omar's fear pulsed with life. It was a newborn tadpole wriggling its way to survival. Metamorphosing, eating its way from egg to Lilly pad relentlessly. It climbed up Omar's throat like bile, growing arms and legs, eyes and tail and, with each feeding it grew stronger, surer, relentless in its search for life. Omar tried to swallow down the full grown frog in his throat. The moment Jeffrey and Chicken had left, his fear magnified tri-fold. Wolves jumped out at him from the shadows of the tree branches. The creaking of the old house as it settled down for the night became the unknown coming to get him...but worse than that was the buzzing of scores of flies in the room next door. One, had been joined by two, and two by six, then more and more. They had become a veritable choir. Omar tried closing his ears to their chorus but it was useless. They were coming for him. He knew it. It was because he had told his mother. It was going to happen to him just like it had happened to the 'Lodge man'...only worse, he wouldn't disappear. His mouth felt dry and fuzzy as if stuffed with a cotton ball. He tried to swallow again...maybe if he drank some water or brushed his teeth the feeling would go away, but he couldn't risk passing her room. Except for the occasional buzz of flies, the house was dead silent and in complete darkness.

Omar pressed his lips together and pushed his bedroom door closed with quiet resolve. *There was a fly in his room!* It buzzed from wall to wall brushing feelers over every surface. Was it looking for a place to sleep, or for him? Omar didn't want to know. The moonlight spilled through the open curtains dropping long shadows everywhere, making the fly appear larger. He stood in the middle of his room for countless seconds, motionless. Finally he moved cautiously towards his bed and lay down as quietly as he could. He pulled the covers up slowly, tucking them under his feet, and pulling them over his head, creating a safe cocoon away from the fly and all other potential threats. If he kept his mouth closed, and his body covered, maybe... maybe it wouldn't happen. His nostrils flared with each erratically-inhaled breath. He prayed for sleep to come, for the darkness to end, for everything to go back to the way it had been.

Just off the coast road at Cattlewash, a few lights dotted the hillside like fire-flies in the night. The group of young people had spent the last few hours contemplating the immensity of the Atlantic Ocean before them. At one point they had entered the water disdaining the currents and frolicked like newborn lambs in a field. Now they were headed back to the beach house where the party was in full swing. From the number of cars lining the road, it was evident that many more people had arrived in their absence. If Junior hadn't been long past the point of caring, he would have noticed the red L200 back in the driveway.

People spilled out onto the veranda in the front and in the back yard where the abandoned barbecue still waited. A few talked, but most danced. Just as the party of eight returned, the D.J. started to play a back-in-time session featuring the best of Earth Wind and Fire. Junior who had consumed vodka, whiskey and endless quantities of Guinness was in his element. As soon as he'd walked through the door, the tireless Ms. Rhythm grabbed hold of him, determined to keep him occupied the remainder of the night.

It was only when the Sunday morning sun had risen high in the sky, that the D.J. and crew began packing up their belongings. With the exception of a lone dog scrounging around the party remains, the house was dead quiet. People lay scattered all over the floor and furniture in varying states of drunkenness. Among the semi-dead, Junior lay sprawled on the sofa with mother and daughter duo for a blanket. Someone snored loudly on the veranda, while from one of the bedrooms intermittent squeaks could be heard as bedsprings gave way to the desires of some unknown couple. For them the party was just beginning.

It would be two in the afternoon before any among them would stir, and then only because they were startled out of sleep by shrill screams. For Junior the screams were loudest because they came from right above him. Miss Rhythm who now stood high up on the sofa was in a fit of terror over the sight of a young lizard that had chosen to explore her print sarong for his early morning walk. It had in its travels eventually crawled up her arm to her face before greeting her eyeball to eyeball.

"Pearl!" Junior shouted as he was startled into wakefulness. "Oh God what happen?" he rubbed his eyes trying to make sense of his chaotic surroundings.
"A lizard! A lizard!"
"Kill it! Kill it!" Mother and daughter screamed as they jumped from chair to table, scaring the lizard more than anything else. Everyone came running to see what was the matter; the toll of a full night's drinking written all over their puffy faces and in their blood-shot eyes. One of the more-coherent individuals was eventually able to remove the terrified animal, carrying it a safe distance from the house, where it was certain never to return to again.
Junior now completely awake, rummaged frantically around the beach house for his possessions. "Michael!" he shouted.
"Yeah Junior I here."
"You know what time it is? Is two o'clock in de frigging afternoon!"
"You lie! I cyan believe we sleep so long. All right come leh we lef now! Fellahs you ready, everybody awake?"
Among the echoes of 'yeah we ready' one person grumbled, how could they not be? after all the commotion the two women had made.

The truck full of young people finally drove off around two-thirty headed for town. This time Junior rode up front with Michael and Lisa, the Black Bird securely strapped in the back of the pick-up. He pulled on his goatee trying to decide how best to organise the rest of his day and whether it was worth his while to let Michael take him home first...but then what would he do with the bike, he needed to get it fixed... he also needed to get out of his funky clothes, the idea of walking through town looking and smelling as he did...but he needed to fix his bike, otherwise how was he going to get around this evening... and he still had to buy the tickets for Cohoblopot...and what about Vanessa? He had to find a way to get her number...and say what? One thing was sure, as soon as he got home he was going to find out what the hell was up with Omar and what it was they were teaching him in school...it was time to tell Loretta to sort her son out because his lying and scheming were getting out of control...shit, now that he thought about it, he hadn't slept well at all for dreaming about Pearl...something to do with body parts. As a matter of fact he was going to yank that little boy by the ears real hard when he saw him. He could actually blame this whole episode on Omar, because had he not been trying to escape his nephew's foolish antics there's no way he would have been caught out in that rain. Yes, if there was anyone to blame it was that little trouble-maker.

Omar finally wore himself out and fell to sleep in the early hours of the morning. It was a sleep little more restful than the daylight hours had been, but it was at least a momentary reprieve from consciousness. When the sun rose Omar jumped up from his bed and whipped shut the curtains hoping to delay the day's arrival for as long as he could. He flopped back into bed and once more pulled the sheets over his head.

* PEARL *
12

The truck made fast work of the country roads. It drove quickly along, bypassing a green blur of scenery. Those in the back hollered in protest whenever Michael dropped into a pothole a little too roughly. Unlike the rains of the previous day, it was turning out to be a lovely afternoon - not too hot, with a cool breeze blowing. There was a sense of expectancy in the air, as if something memorable were about to happen. Junior propped his arm on the front passenger window regarding the scenery. There was just one more day to go before countless weeks of mad partying and spending climaxed in the ultimate day of revelry and abandon: Kadooment Day. He could not wait. He forgot for a moment all the things that had gone wrong in the last twenty-four hours; his spirits were high and not even his total state of uncleanliness, the missed date, or damage to the Black Bird could mar his present state of euphoria.

It made sense to get the bike fixed first. It might not look cool, but maybe he could substitute the damaged tyres for a pair of temporary replacements. At least then his transportation would be organised for the rest of the weekend. He hated having to depend on anyone - friends included - to get around. It must be a trait he'd picked up from his sister because as generous as she was, Loretta hated to be in a position of dependence. In any case his friends weren't reliable. Junior reached around in his back pocket for the comb he knew he always kept there. When it met resistance from the consolidated mass of curl at first try, Junior knew that to continue would be futile. It was a good thing he didn't have a mirror to look at, otherwise he might not even have the courage to go into town. With his luck he'd butt into some gorgeous female and make an unforgettable impression on her as the town paro - stumbling around wildly looking for his next high. Junior chuckled to himself at his out-of-control imagination. Clearly those four or five hours of sleep had done little to eliminate the last effects of alcohol.

In what felt like minutes they were arriving in town. First Michael took Lisa home, then, making a slight detour through Princess Alice Highway he dropped off the remainder of the group just outside Fontabelle. From there, they would walk to Bridgetown market where the fun and festivities had been going on non-stop since Saturday morning. Cars were parked everywhere: on sidewalks, grass verges, even on the round-abouts. The only other time of year Fontabelle saw this much confusion was cricket season at Kensington Oval.

"So Junior, we going get the Black Bird back in shape?"
"Yeah den. Got to have my girl working by tonight."
"You figure out what you going say to Vanessa when you see her?"
"There ain really got much that I could say man."
"You ain'going tell her 'bout the bike?"
"Nah dread, she ain going never believe that. Women don't believe them kinda stories, how it going take me a whole day to get home from a flat tyre. I got to mek up something man."
"Fuh real? If I tell Lisa she would always believe me."
"Yeah? Well the people I know does operate differently. I would got to tell she that my dog dead or my grandmother had a stroke or something...make the heart bleed lil' bit you know? Women like to feel that yuh real break up bout them things yuh know?"
"If you say so..."
"Turn left here Michael." Junior spoke quickly, but not fast enough to prevent Michael flying past the turning he'd just indicated. The L200 screeched to a halt and backed up a few metres before it tumbled down the narrow avenue just off Tudor Bridge. Their bodies jerked forward as the truck struggled into gear.
"I want to see if this tyre-repair shop I know here open."

Michael made a few more lefts then rights before he pulled up outside "KG's Body Works & Tyre Repair"; a galvanized shed with different-sized tyres, including four massive tractor tyres piled high one atop the other. You could hear the steady hammering of metal on metal coming from within.

Through the half open doorway, a man dressed in blue oil-stained overalls could be seen, the source of all the hammering.
"KG!" Junior called out. The man looked up with a ready smile.
"Hey Junior, how you doing?" they pounded fists. "How come you ain at Bridgetown market like everybody else? I going there just now."
"I cyan do that today man. Listen KG, I pass by here because my girl got a flat, she mess up fairly bad man...I need to know if you could fix her for me now."
"Yeah? Wha' happen?"
Junior's voice became low and subdued as he retold the tale of the motorcycle's tragedy. "Man, like I drive over some serious glass bottle and t'ing, and now the chain guide slider pop and all my tyre tear up. I feel the front suspension off too. She in the back uh de truck. This is my man Michael." Junior paused to introduce his companion. KG and Michael nodded at one another in acknowledgement. "You want me to take it down an' show you?"
"Yeah Junior, you could do that."

With the help of the two men, KG placed the Black Bird on a large workbench. His expression, one of humour, as he watched Junior run a reverent hand over the bike's damaged body. "Boy you like you like this motorcycle real bad nuh?"

Michael chuckled. "You could tell too?"

"How you mean if I could tell when he here feeling it up like if is woman! Junior you sure you don't carry this thing to bed with you?" KG guffawed at the sour look Junior threw him.

"Nah dread." Michael came up from behind giving Junior a supportive slap on the back. "I could vouch for him. He like the other kind a woman too."

Junior unimpressed by the men's jokes gave a long chupse. "Why the two uh wunnuh don't carry wunnuh tail. KG man, tell me wha' you could do for my bike so I could go out and have some fun tonight."

"I cyan do nuffing fuh you Junior."

"You wha'?"

"This bike got to stop here overnight."

"But you just tell me that the engine sound."

"I tell you I think so, but I ain no mechanic. I would got to let my man Capleton look at it first and I don't think he passing by today. In any case, motorcycle don't run 'pun engine alone."

"Look man KG, just gi' me two tyres and sort me out nuh man."

"Junior I going tell you again 'causin you like you ain understan. Tyres cyan fix - too rip up. I ain got no tyres to fit this bike, and the way you does race bout, I ain giving you no scooter tyres for you to pop your ass and them come back an' sue me like how them foolish people doing in 'Merica"

"Shoot! So you mean I ain going got no transportation tonight?" Junior muttered to himself. "And to catch bus home at this sorta hour going be bare hell."

"Don't worry about it Junior, I could still drop you home, I ain really had that much plan for today."

"Thanks Michael." Junior watched Michael for a while, not quite sure how to respond to his generosity.

KG spoke again, his tone indicating scepticism. "To tell you de truth, she might got to sleep over more than one night 'causin, tomorrow is Kadooment day and I ain going be here. Me and the wife jumping in a band. Then Tuesduh...." KG adjusted the crotch of his pants "Tuesduh I going be recovering from Kadooment, so I really cyan guarantee you anything before Wednesduh or Thursduh.

"Thursday!?" Junior was appalled.

"But even so, I going see if I cyan call 'bout an order a new side mirror and chain guide slider for you first t'ing Tuesduh morning, cause it too late to do it today, you call me and remind me though, cause waking up ain going be so easy."

"Alright KG, look like I ain got much choice. I going call you Tuesday. Come Michael, leh we go."

Junior stretched out his legs in the truck, crossing and uncrossing them at the ankles, trying to get comfortable. He watched Michael tap the steering wheel, playing out the beat to some unknown tune. Both men looked at each other with somewhat tentative smiles. To each it was obvious that the other was uncomfortable. With no one else in the car and nothing else to worry about they lacked a common focus around which to direct their conversation.

"Want to hear some music Junior?"
"Yeah sure."
"Calypso, Reggae?"
"Man I cool, whatever you choose."
"You choose it then, I like I can't find a good reception... got so much bends in the road, probably better if I just keep my hands on the steering wheel anyway."
"No problem. Yuh know what Michael? Better don't drop me home, drop me by my friend Trevor in Wildey instead because I still got to get my tickets for Cohoblopot tonight, and at least by him I could hold a fresh and borrow a spare shirt before I go and shame muhself in the people town."
"So just drop you off by your friend then?"
"Yeah, I was to hook up with him later this evening anyway, so may as well do it now since I in town." What Junior had said was true, but he also didn't relish a long drive back to the country with only Michael for company.

"Michael nodded thinking he should say something more. "Listen Junior, I real sorry 'bout keeping you out all last night though."
"Nah is alright, don't worry 'bout it no more."
"Sure I can't help you out more, take you home to make up for it? I don't mind dropping you to get the tickets and I would still drop you home too. Is not like I doing anything right now. If anything, I was going go back to Cattlewash afterwards anyway."
The truck lost momentum as Michael geared down to accommodate the slow-moving traffic ahead of them.
"Wha' happen?"
"I don't know. If you stick your head out you could probably see better than me. They had turned right by Welches Post Office following the road up to Government House and were now stuck behind an unseen vehicle, just metres from St. Winifred's School. It was not until they reached the little straight by the agricultural station at the bottom of Pine Boulevard that they were able to pass.

During the long and painful wait both men took turns cussing the unknown driver who carted heavy farm equipment in the back of his rusted blue pickup. Junior leaned forward as they made to overtake, ready to ask the driver if he didn't know that country road was made for slow driving and tractors, not public thoroughfare. But before he could get his first sentence out, the driver sped up. They were back behind the truck just in time to avoid being nicked by a rapidly-approaching Transport Board bus.

"Wait Junior, he just speed up?"
"I can't believe he just speed up."
"But look, he looking through the rear view mirror too, I swear to God he laughing."
"You got another chance after this red car."
Engine in second gear, as they turned up towards licensing authority, Michael made a second attempt at overtaking but once again he was forced to fall behind.
"You could believe he do it again?"
"Wait! I know that driver." Junior peered hard at what he could see of the driver's reflection in the rear-view mirror.
"Michael honk that horn."
"You know him for real?"
Completely ignoring the urgent sounds of the horn, the driver refused to acknowledge the pair behind until they signalled to him that his door was not properly shut. Of course it was a lie, but resulted in the desired effect. As the truck slowed down, Michael pulled up beside it once more.

"Patterson! Junior called leaning out the window."
"Junior! Muh man! How you doing? I ain realise that was you behind me so."
"Man wha' you doing pun de people road keeping back traffic so?"

"I only trying to get home like de res' uh wunnuh. Hey you find the doctor yet?"
"The what?"
"If you find the doctor?"
"What doctor?"
"For Pearl."
"What? Pull over. I ain know what you talking 'bout. Michael you could pull over for me a second?" Before the vehicle could come to a halt Junior was out and by Patterson's side. "What doctor you talking 'bout Patterson?"
"The doctor you supposed to get for Pearl."
Junior shrieked inwardly. "What happen to Pearl, she sick for real?"
"If she sick? Pearl dead!" Patterson paused, suddenly realising that his badly delivered news was having an overwhelming effect on Junior. After all he was not some random passer by. "Oh Junior, I thought you know. I coulda swear you know." Patterson's at once serious face regarded Junior's. "Man I sorry, I thought you know. I coulda swear Loretta tell everybody that you was going deal with the doctor or the police for she."
"Police?"
Yeah well it look like Pearl commit suicide. You's don't have to call police for that?"
"Suicide?"
"Yeah, Omar is who find her. The poor little boy... like he can't even talk now he so frighten."

Later, not until the strong scent of gutter filled his nostrils did Junior realise he'd been sitting on the sidewalk. His thoughts were a blur of disjointed images; images of Pearl lying in her bed as he had seen her the previous morning. He was only vaguely aware of Michael and Patterson helping him to his feet. As the story unravelled he became faint at the thought that he might have been able to save his niece's life had he not ignored the pleas of his young nephew. What kind of uncle was he? What kind of brother was he? Why had Loretta led people to believe he knew something about a thing he knew nothing about? How was he supposed to deal with this death? He had never dealt with death before. He was young. His friends were young. Apart from his mother, no one close to him had ever died, and then he'd been too young to remember.

Sixteen year olds weren't supposed to die. Ten year olds weren't supposed to find dead people. Mothers weren't supposed to turn their backs on their children. How had he ended up this way sitting in a passenger seat of a truck next to someone he hardly knew...and his family needed him?
"Junior you want me to turn off the air-conditioning?"
"Huh?"
"You told me you were hot remember? That is why we put it on."

"What? I don't feel hot. I feel cold." He rolled down the window trying to warm himself up. "Where we going? This ain the road to Trevor house"
"Right, we going to the police station."
"The what?"
"The police station? Remember we decided to go to there so they could help us figure out what to do about Pearl?"
"Oh. Where Patterson gone?"
"Patterson gone home, but he say he might check by your sister later. He gave me a number that we could call him at after we get through with the police."
"Oh good."
"You alright?"
"Yeah man, I good. Which station we going to?"
"The one just down the road, Central. See? We almost there."

Junior remained subdued as the truck pulled into the empty parking lot. "I don't know Michael, I never do anything like this before. You sure this is the right thing to do? Maybe we supposed to call the hospital."
"I never do anything like this before either, but Patterson say he sure that when a person die like how your niece die, that the police is who normally deals with it. In any case, they got to be able to help us one way or the other."

Decision made, they pushed through the doors of Central Police Station to report Pearl's demise. A lone officer sat at one of the wooden desks. He'd just gotten off the phone and was writing notes in a large blue book. The place looked liked a ghost town. A random thought ran through Junior's mind that the Crop Over season must be putting a real strain on police resources. He knew for a fact that many - and he had quite a few friends who were officers - worked double shifts during this period. For sure there would be tons of them patrolling the streets at Bridgetown Market.

Junior cleared his throat. "Uhmmn...afternoon..." The officer looked up only after he was good and ready. He looked at the odd pair in front of him, taking in the half-white fellah's surfer shorts and expensive Reef sandals and equally expensive Oakleys... 'pretty boy'... he thought to himself. Then his gaze travelled over to the black fellah, noting the very closely cropped hair and finely chiselled moustache and goatee beard... musee does put down nuff horn pun he woman. The Polo shirt revealed salt stains under the arms and his jeans were marked with motor oil...but he didn't recognise the shoes. He couldn't imagine what these two could want, must have been an accident...then again, that didn't explain why they were here in front of him instead of calling from a phone near the scene of the accident. And no way would 'pretty boy' come over to a police station if he didn't have to. They both reeked of alcohol and a stale sweat...must be friends... probably been smoking nuff herb and partying all

night. He closed his book with a resounding thud. "Yes sirs may I help you?"
Junior stepped forward. "Yes. Good afternoon, I would like to report a death..."
"A WHAT!" Junior's words completely shattered the officer's indifferent posture.
"I said I would like to report a death...Sir."
The officer sat erect in his chair. "I am not deaf, I hear you." He abruptly picked up the phone and called for another officer to join him. Junior and Michael stood there in shock, unsure whether something they'd done was about to get them into trouble. The footsteps of an approaching policeman echoed down the hallway.
"Yes Sergeant?"

The officer leaned back in his chair, resting an arm over its back. "Look here Constable Best these two young fellahs want to report a death."
"A what?" The officer's businesslike air immediately changed. His body relaxed, an amused grin spreading across his face. He too had assessed the young men, but was unable to figure out the association. He leaned in closer, curious. "You say you want to report a murder?"
"A murder?"
"You kill de body?"
"Huh?" Junior was apoplectic. He gaped at the two policemen wondering if he had come to the wrong

place. “NO!...ahh..ah. my, my sister daughter just died.”
“Ahhh.” said the seated officer seeming to understand it all. “Your niece.”
“Yes, my, my niece.”
“So why you come here, somebody kill her?”
“You were in a car accident?”
“No. Look like she died in her sleep.”
“Ahhh. When she die?”
“You live near here?”
“You call the doctor?”
“How you know she dead?”
“She not breathing sir.” Junior’s head bobbed back and forth trying to keep up as constable and sergeant threw question after question his way.
“If she dead since Saturday, how come you take till Sunday to look for help? They ain got no phones out by where you live boy? How you mean they ain working. They got someplace in Barbados where you can’t find a phone to use Constable Best?”
“I don’t know Sergeant Smith, never heard of it yet. You feel these boys mekking mock sport ah we or what? It take you two days to make a phone call, find a doctor?”
OH! You ain find the doctor yet?”
“No. We thought we’d come here first.” Volunteered Michael, trying to help Junior out under the officers’ barrage of questions. A penetrating look silenced him immediately.
“Is your sister chile that dead or his?”

"Is mine," responded Junior.
"Oh, I thought you couldn't answer for yourself. What time you say she died?"
Junior felt really stupid now, how was he to explain, he hadn't known. Omar's tales, the motorcycle, the rain... they were all a confused blur in his mind right now. It would be even worse if he told them that his sister had known since early Saturday afternoon and hadn't done anything about it. "I not sure, I guess some time last night...ahmn we find her late this morning."
"And what he got to do wid it?" Sergeant Smith nudged his chin in Michael's direction. "He live wid you? Oh, just for moral support! No. He give you a drop into town. I guess the transport Board buses don't work out where you live neither huh? I ain even going ask how you manage to bypass all the other police stations and come straight down to Central." Junior tried to explain about meeting Patterson on the road and only then being told about the incident. Sergeant Smith cut him short. "Nah nah! We don't need to know them sort of details"

Opening up another book Sergeant Smith began to write profusely for several seconds before returning the pen to the table. "Listen young fellah. Sorry to tell you, but you shoulda call before you come. We don't collect bodies here. This is a police station. We maintain law and order and catch criminals. Are you a criminal?"

"No Sir." Junior squirmed beneath the officer's intense gaze. He held his clenched fist tighter; fighting the urge to respond to the unkind treatment that he'd received so far, because one thing was for sure, reacting violently in a police station would get him nowhere.
"We don't pick up nobody that dead. That is the job of a Police Medical Officer. You know what that is?"
Junior shook his head.
"Quincy – remember him - The coroner? He's the only official that can certify a person's death. You know of any other Constable Best?" Smith turned to his colleague for confirmation.
"No Sergeant Smith, I would have to agree with you."
"If however, the doctor diagnoses your niece as having died under suspicious or unnatural causes," Smith continued punctuating each point with his index finger. "...then and only then would the police come into the picture. Is that not so Constable Best.?"
Constable Best rocked back and forth on his heels nodding his head importantly. "I would have to agree with you there again Sergeant Smith."

The four men stared back at each other, silence filling the room. Junior was unsure whether the interview had actually been brought to an end or whether he should await further instruction. Michael finally broke the silence by slapping away a mosquito which hovered annoyingly near his face.

Sergeant Smith leaned forward hands clasped on the desk. "One of our responsibilities as police however, is to take seriously every single claim of every single person who walks through that door, no matter if they stink like pigs, are stark raving mad or devoid of clothing. It is our duty and responsibility to the community. So even though neither of us believes anything that the two of you have said, we're going to follow up on this report and have a coroner dispatched to your home immediately. Now where exactly do you live sir?"
Just as Junior was about to speak, the sergeant raised his hand to silence him. Not giving any more of an explanation he just picked up phone and proceeded to dial a number.

After a long pause he finally spoke to what was evidently an answering machine. "Dr. Branagh, Sergeant Smith calling from Central. We have a death I'd like you to investigate. The time is now fifteen hundred hours. Thank you." With the receiver still in hand the sergeant looked up acknowledging Junior and the others briefly before dialling again. "He's not home. I will try to page him. Yes maam I would like to have Dr. Branagh paged – please tell him it is urgent. Sergeant Smith, Central Police Station."

While the sergeant spoke, Junior's eyes roved his surroundings. It was much more preferable to maintaining eye contact with the other officer openly evaluating him. Was it as obvious to the officers as it was to him that their clothing reeked of stale herb and liquor? Junior tried to ignore Best and continued his perusal. As police stations went, he had hardly been in any. But if Central was anything to go by, he wasn't missing much.

Central's only decoration was the lone tree in its courtyard. With several stairways leading to as many departments, Junior was certain the building had been designed to keep a person confused. Seeing them on the outside, functional two-storied rectangles with nothing but long rows of windows gave little indication of what to expect inside. Sparsely furnished, with old wooden tables and chairs placed randomly about the room; rusted filing cabinets so old and overused their drawers overflowed with paperwork, their painted surfaces completely worn to black. Recent cases remained propped inelegantly upon cabinet tops, while long defective staplers and rubber stamps crowded an area alongside dried-out pens and stubby ends-of-pencil. It was not a room that instilled confidence in the island's law enforcement system. For how could anyone function efficiently under these conditions? A musky scent of lingering damp permeated the room. Junior's mind was suffused with images of decades of cleaning ladies trying to keep up with the countless layers of grime that accumulated faster then their strong hands could remove. Suddenly he was no longer so certain he trusted the officers to help him with his situation.

"Ok, so I've had the doctor paged. Once we get your address you'll be free to go."
"Just my address? You don't need me to show him where I live?"
"Well he should most likely call back within the next few minutes. So you can give him the directions yourself if you want."
"Yes I prefer to wait."
"But I still need to take it down for our records. You live in the country right? I know out there does have a lot of little back roads. In any case, we'll have to refer your case to Belleplaine. Because you live in that district your case will have to be registered there.

Junior looked around at an empty bench and the few empty chairs scattered around the room. Would it be alright to sit? Michael shrugged his uncertainty, his eyes reflecting similar thoughts. Very tentatively they both moved towards the bench hoping it would not be cause for censure. Heads bowed, arms resting on their knees, they waited silently while the officers went about their business. As the minutes passed, Junior singled out the loud ticking of a wall clock and the even louder humming of a faulty florescent bulb. It seemed the more he tried to ignore them the louder they got. For the next 45 minutes he would sit there contemplating ways to avenge his treatment at the hands of these officers.

It angered him that the officers had put him through that entire rigmarole knowing full well that they had to help him anyway. He found their lack of sympathy insulting. Now he was also worried about what Patterson had said regarding Loretta's reaction to Pearl's death. Why did people always have to jump to conclusions and spread rumours and encourage negative thought so? That's why he didn't have none of them in his business. If he not home, nobody need to know where he gone. And now he just vex with Omar, because if the foolish little boy wasn't always crying wolf and doing what he shouldn't be doing. He would never have driven away and left him so. Junior chupsed to himself. This was supposed to be a festive time of year, one that he had been looking forward to for months but instead of partying with his friends, he found himself in a ratty police station feeling guilty over something he didn't have any control over. Just like Pearl to go and dead when people most want to be happy and forget the stress of daily living.

Michael looked up when he heard Junior chupse for the umpteenth time. "You alright Junior?"
"Yeah, don't bother with me man, I just thinking 'bout this thing. Is something I got to go through you know?" Suddenly impatient Junior got up to ask

what was the usual response time for a police medical officer and if there wasn't a way to speed up the process. The sergeant chuckled. "Oh after waiting two days to contact us you now decide you in a hurry to get rid of the body. It starting to smell nuh?"
Junior didn't grace him with a response. He happened to know nice policemen. This man obviously had the job because no one else would hire him. Either that or he was vex 'cause he didn't get the chance to go down to Bridgetown Market and look at all the pretty girls. Realising he might soon cross the line of acceptable conduct, the Sergeant continued in a more business like tone. "Truth is usually by now he would have called, but today is a funny day." Sergeant Smith stretched and rubbed his belly before continuing. "I wouldn't be surprised if Mr. Branagh just don't want to be found and enjoy his Sunday like everybody else. Because really and truly he should still be at the hospital all like now. It wouldn't be the first time he's done it."
"So you can't go down there and get him?"
"And who would man the station, you see only two people here? You'll just have to wait until he calls. If he does not contact us within a reasonable period of time we will have to find someone else."

As Junior became more anxious he grasped at alternative solutions to the problem. "So what is a reasonable period of time? If you know he at the hospital we can't go there and get him ourselves?"

"I don't suppose I could stop you, but why you think that Dr. Branagh would drive all the way out to the country with two people he don't know. Just let the law take its natural course man."

"You say Dr. Branagh, Peter Branagh?" Michael who had remained silent all the while suddenly jumped up, an idea clearly taking shape in his head. "I know him, my family knows him. Junior, I sure if we ask him he would come."

"Well go then!" responded the policeman irritably. "I got enough work to do around here. All wunnuh really doing is keeping me back from filing this report"

The officer pulled the big heavy book back out of the drawer and proceeded to write, leaving Junior and Michael staring agape at their apparent dismissal.

Back within the relative safety of the vehicle, they let out deep breaths.

"Michael you believe how them people treat we?"

"Man! I glad enough I ain never commit no crime hear!"

"Yuh telling me!"

"You could imagine butting up pun the two uh them in jail? Man, you guilty before you declare innocent!"

"You think they could smell the alcohol on we?"

"Nah man!"

"Wha' 'bout the herb we smoke last night?"

"Nah, them cyan smell that. We was out on the beach, the wind woulda blow that way."

"You sure?"

"I ain sure, but at least them ain arrest we!"

"Yeah. Leh we clear out a here quick before them change them minds."

Michael started revving up the engine with his usual enthusiasm until he remembered their present location and that the officers were well apt to change their minds and cite them for noise pollution. He virtually rolled the L200 out of the station's parking lot, driving below 20Km until he was well out of their range. "So Dr. Peter Branagh is who we looking for?"

"Yep."

"You know where we supposed to find him?"

If I remember correctly he works in obstetrics and gynaecology or something so, I'm not sure what ward it is though."

The truck wound its way through the Queen Elizabeth Hospital parking lot, leaving the left lane free for emergency arrivals. Moments later Michael and Junior would follow a similar path back to the main doors and reception. Their solitary footsteps echoed down empty corridors. After being directed to about three different wards, they eventually ended up at Accident and Emergency, where Branagh had reportedly last been seen. They had bypassed the waiting area, which overflowed with Barbadians in varying states of ill health. Junior watched as nurses and doctors bustled left and right in the emergency room. It was clear that if they joined that line of people waiting for attention, they would never leave before dark, so pretending to have legitimate business at the hospital seemed the obvious solution. Behind the glass booth the lone attendant didn't even blink when they pushed through the large double doors with purposeful strides.

Junior approached one of the male doctors who appeared most likely in charge of the situation.
"Excuse me, but can you tell me where I might find Dr. Peter Branagh? The security guard told us that we should find him here."
The doctor, who was typically wearing a white coat, continued filling out the chart he held in his hands, and responded without even sparing Junior so much as a glance.
"Whoever tell you that was wrong, because he is not here."
"Do you have any idea when he might be coming back?" Junior knew how stressed these people tended to be and figured he'd catch more flies with honey than vinegar, so he put on his humble voice. The doctor walked away from the two young men, bending over a counter to put away the chart. Not only was the white coat stained with blood, but also very visible were ten bloody fingerprints streaking down to the hem of the coat, as if it were the only place some very sick person had been able to hold. God only knew what had happened there. The doctor

grunted with the effort of leaning so far over the counter.
"No".
This man was clearly very busy and not in the best of moods. Trying to sound even more polite Junior braced himself for a monosyllabic response. "Sorry to bother you, but do you have any idea where we could find him?"

Two nurses ran by almost knocking Michael out of the way as they tended to a serious accident victim. One signalled to the same doctor for help.
"I know for a fact he was here this morning, but I'm sure he's already gone. To tell you the truth I really don't know anything about his schedule.
Junior groaned, feeling his hopes rapidly deflate. "The problem is I need to find this doctor really urgently for my niece...We think she died in her sleep, at home... and we're not really sure what to do."
"My friend, you see in here? I got a lot uh sick people and dead people in here too, so I guess you come to the right place, but right now we working overtime on a skeleton staff. Everybody choose Kadooment weekend to take their vacation or get sick, so we really cyan help you."

The man, whose badge identified him as Dr. Gooding, held up his hand in response to the two nurses, signalling that he would be right with them. The patient didn't appear to be getting much better. "Yeah,

I coming there now, wha' happen? Through a series of hand signals and incomprehensible medical jargon the patient's problem was made clear, along with their need for immediate assistance. More agitated, Gooding turned back to them looking at Junior directly for the first time. "...yeah what was I saying? Look, we really short staff right now. I sorry 'bout your family, but we got people in here who at least we could still help, the only thing I could tell you is, try calling him at home."

Gooding walked behind the same counter, this time pulling out a series of packages filled with tubes and medication. Finally, as if sensing Junior's frustration, he stopped long enough to try and figure out a way to help the two young men.

"Listen." He signalled for them to follow him over by the patient as he started working on saving another life. "Nobody here has the time to help you, but I know that Dr. Branagh usually works at Bayview on weekends after leaving the hospital, but don't tell anybody I told you... if not look in the yellow pages and you should find him easy enough at his private practice, or in the white pages listing under Belgrave, High Gate Gardens Christ Church. Don't tell nuhbody I tell yuh dat neither! If you can't find him, I think the acting P.M.O is now Dr. Cummins."

"Doctor who?"

"Owen Cummins. You could use the directory over there to look it up but not the phone, that is for staff

only. These last words were said with a grunt as he tried to shove a needle into a resistant vein.
With the doctor's unexpected demonstration of humanity, Junior felt his hopes rise again, making him able to smile with sincerity "Thanks man!"
"Yeah nuh problem, good luck, yuh going need it..."

And they did need it; Branagh hadn't been at Bayview either. When Junior tried calling for Sergeant Smith at the station, it was to find that both he and the constable had left for the day, after more than twelve hours on the job. While the new officer had been far less surly, he had been no more helpful, explaining that neither officer had passed on much information, but that he was certain the district D station was responsible for follow up. The Belleplaine station, when Junior called knew nothing about this report. The Action Post Mortem the sergeant had preached so royally about had never taken place.

Tired and frustrated, both young men were starting to feel as if they were on a never-ending wild goose chase. When Michael suggested they go back to his house to regroup, Junior readily accepted. The idea of a warm meal and a cool shower, even if he had to put back on the same dirty old clothes was indeed a welcome one. At well past five in the evening Junior had now been in the same clothes for more hours than he wanted to count.

Omar watched the woman dully. She stood over Pearl in a faded floral print dress running her hand over his sister's body like a blind person reading Braille. Did she think that if she stood there long enough Pearl would start talking? What was the attraction these people had to his sister's body lying stiff, unmoving in a bed? Her skin was a sallow shade, the blood having already drained from her veins and settled at her back. It divided her exposed arm like a grey and purple candy cane. And this woman had come here to see that. On closer inspection he realised she wasn't actually wearing a dress, it was a matching shirt and skirt, the kind of ensemble Pearl would have scorned. With her heightened fashion sense his sister had deemed people like this woman to be as dangerous to stand next to as a five year old with the flu. What they had was catching and they should be avoided.

Why didn't she go home? Didn't she have anything better to do? He didn't even have a clue who she was, or half the other people who'd trekked through his house lately for that matter. More people had visited in one day than had ever visited in countless years of television watching. His house had suddenly become the stage for a real life soap opera. Days of Our Lives had long been forgotten...it had been replaced by something far more intriguing.

The idea of half the neighbourhood viewing television in his house on a nightly basis had never been much of a problem for Omar. He'd liked hearing what people had to say. He'd liked the jokes they made and the disagreements they'd had when the plot didn't go their way. It was Pearl who had often complained that she lacked privacy and that coming home in the afternoon should never have been more stressful than being around the teenagers she'd left behind at school. After all how was she to do her homework when she could hear people arguing that little Johnny couldn't really be his father's son, especially since his mother was nothing but a drunk who had gone through twenty men in as many years and all the while she still looked seventeen even though little Johnny who'd started the show two years ago at the age of five was already fifty.

Omar was ashamed that he'd turned his sister's life into a soap opera and imagined her tearing at her hair in frustration. The vision haunted him as surely as if Pearl had been right there expressing her disappointment in him for getting into more than his usual share of trouble. He turned away before the woman sensed he was there, the creek of the floorboards her only indication that she'd been watched.

* PEARL *
13

There was no doubt about it; Michael lived in a big house. From the moment Junior walked through the door, he felt poor and uncomfortable. From the garage, they'd passed through some sort of flowered entryway and right into a large open space. This, Junior could only assume, must be the living room because it boasted two large white sofas which met in a curve at the corners. There was an equally white-three-inch thick carpet, occupying the space in the centre. The floor was laid with large white tiles opening out onto an inner patio. On the wall, were hung three massive paintings, splashed with various shades of pink and green depicting vague impressions of human beings. He couldn't imagine ever wanting to have something of that nature staring back at him every day of his life, first thing in the morning, before he'd hardly woken up properly. He was sure he could even make out two naked people kissing in one of them. Junior muttered to himself. *"...man, Adam and Eve sure come a long way."*

"What you say Junior?" Michael was right behind him.

"No nothing, nothing."
"Oh, I coulda swear I heard you say something. Sit down though Junior, I coming back in a minute."

Junior massaged his goatee unsure whether to sit or remain standing. After having been in the same clothes for the past two days, he was certain any dirt would rub off on the pristine sofas if he sat down. He went over to inspect the paintings more closely, reasoning to himself that since there was no doubt that these people had money...and lots...those things on the walls must be art, and since all the walls were white, it was like living in an art gallery. He remembered going to an art gallery once when he was still in school. It hadn't been bad, he'd actually understood what the artist had been trying to say in those paintings. Back in those days the fellahs all used to call him the 'art master', though he could never have imagined doing that sort of thing all day and calling it work. "*But it seem like you's make good money doing this shite.*" Junior mumbled to himself again.
"Uhh?" Michael turned around from checking his phone messages at a little corner table. "What you say Junior?"
"Huh? Oh. That the paintings at a good height!" ... he was sure that he could draw a woman lying down much better than that one. All the arms and legs were out of proportion. There was some name in the corner beginning with a *C*. Junior peered closer trying to decipher the script. He could make out

what looked like the letter *Z* and then *e*. It wasn't a Barbadian name thank God! At least that was a relief! Junior stepped away from the painting losing interest. Michael looked up from the little corner table where he stood.

"You like that Cezanne? My mother don't usually put up prints, but when she saw that one she liked it so bad that she had to buy a frame for it."

"Yeah it real nice man" enthused Junior "I could see how well it blend with the rest of the house!"

"Yeah I think so too. 'Scuse me a minute Junior, I got to return a phone call. You want something to drink? I'll fix it for you as soon as I done here."

"Thanks man, that cool."

When Michael came back he set them both up with two heaping plates of baked chicken and rice topped with a serving of stewed sweet potatoes and vegetables on the side. They settled down in the TV room - which was much more to Junior's liking. This room at least felt lived in, not like some museum piece. The sofa was well worn and faded, its throw cushions lumpy and slightly ragged. Michael sat there with the plate on his lap, eating to his heart's content while simultaneously flicking through the TV channels with his free hand. They even had a satellite dish. Junior sat next to him using the coffee table as a prop for his plate - which was filled with an equally high portion of food. He ate while scanning the yellow pages for doctors. He'd already tried calling

Dr. Branagh, however as predicted the answering machine clicked in explaining that he wasn't home, but that he could be reached on his cellular. This information would have been useful had the good doctor also left his cell number. All he could hope for was to have better luck with Cummins.

But with each call it was the same. An answering machine would announce his unavailability, or the phone would simply ring. The thoughts of a cleansing shower foremost in their minds Michael and Junior deliberated whether to bathe first or make one final attempt with Branagh and pass by his house unannounced. In the end Junior accepted Michael's offer to take a much-needed shower and change of clothing. Dropping by the Branagh home could wait until after they'd cleaned up and looked a bit more presentable.

Junior couldn't help it; for as long as he'd known himself he'd been a fanatic about personal hygiene. He marvelled at how other people could stand the stench of their own dirty bodies for so long, while he just couldn't imagine going through life without having a bath at least twice a day. He most certainly couldn't go out with a woman unless she was at least partially on the same wavelength. He had hardly been able to relax for constantly turning around in surprise whenever he caught a whiff of his under arm. Spending an entire weekend in the same underwear would not end up on his list of ever–to-be-repeated experiences. He was so glad to get out of his rotting clothes which smelt of sweat, alcohol and salt spray, an unimaginable combination - If he could capture it and bottle it, he would definitely call it 'au de skunk' or 'dead cat'. Junior shook his head laughing at his own ridiculous thoughts then turned on the shower full force. He stepped under the water quickly working up a lather with the sweet-smelling soap... cinnamon...not exactly what he was accustomed to. He knew Pearl liked to bathe with those kinds of frilly fragrances, but it was not exactly his style. Pearl...he remembered, but didn't want to. He scrubbed himself vigorously, just letting the water wash over him and soothe him. He let the hard spray of the shower run over his face and into his mouth, the heat relaxing and cleansing. By the time he got out, Junior felt like a new man. Thank God he and Michael were the same size, Junior thought as he held up a borrowed shirt. Of course he had a slightly bigger package in the front, but the pants still fit. He trotted around for about half hour with a mere towel around his waist while his briefs rolled around in a dryer. A dryer in the tropics! Man only when you were rich.

Mrs. Peter Branagh, tall, slim, and *very* sexy, stood sleekly poised against her doorway. One arm stretched along its length, she wore a gloriously revealing ultra red teddy and matching garters. Her long shiny blond hair hung in waves down her back and shoulders, and she smiled in contentment while humming some familiar tune. All Junior and Michael could say was "WOW!"

The next thing they saw was the door in their faces accompanied by a loud bang! On the other side of which Mrs. B could be heard screaming and hyperventilating alternately. She clearly hadn't been expecting them. Michael waited a while then knocked on the door again. When Peter Branagh's wife came back to the door, she was much more discreetly covered in a plain blue terry cloth robe, her face revealing none of the trauma she had so recently experienced.

Michael knew the Branaghs well enough to know he didn't even want to speculate on why she should be answering the door in such a state of deshabille. Junior not so encumbered, was literally biting his lips to prevent the big grin from spreading across his face. When Michael looked at him, he sniggered causing Mrs. B to turn a delicate pink.
"Michael, what a surprise! I didn't know you'd ever come to our house before." She plastered that smile on her face determined to keep up the front. "I was expecting my sister; we're supposed to have dinner together..."

While Mrs. Branagh floundered for words to explain her lack of clothing and unusual behaviour, Michael studied the ground, not trusting himself to look anywhere else. He could feel Junior's body shaking with repressed laughter next to him. It was all he could do to position himself just in front and save her further embarrassment. "Uhmn that's nice, were you going out?" The sound of an engine hummed in the background causing Mrs. B to look out the door over Michael's shoulder anxiously. She fidgeted with the tie at her waist.
"We haven't decided yet, are you looking for Peter? He's not here." Hearing this, Junior still fighting for control, let out an enormous laugh, which came out more like a roar of pain when he received a hard kick in the shin from Michael. He tried to disguise it by coughing but Mrs. Branagh was no fool and understood that they had seen through her ruse. She turned a shade of crimson so bright, that it could have rivalled the undergarments she'd so recently covered. "Yes actually, I was looking for your husband because my friend needs to find a doctor for his niece quite urgently, we were hoping that he was here. Is there anyway for us to reach him, or is he coming back soon?"

Mrs. Branagh couldn't stop looking over his shoulder, evidently worried that whoever she was expecting would arrive while they were still there. She spoke to them now in rapid bursts, hoping to speed up their departure. "Peter went sailing. I don't think you will find him till tomorrow evening. Better to come back then. Unless of course you go to the pier and see if he's still there. Why don't you do that!"

Neither Michael nor Junior was sure about the last suggestion. She read their faces and made a last attempt. "I know! We can call him on his cell!" She hurried inside for the cordless then came back to the door dialling her husband's number. The two young men stood waiting and watching as she paced back and forth guarding the massive doorway. A recording finally came on indicating that the cell phone they were trying to reach was out of range. "I'm so sorry. I guess he's already out to sea. Why don't you go home and try looking in the yellow pages for other doctors, I'm sure you'll find someone who can help you." She smiled her first real smile.

"Yes I guess we'll have to do that. Thanks anyway." Michael stepped back ready to leave. Mrs. Branagh already had a firm grip of the door and was about to push it shut, when some stronger force prevented her. "Wait! Hold on a minute, I could make a phone call real quick?" When she looked down it was to see one of Junior's black metal tipped boots, standing between her, the door and getting rid of them.

"Why?"

There were no words to describe the expression on her face, she could no longer pretend at politeness.

"Come Junior man leh we go."

"Wait Michael, I got a good feeling 'bout this one, jus leh me call Dr. Cummins real quick."
The woman reluctantly relinquished her tight hold on the door and handed over the cordless.

By now after so many attempts, Junior had memorised Dr. Cummins' number. He dialled the seven digits with his right hand and crossed the fingers on his left. A little girl answered after the first ring.
"Hello Cummins' residence, may I help you?"
"Hello, may I speak to Dr. Cummins please."
"I'm sorry Daddy is not here right now, can I take a message?"
"Can you tell me when you expect him back?"
"I don't know...but not long."
"Is your mother there, can I speak to her?"
"Mummy's not home either."
"So who are you there with?"
"Granny, but she's sleeping...Can I take a message?" It was the second time the voice had asked, her parents had taught her well, Junior was impressed.
"Listen sweetheart, what's your name?"
"Rebecca..." She breathed into the phone.
"Ok Rebecca, could you do me a favour?"
"Yes..." She sounded so cute. Junior could just imagine the lovely round face and ponytails that could only go with such a voice.
"Rebecca, my name is Junior Walcott; you think you could remember that?"

"I don't know, let me go and get a piece of paper." She put down the phone with a thump and ran a few steps away before Junior heard her run back, picking up the phone again just to say, 'Hold on a minute' then she was gone again. This time he could hear her pulling open, then rummaging through some drawer not far away, looking for pen and paper, he presumed. Before him loomed Mrs. Branagh, checking her watch conspicuously, and still guarding her door like a lion its lair. She and Michael were engaged in some mundane conversation about gardening and swimming pools. They were both uncomfortable with the situation in which they found themselves, of guilty perpetrator and unfortunate witness. Each time she looked out the doorway to see if her friend had arrived, Michael would automatically look over his shoulder too, only making the situation worse. Now he called out to Junior somewhat impatiently.
"Junior you ready yet?"
Junior whispered back, covering the mouthpiece. "Almost, the daughter got me on hold."

When little Rebecca came back to the phone, Junior left her his name along with Michael's number where he could be reached at any time.
"Ok, so don't forget now."
"I won't forget. Bye."
"Thanks love bye." When he hung up both Michael and Mrs. Branagh looked at him with absolute relief. "Ok Michael we could go now?" Junior summoned up

a polite smile and held out his hand. "Mrs. Branagh, It was a pleasure meeting you..." She took it limply "and thank you very much for letting me use your phone."

Michael had his keys in his hand and was halfway to the pick-up before Junior added on the bit about being sorry for the inconvenience. Meanwhile the relieved Mrs. Branagh was all false smiles insisting that it had not been an inconvenience at all, that she had heard of Dr. Cummins before, and he was indeed a good choice since her husband couldn't be found. Then she called out to Michael suggesting that next time he pay a real visit with his mother so that they could discuss the pool and landscaping issue over tea. Michael responded with a sound that was neither yes nor no. In the pick-up he grumbled to Junior, that never before this day had his family ever received any invitation from that woman to drink even a glass of water and that she knew who he was only because she and his mother happened to come from the same town in Massachusetts and had one very rich friend in common causing them to meet socially on more than one occasion...and that his mother always said she was an opportunist bitch and now he believed her, and pity the poor foolish husband that didn't know she was horning he. "I should really park down de road there and see who it is she waiting for." With each sentence that Michael spoke, he tore from first, to

second, then third gear. The L200's gearbox protested at the rough treatment.
"Nah man, don't worry 'bout dat. Dat ain got nutting tuh do wid you. Barbados is a small country he going find out soon enough."
"Fuh real! Barbados suh small, somebody wud eventually tell he."

Once again, Junior drove back with Michael to his house. The young man was much calmer now and treating the vehicle with the smooth ease and expertise to which it was accustomed. Junior sat back in his seat and mused to himself. It was strange; in these last two days he'd spent with Michael, they had become... friends. It was one thing to work with someone and joke with them every now and then, or on the rare occasion share a drink at happy hour when the staff wanted to celebrate some big event. But he'd never considered that he or Michael could have anything in common beyond work. Michael was the 'pretty boy' from the 'heights' and 'terraces'; while he was the 'country boy' whose favourite meal was Cou cou and flying fish, and for whom eating out meant Kentucky or Chefette. The experience over the last two days had revealed to him that just because they were not from similar backgrounds, didn't make either of them any less real, or human. Obviously there would always be unkind people like Branagh's wife, but then he guessed they existed everywhere in the world, and Michael had reacted as strongly. Junior sniggered, remembering the woman's embarrassment at being found half dressed.

"Wha' you laughing at, that foolish woman?"

"Michael, you see how she had all she bubbies at de door? Wha'! Dem didn't even look good, neck half brek an' all." Both men laughed uncontrollably at Junior's demonstration of the woman's drooping breasts.

"Ain true though Junior, she didn't look bad at all in the piece ah lingerie though nuh?"

"Fuh real she didn't look too bad, yuh tink them real? I know nuff women younger than her, who bubbies don't stand suh tall..."

"Man nowadays yuh cyan tell, and I ain care, I like all! Big, small, long, round..."

Junior sighed, his thoughts drifting to more serious issues. He felt positive about Cummins though; the little girl had taken down his message and said her father would be home soon. He'd much rather take his chances with a man whose daughter answered the phone politely, than with any of those policemen he'd dealt with so far. Most probably when he got back to Michael's, the doctor would've called, then he'd finally be able to go home. He just couldn't imagine what things must be like, having the dead body still in the house; it had been almost two days. Not since the old time days when the coffin was built right outside the yard had he heard about anything like that happening.

Now that it was night, more cars could be seen on the streets, their lights blinding Junior as they passed. Everyone seemed to be in such a hurry. He guessed they were either running home to cook dinner after a long day's play, or rushing out, late for one of the many Crop Over events. Performances at all the calypso tents were over, but there were still the Cohoblopot kings and queens of the bands to watch dance across the stage in their glimmering costumes and perhaps a last chance to hear the season's top calypsonians. He should be there now. Good thing he hadn't bought his tickets before as planned, otherwise he'd be out some sixty dollars. He would have to call Trevor and the others to let them know he couldn't make it. For the moment Junior would have to console himself with the knowledge that he was doing everything he could to find a doctor for Pearl.

The pudding and souse was good. The souse had just the right combination of salt, lime, hot pepper and cucumber that Patterson liked. He swallowed a satisfying mouthful savouring the tangy flavour as the pickled cucumber and spicy juices of the souse slid down his throat. This cucumber had been grated, not cut up into little cubes as mediocre chefs were often apt to do. If Loretta and Annie had made the dish, then his two year search for the person who could replace his dead mother's cooking was finally over. The pork was so mellow, it slid off the bone; feet, tails and ears practically melted in his mouth. The award worthy pudding was sweet not from sugar, rather from the careful selection sweet potatoes stuffed in good old fashioned pig's intestine with pig's blood. *Even the breadfruit was superb!* Firm and meaty, it was obviously picked from a tree nourished by country soil and weather. This was a meal that would have done his mother proud.

Completely ignoring his knife and fork, Patterson picked up a wedge of breadfruit and shoved it whole into his mouth. His fingers were moist from sopping up the juices in his plate. He was in heaven. It was the kind of joy that would have been inappropriate to share with the people around him. How could he express his gratitude for this meal knowing that without Pearl's death he would never have had the privilege of tasting so wondrous a dish? Since his mother had passed he'd suffered; searching parish after parish from St. Philip to St. Lucy asking anyone who cared to answer, where he might find the best pudding and souse in Barbados. Little had he known the dream had been right under his nose all along... maybe *if he married Annie, he could eat like this all the time!* Patterson stopped, shocked at himself, at the direction his thoughts were taking. Was he actually contemplating marriage just to get closer to a good souse? He who had guarded his freedom so dearly all these years? He who had sworn that his mother would forever be the only woman who ever need know where he was going and what he was doing? *Hell yes!* He missed the crisp, starchy feeling of a well-pressed shirt and the daily blessings that were bestowed upon him. When was the last time someone had said a prayer just for him? Corned beef and biscuits were good, but a man couldn't eat the same thing everyday. Annie was a good woman, easy on the eyes and better yet, he saw no Big Davies hovering around her. *Maybe it was time to settle down.* Loretta's friend was probably a wee bit older than he...but *then that should only make her more grateful for the attention she was about to receive.* After all if she could make such a good pudding and souse for a bunch of old ladies going on a church picnic, what wouldn't she do for her husband?

Patterson ambled over to the dining table where the food was spread out invitingly, and helped himself to his third portion of souse. Omar sat in a corner of the room, watching the man who had laughed last with Pearl. He wasn't sure he wanted him here. It was the first time Patterson had actually ever stepped foot inside their house and it felt strange. He watched Annie preen and let out a girlish giggle as she added a few more slices of breadfruit to Patterson's plate. She was embarrassed to be complemented so ardently about her cooking. Something about the scene reminded Omar of those times when Pearl and Shelly talked to boys, but he wasn't quite sure what, since these two had never spoken before today.

From the moment Junior first walked into Michael's house, he'd noticed how often the phone rang. It rang constantly for Michael, and for Michael's parents. It rang for the sister he hadn't yet met and for the cousin who didn't live there. If it wasn't Michael's girlfriend Lisa calling for the hundredth time that day, then it was someone who wanted to speak with her and assumed she lived there. Junior didn't like assumptions. That was not his style. Most of the girls he went out with didn't have a number for him, or know where he lived. The last thing he wanted was them calling every five minutes, or worse yet, getting friendly with either Pearl or Omar and discovering that they weren't his *'one and only'.* Fortunately he didn't have to worry about Loretta. His sister had figured him out years ago and did not interfere. Still, he guessed as long as Michael seemed happy, who was he to judge? When the call came through for Junior, it took him completely by surprise. Michael held out the receiver, it was Patterson on the line.

"Junior, how yuh doing man? You find de docta yet?"
"Hey Patterson, Yeah I find the doctor, but I got to wait for him to call me back. How things going over

there, how Loretta? I guess if you calling me it mean things still the same."
"Junior boy, you ain know de half uh it! The other man's distress was palpable even through the phone lines. "Listen, your sister like she gone off you know."
"Loretta? How you mean she gone off?"
"Is not even just your sister, is the whole house, de whole neighbourhood Junior! I call you to tell you, hurry up and find that docta real quick!"
"That's what I here trying to do; he supposed to call me back any minute now...but how you mean Loretta going off?"
"Junior, if I tell you that you sista 'bout there cooking fuh de whole neighbourhood like if it was a wedding party, you would believe me?"
"How you mean she cooking?"
"My man! From de time I get there till when I lef' I mussee see 'bout fifty people walk through that front door. De people eating and drinking like is a party and everybody going in to look at Pearl and talking to the girl like if she still living. No offence Junior, but that girl body done starting to smell and like nuhbody don't care! It ain normal, hear what I telling you?"
"For real?" Junior dragged his fingers across his brow, the long-fought-for-calm shattered by Patterson's last words.
"For *real!* You ain seen how hot it been lately? Flies 'bout de place man. The only body who getting on normal is Omar. He lying 'bout in the bedroom and

wouldn't talk to a soul. Not a body cyan get that boy to open he mout' since it happen."

"Oh no!" Junior expressed his dismay. "I should know he would take it bad."

"And them two disgusts Sandra and Belinda 'bout here telling everybody how Pearl gone and kill she self just to spite she mudda."

Junior ran his hand through his hair repeatedly. What he was hearing was too incredible to believe. His sister was practically having a party at home while her daughter's body lay stiff and smelling in the bed? The fact that the only near-normal behaviour was Omar's not speaking, did not ease Junior's worries in the least.

According to Patterson, Pearl's friend Shelly had even fought with Loretta about it. The girl had come over to the house late that Saturday evening after having been in town all day. Someone had already told her the bad news so she had rushed over distraught heading directly for Pearl's room. She'd started screaming and crying hysterically the moment she saw the body. To find her friend's mother entertaining guests and acting as if nothing were out of the ordinary was too much for Shelly to bear. And then came the hurtful exchange; Loretta had walked up to Shelly offering a glass of rum, advising that she calm herself down. She saw no reason for such hysterics especially considering that her good friend Pearl had clearly not been thinking about either of them when she decided to kill herself.

This callous indifference so incensed Shelly that she'd knocked the glass out of Loretta's hand and had a stranglehold on the woman's throat before one of the onlookers could pull her off.

Junior got off the phone from Patterson in a daze. Michael looked on, concerned.
"What happen Junior?"
"Things brown Michael man, things brown."
"Wha' happen?
"That was Patterson. He say that my family acting real strange. My sister have all the neighbours over like if is a party."
"How you mean a party?"
"I mean like serving drinks and everything."
"Serving drinks!" Michael was incredulous "So why she doing that?"
"I can't believe it myself." Junior gave a distressed laugh. "Apparently she feel my niece do it to spite her so Pearl body could stop there and rot for all she care."
"She say wuh?"
Junior scratched his head confused. "...and to think I was here worrying because I tek suh long to find one doctor, and she 'bout there cool, ain worried 'bout a thing."
"You sure it isn't a wake she's having? Maybe your friend didn't understand what was going on."
"A wake? My family never had a wake before! If is a wake, is the first time my family ever hold one."

"Junior you know that sometimes death does mek people act in really strange ways."

"Yuh telling me!"

"I remember one time my father tell me how he went to this funeral when he was a little boy growing up in St. George."

"Your father come from St. George? My family come from out there too!"

"For real? Shoot but this country small...you never know we might even be related..."

"Anything is possible, Barbados small. So you were telling me about a funeral?" Junior needed to hear Michael's story, anything that could get his mind off this crisis, if only for a minute was worth a shot. So he stopped pacing and encouraged Michael to continue.

"Daddy say he remember that day good because everything he had on was new. New suit, new tie, new shoes, everything was new! The shoes was so new, them was hurting he foot." Junior chuckled recalling similar days. "The funeral start round three and my father swear come six o'clock they was still in there."

"Wid the body open in the church?

"Wid the body open. Flies hovering and this man boring sermon wun done!

"Wuh laaws!

"He say they had this woman name Miss Mazy, a real character man. The people already used to laugh at she, 'cause she musee was 'bout forty and still couldn't married yet. All the men say them cyan afford she belly. Mazy fat fat fat! And when she sit down, they say she botsie used to take up enough space for three people!" Michael spread his arms wide in demonstration of Mazy's ample girth. "Well didn't nothing Miss Mazy love more that to go church. My woman used to go church every chance she get especially if it was somebody funeral...and think she care whether she know the body who dead or not? My woman could cry louder than family! The only thing Mazy interested in, was singing the people hymns as loud as she could - mek sure ever body hear she pretty voice – and eating up the people food when the funeral done. As for beef stew don't leh Mazy know yuh got beef stew sharing!"

"Mazy pun a regular basis could mek it to as many as three funerals in the same day... Presbyterian, Anglican, Jehovah's Witness, Mazy was there! Well this one day, my lady turn up at my father-great-aunt-husband funeral..."

"Your father-great-aunt-husband-funeral?" Junior paused trying to make sense of Michael's family tree.

"Yeah. So since Daddy was part of the mourning party, that mean he was sitting in the front pew right? Well when Mazy get there, my woman had done gone to one funeral in the morning and to the wake after. Seem like she eat suh much, that like she get de belly. Thing is Mazy like the preacher and she really only going church to see if she could snag he for a husband. So even though it killing she, Mazy cyan walk out without him noticing. This time now she brekking out in cold sweats with the effort!"

"Uh huh,"

"So Daddy now, he sitting down between he mother and he grandmother, right in front the preacher. You know what that mean? That my man can't move... and this preacher wouldn't stop talking! Then all of a sudden he hearing this moaning coming from down back, but he thinking is the wind blowing the church doors or something. Till he notice it coming more regular and everybody else peeping back. So he want to look back too...but all he see is that people in the pew next to Mazy got them face screw screw screw. Daddy trying to ignore it 'cause granny done tell him he got to report on what the preacher say after. But every time he try and concentrate on the sermon he hearing this moaning coming from down back again. The more Mazy try to hold it, the more noise this thing mekking when it come out...and my woman fanning hard yuh know trying to blow way this smell. Next thing, Daddy say all he hear is bruggadown! Sprrugggullacks! backattacks! Like if somebody car muffler backfire ...Mazy leh go air!"

Junior started to laugh. "Mazy poop in the people church?"

"But you ain hear the best Junior! My woman like she frighten she self suh bad that she jump up and holler fuh 'Jesus Christ!' Well now when the people hear that everybody turn round, cause the timing didn't exactly right to holler fuh Jesus Christ. So Mazy start to think quick quick and add some Hallelujah praise Jesus pun the end uh that, and start clapping she hands like she testify to wha' the preacher saying. This time the smell hovering over the pews like a pit toilet. People pulling out fans, covering dey nose with 'kerchief, and Mazy cyan stop pooping. The only place the scent ain reach is the pulpit. Each time Mazy poop she hollering fuh *Hallelujah!* and the foolish preacher at the front ah the church getting all excited cause he feel somebody like he sermon. Mazy jump up and holler for hallelujah? He hollering for hallelujah too.

Junior sniggered. "I bet they had nuff people calling the Lord name in vain that day"

"Not in vain Junior, not in vain. Daddy say he wanted to pee so bad, he had to cross his legs to stop water from running down...he say he would never forget how hard his grandmother was cutting her eye at him and how his mother had her spike heel rest pun top he shoe, and if he even think to move, she pressing it down firm 'pun top the big toe...wuh! You could imagine living in them days?"

"Not fuh joke dread. *That is pressure!"*

"The clothes got you hot, shoes burning, and to make matters worse yuh got to sit down pun them hard pews for hours and ain't got nuhwhere to rest 'pun cause yuh shoulder keep falling through the space in the back."

"...space in the back!" Junior couldn't stop laughing. The way Michael told the story was so funny..." Lord have mercy Michael, You had Sunday school days too?"
"How you meaning! I used to hate Sundays boy!"
"You telling me!"
"Well from that day on, anytime people see Mazy or the foolish preacher passing, they hollering for 'looka Hallelujah One' or 'looka Hallelujah Two going down the road.' None uh them ever get call by them real name again, you hear what I telling you?"
"And the moral of this story is?"
"Never poop in church!"
"Or somebody might laugh at yuh!" Michael and Junior laughed until they were almost on the floor. They laughed at Mazy, the preacher and at their shared experiences. It had been a good distraction. Junior pulled at his goatee, becoming pensive. "You think I should try and call this doctor again?"
Michael looked at his watch.
"Look like you going have to 'cause we been back here an hour and he ain call yet."

Junior called, his fingers dialling the familiar numbers reluctantly. He wasn't particularly eager to be given the run around anymore. He was hardly surprised when little Rebecca answered the phone. Neither could he identify the emotion he was feeling as disappointment when she told him her father had yet to come home.

Was Granny still sleeping? Yes; Any other adults in the house? No.
"Are you the same Junior who is supposed to be working with Daddy at Cohoblopot tonight?"
"No...I don't think so...your daddy working at Cohoblopot tonight?"
"Yes..." Rebecca breathed into the phone "Do you get to ride in the ambulance too?"
Whoever the other Junior was, this Junior was eternally grateful for his existence, because now he knew where to find the father of a little girl named Rebecca. It took a little convincing but he eventually got miss-suddenly-talkative Rebecca off the phone. Michael stood close by nervously biting his nails while he strained to hear the conversation at the other end of the line. It appeared their search party was on the move again.
"So wha' yuh say, we going still tek one last try, and go and look for this doctor at Cohoblopot?"
"Yeah man, I guess that is the plan."

* PEARL *
14

Omar was lonely. There was an ache in his heart. Not the familiar burning of indigestion after eating a handful too many green tamarinds. More, it was a deep ache, identifiable to adults as loss and profound regret – at not having said, not having done, of not having given, acknowledged, with enough love, respect, or attention – that person now recognised as important, essential to one's definition of self.

A jumble of disjointed "what ifs" swirled around in Omar's head, tumbling and spiralling with an irregular pattern that would cause his stomach to suddenly drop and his heart to skip – not dissimilar to that which passengers experience during a turbulence-filled flight. Still, never having flown before, never having experienced loss beyond that of a favourite ball, or missed treat, Omar could not have identified his emotions with such clarity.

At the moment he was effectively ignoring the persistent knocking on his windowpane. This would be Jeffrey's third attempt to attract Omar's attention since his knock on the Walcott front door had gone unanswered that morning. His mother Loretta had departed to he knew not where. Between them little dialogue had taken place.

It was the idea that he was lonely, that would eventually form the impetus for Omar opening his bedroom window; It was this same idea that would lead the trio of friends – Omar, Jeffrey and Chicken, to, as they had so many times before, their usual hang-out spot hidden within a clammy cherry grove. Chicken melted out of the trees, silent except for the crunch of crisp grass under his feet, leading the trio to the central boulders turned blindingly white under the midday heat. Omar, last in the single file, followed Jeffrey across the dry pasture with the understanding that these were the people he had always spent his time with, always relieved his frustrations with, and with whom he had always arrived at helpful solutions to even his most trivial of problems. That these same people now represented the cause of his most recent and greatest predicament; Omar hadn't precisely reconciled his feelings on that issue yet.

The dog Commando was curiously absent as the boys settled into their usual routine. Even he seemed to think there was better action to be had than around the subdued lot. Omar sat with his back propped against a boulder, head tilted up to the sky, eyes closed. Chicken to his left, worriedly picked the scab off a skinned knee. Jeffrey whittled a twig to a fine point with his Boy Scout penknife. The patch of earth in front him bore the marks of restless feet. They sat like this, not contributing much to the idle chorus of life - at that moment punctuated by the grunts of cattle egrets, and lone molested cow, followed intermittently by the sympathetic baas of black belly sheep.

Suddenly Jeffrey jumped up, "I tired of this man!" Feeling hot he yanked his shirt off, tossing it into a ball at his feet. "Why yuh all so miserable? Why nobody wun talk?"
"Omar sister dead Jeffrey." Chicken paused his scab-picking for a moment.
"I tell wuhnuh a'ready nobody ain going suspect we. We clear…"
"And when Junior come with the doctor, he going fix it..." Chicken's derisive tone resulted in a stare down between the youngest and eldest of the friends. Omar looked on, not wanting to participate, not wanting the tension to escalate. "…or you mean the doctor going know it was murder?"
"I ain murder nobody!" a primal force within Jeffrey, jumped up and down beating his chest, rebelling against the accusations.
"That's right Jeffrey," Omar got up, dusting the dry dirt off his shorts, looking back one last time as he walked away, "That's right. You didn't, *WE* did."

For possibly the hundredth time, Omar wondered where his uncle Junior might be. How could it possibly take this long to find a doctor or the police? The unnaturalness of the situation at his home was driving him crazy. He'd been wrong to think that hanging around self-centred Jeffrey could have made him feel any better. While it was comforting to know that Chicken was on his side, he just wished that someone would come, that anyone would take charge of the situation so that this business with Pearl would be all over.

Sunday night: less than a day to go till the big "jump-up", and Cohoblopot was the place to be for any true Kadooment reveller. Many, like Junior, would have planned this special night weeks in advance; who to go with, what to wear, where to park their car, and how to ensure all four tyres remained when the evening was over. This year however, Junior and Michael had other things on their minds. Settling into the L200 once again, their spirits were not so high. The drive was a quiet one, neither of them terribly optimistic about finding the elusive doctor.

With fifteen minutes left to spare till the show's scheduled eight o'clock start; the exterior of the stadium resembled the scene of a minor catastrophe. Those hustling to buy tickets at the very last minute jostled for position with late-comers trying to get in. Cars were everywhere, and even with officials directing traffic, it was still a parking nightmare. Somehow, Michael eased the L200 into a spot seemingly made to the truck's specifications. The men chuckled over their tremendous good luck and hoped it would carry over into the remainder of the evening. Judging from the number of people still purchasing tickets, Junior couldn't imagine the show starting on time. Three jagged lines snaked around the stadium's entrance. Junior and Michael bypassed them hoping to simply ask for the doctor and be let in. Better yet, they could try to sneak in with the fancy car being allowed access through the V.I.P gates.

Eyes focused determinedly on the goal ahead, they walked as inconspicuously as possible alongside the sleek silvery sedan. They were spotted almost immediately by the police officer on duty. Junior tried to play it cool by walking up to the officer, as though he'd always planned on asking him a question. He didn't want to pay if he couldn't see the show. "Excuse me officer, I'm trying to find a Dr. Cummins who's supposed to be on duty tonight. Can you tell me where I might find him?"
"I don't know the person you're talking about, but it would seem to me that if he is working here tonight, then you would have to come inside and look for him."

Junior looked at the long line of people they'd just passed.
"Yeah uhmn...we sort uh got an emergency, you feel you could let us in?"
"Let you in?" The officer laughed. The sound was an abrupt explosive bark. Junior fidgeted feeling uncomfortable with the way the officer looked at them as though he knew they were up to no good.
"Listen, I know you probably hear this one before, but we don't want to see the show, we just need to find this doctor and then leave. That can't take us more than ten minutes, right Michael?" Michael nodded.

A look of passive resistance crossing his face, the officer blocked Junior's vision of the distant V.I.P entry "Sorry sir. I cannot do that. Kindly join the line."
"You can't let us in not even for ten minutes?"
"Nope."
"Why not?"
"You see this?" He held up a clipboard in his hand. "This is a list of names of all the people I'm supposed to let pass through this gate. Is your name on this list?" Junior shook his head. "...because if your name were on this, you could go in and out, in and out, as many times as you pleased and I wouldn't be able to stop you."

Junior scratched his beard, trying to figure out a way to reason with the officer. "Could you call the doctor for us then?"

"Nope." The answer was a simple one. Junior tried again.

"Alright, how about if I go in and leave my friend outside here...to show you that we ain trying to fool nobody. We really don't plan to see the show yuh know!"

Like a true gentleman the officer held out his hand and politely showed them the gate. Junior had to admit, civil though the officer might be, it wasn't the answer he needed. Stubbornly persistent, he tried another tactic. "If I go in and my friend stay outside and wait for me, that won't prove to you that we not trying to pull a trick?"

"And then when I let you in, you going find one of your friends with a ticket, pass it on through one of the gates where I can't see, he won't have to pay, but I going be standing up outside here like an idiot, correct? The answer is still NO."

"But I'm not going to do that, *we're* not going to do that! Junior pushed Michael forward and pulled at his cheeks. Look at this man. Does he look like the kind a person who would do that to you?" Michael shook his head offering up his most innocent expression. They watched expectantly for a breathless second as the officer's lips twitched while he fought to control his amusement. Still he would not budge. Defeated,

Michael and Junior joined the queue. Despite the long lines remaining outside, the show was indeed beginning on time. They listened to the M.C announce the evening's line up and resigned themselves to the long wait ahead as the first of several acts performed. Junior paid for Michael. His unlikely ally had never been to a calypso spectacular like Cohoblopot before, and would probably never attend one again. Had it not been for Pearl's death and his family's bizarre situation - after all of Michael's kindness - he couldn't very well make the man pay for a show they would hardly see.

Half an hour later, they broke through the thick crowd of people buying food and chatting excitedly just inside the stadium's entrance. They stepped up onto the cycle-track and surveyed the sea of people on the grounds ahead. Rising with them was the roar of thousands of voices all laughing, talking, and singing. The stands behind them were packed. Michael turned around in amazement. He looked at the full stands and overflowing grounds, taking in the multicoloured spectacle; Food tents, a double row of bright yellow chemical toilets, dancing lights, excited people and at the very centre of it all, the stage. Large enough to hold several towering glittering structures, it currently supported the weight of six extremely acrobatic dancers, tumbling and cart wheeling around one dynamic performer. Immediately forgetting his purpose there, Michael's eyes roved from one end of the stage to the next, impressed by the energy-filled performance. On the ground level to the back of the stage, he could see a glittering structure of a costume waiting to be assembled. The brightly lit stage shone out from the centre of the field like a beacon in the night. The two men walked forward, drawn to the scene.

"My Lord Junior, I never knew they had so many people in Barbados!"
"Well now you know ma brother...It look like the whole country here nuh?"
The sounds rushed at them in rumbling waves, washing over them and reeling them in. Although right next to each other, they now had to shout just to make out each other's words. "Besides the presentation of the kings and queens of the bands, what else will happen?"
"Music groups and calypsonians like Brown paper bag or Coco tea. My favourite band's performing tonight. We get musicians from T&T and St. Vincent or Antigua too. Last year there was a laser show."
"Oh yeah?"
"Yeah."
"Man, the government must be mekking real money, if this amount a people does come here every year!"
"I would have to feel so too, if they going mek we pay seventy five dollars just to come in for ten minutes..."
Junior led Michael over to a quiet corner, "Now how we going find this doctor?"

Moments later they intercepted a stadium official as she hurried past them. "Excuse me Ma'am, we're trying to find a Dr. Cummins, he's supposed to be on duty with the hospital crew, you know where we could find him?" The woman in question wore a Lions' Club waistcoat, her access-pass pinned there and the walkie-talkie in hand indicated her authority. She was quite petite. "Our hospital crew should be situated with the ambulance near the back of the stage, but you need a pass to get in."

"You going there now? You could call him for us?"

"I wasn't really going that way, but I guess I could help, just follow me."

As tiny as the woman was, the two men found themselves panting with the effort of keeping up with her. She left them waiting by the fence while she went in search of the doctor. As predicted, the ambulance was parked nearby on the grass, ready for any emergency. Junior wondered how long it would be till the doctor was off duty and could go with them to see about his family. With little slowing of her pace, the Lions official was back outside almost as quickly as she'd gone in. Pointing at a figure behind them she fired rapid instructions before jogging off in the opposite direction. Doctor, blue shirt, and food-stand were about the only words they heard, all they saw was a man disappearing into the crowd, wearing a blue shirt.

"What!?" Junior shouted.

Junior and Michael rushed headlong into the crowd doing their darnedest to keep sight of that blue shirt. They followed it past a popcorn stand and several hot dog vendors, the chemical toilets and a mass of electric cables. Then just as they'd started to gain ground, Junior tripped, falling flat on his face. And in that split second, the man in the blue shirt had disappeared.

"Shite! Michael you see where he gone?" Michael's eyes searched the crowd, but it was impossible to make anything out in the thickness of the crowd. "I cannot believe it!" Junior swore stamping his foot and angrily knocking the dust off his borrowed clothing. "How he could be gone so quick?"

"I don't know man...but didn't the woman say something about food? Let's check Kentucky and see if he was going over there..."

They tore off again, this time running onto the edge of the track, thus avoiding the majority of the crowd and any other unseen dangers that lay in wait on the ground. When they came to a halt in front of the Kentucky food tent, they found no blue shirt there. The doctor obviously hadn't gone that way; otherwise he'd still be in the long line hungry souls waiting to make their orders. Junior rubbed his bruised elbow. "Let's check another tent. The man mussee tek one look at this line and decide to go someplace else for food.

"Maybe if he isn't a Kentucky-man he's a Coo Coo Village-man!"

"Good thinking Michael, let's look for him over there!"

They rushed off again, slowing down, only when the thick crowds made it impossible to move faster. Junior groaned. "You mean we got to go through all these people to get over there. He stared into the distance searching for a clearer path. People of all builds and sizes passed before them in a jumble of colour; from black and white to red and yellow, then suddenly through the haze Junior glimpsed a flash of blue.... *Blue!!!*

"Michael, you see that!"

"What?"

"Look!" Junior pointed. "That ain de same blue shirt?"

"Where?"

"Over there! Yes is the shirt, come!" Junior grabbed hold of Michael roughly pulling him along. "Stick with me, we got him now!"

Indifferent to the mashed toes and angry glares Junior and Michael pushed their way through the crowd. Each time the elusive blue shirt appeared, they ran forward in anxious bursts, but as mysteriously as it appeared, a few yards ahead, a little to the left or a little to the right, it would disappear. "Michael, you see where he gone now?"

"Over there!" Michael pointed to his left.

"No look! Straight ahead!" It was impossible to believe that there could be two men of the same height and build both wearing the same blue shirt. They didn't know what to do. Junior beat his head with his fists like a deranged man. "Oh lord what to do? Think quick, think quick...Michael! You follow this one, I going follow that one!"

The chase it seemed would never end. When Junior's man eventually led him to a drinks stand it turned out he was not the doctor, knew nothing about the doctor and really thought that Junior should *"chill out a little and watch the show instead of sneaking up on unsuspecting citizens and scaring them half to death."* Junior's eyes followed the man's meaningful look downwards to where he clutched tightly at a hairy arm. Junior let go surprised at himself, and mumbled an embarrassed apology before melting back into the crowd. What was going on with him? He had to get a grip on himself otherwise he was likely to tangle with someone who might not be as understanding as the last guy had been. He looked around for Michael, not really expecting to find him. The smart thing to do he guessed would be to return back-stage and wait for Michael there.

Michael for his part, finally caught up with his blue shirt by a hot dog cart. "*Doctor Cummins!*" he called, "*Doctor Cummins!*" Michael was sure the man was within hearing distance, but he wouldn't turn around.

"Must be deaf" Michael muttered to himself, running up to the man and touching him just as he was about to bite into a hotdog. "*Doctor Cummins!*"

"Ahh!" The man jumped at the voice so close to his ear, then pressed a hand to his rapidly beating heart. "Who you?"

"Oh, sorry Sir, are you Doctor Cummins?"

"No! The man recommenced eating his jumbo hotdog, then looked at Michael sideways "...But I work with Doctor Cummins." Somewhat suspicious, he moved a little away from Michael. "I does drive the hospital ambulance. What you want?"

"I want..."

"DR. CUMMINS AND CREW PLEASE REPORT TO STAND C IMMEDIATELY." Just as Michael was about to explain, a voice over the loudspeaker interrupted them. Both men looked up and listened. The MC had come back on stage to make the announcement. "I REPEAT. WOULD DOCTOR CUMMINS AND THE REST OF THE HOSPITAL CREW PLEASE REPORT TO STAND C- THERE IS AN EMERGENCY IN STAND C- AN OFFICIAL WILL GUIDE YOU TO THE PATIENT'S LOCATION."

Now in a hurry, the man in the blue shirt shovelled down his remaining hot dog and motioned for Michael to follow as he walked briskly towards the back-stage and the ambulance. He turned to Michael. That's why you looking for Dr. Cummins? What happen in stand C?"

"I don't know...but it must be something fairly serious if they call it over the loud-speaker." Michael hopped agilely over the same cables that had tripped Junior previously. "You know where Dr. Cummins is?"
"Well he lef with me to get something to eat, but like I loss him near the Kentucky stall. They send you to look for him?"
"Ahh..." Michael wasn't sure whether to lie or tell the truth. "I was looking for him because somebody... somebody sick and..."
"Well I guess he must be there by now if he hear the same announcement we hear." They had arrived backstage and Michael was once again obliged to remain outside the secure area.

"Michael!"
The young man turned around to see Junior up ahead, panting and out of breath.
"You find Dr. Cummins? That is him?" he quizzed excitedly.
The ambulance driver turned back when he heard the exchange, not particularly thrilled by Junior's presumption. "Why everybody tek me for Cummins. I look like Dr. Cummins?"
"No Junior, this is the ambulance driver."
"Yeah, I is the ambulance driver and I got an ambulance to drive, so *excuse me*."
"We could come with you?"

"Come wid me! Wha' you feel this is, Coney Island? Is wukking I wukking!" The driver jumped into the ambulance and was on his way sirens blaring before Junior and Michael could follow him beyond the small exit gate.

"What to do now Michael? You know for a minute I thought it was you who call the doctor on the loud speaker you know."

"No it wasn't me."

"That would have been a smart thing to do...you think we should go over to stand C?...but then I guess the doctor ain really going have time to talk to us if somebody really sick though. You think we should wait here?"

"I don't know what to think. Maybe if we hang around a while they'll come back."

With little else to do Michael and Junior walked towards the side of the stage and watched the "Queens of the Band" parade in front of the audience. One queen in particular caught Junior's eye. After seeing her, Junior found it impossible to recall any of the other contestants who had appeared on the stage before or since that. She was beautiful. Like a dream out of his deepest fantasies. All glittering gold and silver, her costume literally danced with life. She was "Spectacular Sensations" from the band 'Speechless Rhythms'. She represented love and life entwined. Junior stood with his mouth agape. On her back rested four large transparent silver wings trimmed

with gold and multicoloured sequins. A butterfly: the link between earth and sky - plant and animal - as multicoloured as love and life. Bright red hibiscuses bounced at her ankles as though she were amidst a field of wind blown flowers. From her head-piece protruded the bright gold and silver rays of the sun. Around her eyes diamond studs twinkled, and to Junior her bright red smile, beckoned him come. He was in love. Junior shook his head like a wet dog, trying to clear his muddled thoughts. "It must be something in the air", he muttered to himself. "You want a drink Michael? Michael!" Junior looked over at his friend, surprised to see eyes transfixed on the stage with a similarly dazed expression. Waving a hand in front of Michael's face, Junior searched for any traces of mental activity. Finally he blinked. Junior chuckled. "Come Michael man, leh we get a drink. My treat... but you got to promise to pick you jaw up off the ground before people start looking at we funny."
Michael looked at Junior, eyes wide. "Jesus Junior! You see that girl?"
"Wha'! She pretty nuh!"
"Yuh telling me!"
"I got to find out who she is boy!"
"Find out who she is? You outa luck Michael. That woman is mine and you got a girlfriend."
"Girlfriend?"
"Lisa, you remember her?" They walked towards one of the bars.

"Leh me tell you! Anything that woman ask me to do, I would do." Michael pointed towards the stage, the image of their last queen, Love and Life still vivid in his mind. "I would be her love slave. If she tell me to get down on all fours and bark like a dog, I there!"
Junior howled. "Bark like a dog?"
"Yeah man! *Ruff Ruff! Just so.*" Michael stood in front of the bar doing his interpretation of a foolish dog, hands curved like paws, his tongue hanging out of the side of his mouth as he whimpered like a puppy. Junior almost choked on the beer he'd ordered.
"Boy how you get so foolish though? I can't eat nothing round you. You always talking junk and making me laugh!"
"But you ain see that girl! You didn't think she look good Junior...boy Junior, don't even talk to me no more if you didn't think she look good, cause something would got to be wrong with you!"
"Of course I think she look good, and that is why next time you see me, I going be *Mr.* Spectacular Sensations!" Junior strutted around like a peacock while Michael slapped the counter top uncontrollably. The people around the bar just watched the two men making idiots of themselves and shook their heads in wonder.

Two white men exchanged comments with each other as they observed the duo's antics.
"Boy, Kadooment does mek people real foolish hear?"

"Yuh don't lie" replied the other taking a glance at Michael. He projected his voice loud enough for the young man to hear.
Michael looked up recognising a familiar voice. "Ray Thompson! That is you? Man I ain see you in so long, how you doing?"
"I good man."
"But I didn't know you were back in Barbados. I thought you were living in Ontario or someplace so."
"Man I come back for Kadooment! You think this could miss me? Kadooment couldn't miss me at all dread!"
Michael turned to Junior all excited. "Junior, you know who this man is? I ain see this man in years! Michael hugged his friend round the shoulders and introduced him to Junior. "Man we had some school days nuh. What you doing now, Rachael here with you?"
"Yeah man, I just come to get us some drinks. Come back with me and say hi nuh."
"Yeah man, we got to talk!" Junior I going over here with Ray a minute, you cool here, or you coming wid we?"
"I cool here man, got my beer. You go along."
"I coming back right now though."
"Nah man. There ain no hurry. Take yuh time, tek yuh time. I might move around a little bit though...see if I find my posse. How 'bout if we meet back behind the stage in about..." Junior looked at his watch."...In about half an hour?"

"Yeah that sound good man. Check you later." Junior saluted Michael with his half full cup and watched him push off into the crowd with his friends.

Ausencia Delgado observed with shrewd eyes as her grandson walked into the house through the front door. His usually sprite steps were slow and heavy. He seemed to carry the weight of at least half the world on his shoulders. For her that was several pounds too many…She dried her hands from the sink full of dishes she'd just finished washing and met Antonio halfway across the floor. He was a brave and strong boy, (much unlike the nickname his friends had given him) Abuela thought to herself. She saw determination and resilience vibrating through his wiry frame.

Chicken loved his grandmother. He could always count on her to be there. Now, as he put his hand in hers, he allowed himself to be lead over to the three-seater.

"*Mi hijito, qué te pasa? Algo te molesta?*"

Chicken leaned into the rhythmic rumble of Abuela's voice as she pulled him close to her breast. He had no idea what the words meant, but her soothing tones were just what he needed. He felt sad. He felt an achy pain that was worse than any skinned knee; worse than lashes from his father when he came home too

late; much worse even than the shame he often felt when others made fun of his stuttering at school. Shame? Maybe so.
Somebody take your marbles again? You can't get so attached to *theengs* you know Antonio.
"No." Chicken shook his head. That wasn't it.
"Well don't tell me this have *notheeng* to do with your friends," Abuela persisted. "*Ay mi vida*...you so young...so much to learn...so much Abuela can't teach you." Abuela peppered Chicken with kisses from his brow to his cheek. You know how you know you alive?
"No." Chicken sat up, peering into Abuela's eyes trustingly.
"*El dolor*...the pain. You know cause you feel pain"

Abuela grabbed Chicken's hand in hers, rubbing it against his belly. "Remember how *eet ees* when you hungry? You'll eat almost *anytheeng* no?" Chicken nodded. He knew that feeling well. When he played too long and too hard and forgot to eat until the bad feels would get him. Abuela continued, "Scared, hungry, angry, or *een* love...*ees* all the same *theeng*. Sometimes in between, you feel happy too.
Ser Feliz es gran cosa!" Abuela's chest heaved with a great big sigh. "*Estar en armonia con todo*"...
Chicken knew those words - be in harmony; happy – Abuela repeated the phrase often enough over the years.

"...*eef* not to everyone else, be honest with yourself." She touched a finger to his heart. "Be true here, know you. Si?"

Chicken nodded. His heart thudding with a faster beat. He would remember, until he could make sense of what his grandmother had said. Something profound, which he almost thought he understood. For now he was relieved to be only nine, relieved that it was still ok to let his Abuela tuck him into bed. There was time enough to act grown-up like Jeffrey.

"No te preocupes mi vida. Everytheeng will work itself out. I ever tell you about the time I fought the great serpent?"

"No." Chicken chuckled, his mood lifting just a little.

Throughout the household his grandmother's stories were legendary. Tales of her journey across the hills and valleys of Central America were so plentiful and well embellished, no one knew when or how fact merged with fiction. Some days Ausencia flew across oceans as a giant winged bird, other times she fought a mysterious black panther, pitting diamond sharp claws against her iron clad will. There was Chicken noticed, always a common theme in each telling and retelling. Abuela victorious, Abuela the survivor, the small, weak, outcast - overcoming – against all odds. Yes Chicken thought he knew what his grandmother was talking about.

Well over an hour had gone by before either Junior or Michael remembered their interrupted search for the doctor. The former had in that time also managed to catch up with his posse and had spent the moments trying to regain favour with Vanessa. His chickens, it would seem, had finally come home to roost. She did not believe his tale of sudden torrential rains, that caused a flat tyre leaving him stranded in Bathsheba, and, she certainly could not believe the saga of his two-day-long quest for a coroner following the discovery of Pearl's sudden and untimely demise. "A *girl had to draw the line somewhere!"* The irony of the situation did not escape Junior. Indeed it was poetic justice, because for the first time in his life, just when he'd found a woman with whom he could be in a stable relationship, his reputation as a player, had finally gotten the better of him.

It was not until almost the last performance that he suddenly remembered his appointment with Michael. He raced back to their meeting point outside the gate, only to spend the next ten minutes wearing a path in the patch of grass while praying that Michael hadn't already left without him.
"Junior, you still here! Jeeze on! You know I completely forget the time. I was having so much fun. I sorry man, this is the second time I got you waiting on me so long."
"Don't worry, I just get here too, I actually thought you had left already."

"What about the doctor. You speak to him yet?"
Junior rubbed his eyes tiredly. "Michael if I tell you, I forget all 'bout that too and when I check just now, they tell me that the man gone 'long ever since. Is a miracle if we find he now, I starting to feel tired and ain really feel like going back to that hospital again." He yawned and stretched. "Police or doctor, that got to wait till tomorrow."
"Yuh right man, we had a long day, I ready to go home too...You could sleep by me if you want and then try and reach him again tomorrow, 'cause right now a few hours ain going make so much of a difference."
"Yuh don't lie. You sure your parents wouldn't mind though?"
"Nah man, they cool. Besides they still in Cattlewash. So is just me and you in the house, 'cause my sister sleeping over by friends, she jumping tomorrow."
"Alright, I ready. Let's go then." Maybe it was because he hadn't been there, but to Junior, Pearl's passing and the events surrounding it, hardly seemed real. It was difficult to feel sad when so much happiness was going on all around you. He was meeting new people and enjoying the experience. Even in spite of his discussion with Vanessa he felt hope. He wasn't quite sure what to make of it, but he did know that he'd done more than enough thinking to last an entire year. Junior shook his head in wonderment; the direction his life had taken in the last two days was all too strange.

Junior knew he was dreaming. He was certain of it. But he was enjoying himself too much to leave this place. It felt good here. Butterflies fluttered all around him in this warm dark space, their soft wings caressing his face. His head was filled with the fragrance of flowers, of grass and morning dew – dew so misty he watched it move each time the gentle breeze blew. In a room somewhere beyond the mist, there came the faintest tinkle of bells. He walked towards it, his steps unhurried. As he drew nearer, a faint melodic voice joined it calling his name. He followed, mysteriously drawn like a moth to a flame. It was she...the girl from the stage. She looked even more beautiful than he'd remembered. Soft waves of light radiated from her body and filled the room with an ethereal glow. Junior felt a rush of love warm his insides when her lips curved upwards in a smile. He stopped, transfixed by her beauty. She floated just beyond his reach, her almost transparent wings keeping her inches off the ground. Her eyes glittered like dark jewels, deep and full of mystery. Under her skin twinkled all the stars in the universe. Blue black she seemed to simultaneously absorb and give off the light which filled the room, and without which he would have stumbled in utter darkness. Her entire body was music. In his head played a symphony of bird-song, the trill of flutes, love and truth. When she held out her hand beckoning, entrancing, Junior was helpless to resist. She led him that way, drawing him out of one space and into some deeper darker place.

Sometimes he lost sight of her and had only her voice calling "*Junior, Junior*" as his guide. And each time he caught up with her, she had changed...just a little. First the tinkling became fainter. Then even though the mist continued to swirl around her, even though her feet never touched the ground – he could tell her wings were gone. Then for one brief moment the mist surrounding them swirled so thickly, he thought he'd lost her forever. Junior held out his hands desperately, grasping at fingers of no substance. His heart pounded in his chest, the loss too painful to bear. Suddenly just when he thought all hope was lost, the mist cleared. She was there. Pearl was there. They were one and the same. She laughed at him playfully. It had been a good game. Did he want to play some more? If so he'd have to hurry, hurry or lose her again. Again...

The buzzing sounded close by, yet he couldn't quite tell where it was coming from. Omar brushed an absentminded hand past his ear, believing that would do the trick. Still...his hand felt heavy. Why did his hand feel so heavy? He tried to lift it again but this time he couldn't even raise it past his thigh. He didn't even remember wrapping the sheet so tightly around himself. Omar looked down as the weight on his arm grew. He was so confused, he was sure he'd covered himself with a white sheet, yet this one was brown... and black.

As early morning sunlight filtered through the window it cast shiny golden brown reflections each time the sheet moved. Even as Omar struggled with his obvious paralysis it rippled of its own volition, like a wave lapping a sandy shore. How could the sheet move when he hadn't? Omar looked around in wonderment... and where was all that noise, that constant buzzing coming from?

A thousand angry eyes snapped at him with military precision. Black and shiny they bulged from the hard shells of sleek brown bodies, ruffling wings with sandpapery abrasiveness. There were roaches everywhere. Omar screamed. It was a scream that stretched his lips farther than they had ever been stretched before. It opened up his mouth like a portal releasing *them* in droves. Swarms of flies thick and black like pitch surged forward. They flew out of his open mouth and gathered themselves at the foot of the bed. As the insects exited, their buzzing increased threefold threatening to deafen him. Silver iridescent reflections bounced off rapidly beating wings adding to Omar's confusion. In an angry haze they swarmed around his head filling all the room and integrating themselves with the army already assembled there. As his scream filled the room it ricocheted off the walls, meeting the low drones of the dark cloud of insects threatening to overwhelm him. Omar turned his head helplessly, his tongue burned where it had been cut. *His tongue had been cut!* Real tears rolled down a little boy's face as his suddenly free hands felt the gaping hole that had once been his mouth and where nothing but the blackened stub of his tongue now remained. With a helpless wail, he clawed at his face trying to seal his lips.

Gaining strength, the army of flies and roaches surged above him in a wave of spectacular height. Shrouding the ceiling they prepared to attack, and petrified out of his mind, Omar threw himself onto the floor in one last desperate attempt at self-preservation. He covered his head, shielding his eyes from an encounter with the inevitable.

Loretta came and found him that way, sobbing uncontrollably. When she pulled him out from under the bed, she found that he had wet himself. And though she tried to comfort him, he still trembled; his sweat-lathered skin cold to the touch. Loretta pulled her only child onto her lap and rocked him back and forth. She rocked him till he slept. He wouldn't talk. He wouldn't tell her what had upset him so. But she took comfort in his tight hold on her. He at least was not about to die.

* PEARL *
15

Junior woke up feeling a sense of urgency. It took him a while to recognise his foreign surroundings. He sat up straight in the double bed of Michael's large guest room. Memories of the very sensual dream he'd had the night before brought an instant smile to his lips. He rushed to the toilet to relieve his suddenly overloaded bladder. With his eyes trained on a crack in the wall above, other pieces of his dream also came to mind. Junior washed his face to the sound of the toilet refilling its tank. Today would bring an end to this drama. With determined strides he headed for the living room and the phone. Why was he not surprised to learn that the doctor had already left home? At least this time he was able to get more concrete information from the not so fictitious grandmother. If the doctor was at the stadium, then to the stadium they would go.

Junior and Michael drove up to the stadium, and met absolute pandemonium. There was nowhere to park, and traffic was backed up on both sides of the street.

People had abandoned their cars in whatever position or wherever they could find a space big enough to fit their vehicle. Groups and individuals walked and ran crazily between cars, some in complete costume, others only partially dressed.

Three very pretty girls all covered in glitter, and too excited to think about where they were going, ran right into the L200. They laughed and giggled blowing on yellow whistles that perfectly matched their skimpy yellow costumes. Their blue and orange Indian chief head dresses bobbed up and down as they blew kisses of apology at the car's occupants before continuing on their way. Junior and Michael waved back and grinned foolishly at one another. You couldn't help but feel the spirit, the excitement. Even though Kadooment happened every year, there was always something new and special about the occasion.

"Junior, it look like you better get out and look for this man while I drive around, 'cause I can't see a patch of green to park 'pon."
"Yeah, ok." Junior got out then spoke to Michael through the truck window. "You drive round and see if we could meet up by the lumber yard. If I finish first I going look for you on the road."
"Yeah that cool"
"Ok see yuh."

Junior became simply one, of thousands of Bajans weaving mindlessly through the traffic. Car horns honked, people shouted and were shouted at, friends lost one another and then found one another back. The sky was so blue and the grass was green again after only a day's rain. *It was a kaleidoscope of colour.* Junior snorted at his clichéd thought. Suddenly he felt a sharp jab at his stomach and looked down to see a long wooden pole with a shiny sky-blue flag on the end. Its source, an open car window. Out of the other two windows hung similar flags, one more blue and the rest shiny magenta. A male hand accompanied by a deep voice, reached out and pulled the offending pole away from his stomach.
"Sorry my man."

After Junior was allowed to pass he glanced inside the car and saw three couples, not including the driver, piled in one on top the other. It was not a big car, which explained why there was so little room left for the flagpoles. Their millennium bug headpieces took up the entire shelf behind the back seat. There was no way the driver could convince anyone she was using it to see through. The big black bugs reminded Junior of a scene out of the old 'Arachnophobia' movie. Since no one was wearing the florescent orange of Dr. Cummins costume, Junior continued on his way. When he eventually reached the assembly point it was to discover that 'Generation Ex', Dr. Cummins' band, had been number four in the draw and had long since left the stadium. They would at least be a third of the way down the road by now.

After looking at the traffic, and rightly assessing that it would be no better elsewhere, Junior reunited with Michael and they decided to drive round the back through Eagle Hall to find a park closer to the band's location. From there they walked towards town on roads more or less parallel to the jump up route. Their first attempt brought them just above Strathclyde. In Kadooment time: approximately two hours into the jump-up session. Revellers would be in varying states of inebriation and exhaustion. The efficient work of the band's busboys was evidenced by the many hot bodies discarding more and more of their costumes while leaving a trampled trail of paper cups and colour behind. Dr. Cummins' band had already gone past this point. Junior and Michael hurried to catch up with them. The smell of sweat and drink lingered strong in the air, causing many to hold their heads high in search of oxygen. It was not until near Eagle Hall Market that they caught up with the band.

This Eagle Hall section of the road was narrow. Consequently the band was extended over a larger distance making individuals harder to find. It was also the halfway point, a crucial time for a Kadooment reveller. There were those who would hit the wall like marathon runners: In spite of the numerous water hoses provided by government at strategic spots, the combination of heat, too much alcohol and two months of partying would in the end invariably claim its victims. They would collapse and have to be carried away by friends or by a nearby ambulance. Others would decide that the band was moving too slowly and break ranks in search of food to satisfy an incomparable hunger. Those too shy to pee outside would go in search of friendly smile willing to submit their homes to the service of public lavatory. Junior hoped and prayed that the good doctor was not among that lot. Better he be one of those who had passed the wall into total oblivion, believing Kadooment day to be two days and not one.

It was also a time of infiltration and penetration. Bouncers had their work cut out for them trying to distinguish between and separate their band's members from others with similar costumes. Their worst enemy the male civilian, who having had approximately two months over which to ponder the great Caribbean issue; 'to jump or not to jump' had decided not to, thereby saving some two hundred or more Barbados dollars - which could be put to better use for things like the next month's rent or making car payments - had of course on D day changed their minds, feeling they were somehow still entitled to a free 'wuk up' from a pretty girl in a 'hard' costume who didn't seem to mind at all. The end result was a team of bouncers who became very aggressive whenever confronted by such 'civilians'.

They would throw them bodily out over the ropes to land in crumpled heaps at the side of the road. In short, the halfway point was total confusion, and Junior and Michael found themselves walking right into the middle of it.

Junior sincerely hoped that the fact that he'd supported this same band for the past three years would work in his favour. Hell! He should be jumping right now! Instead his costume lay at home on his bed waiting for its never to come again moment of glory. He didn't even have an I.D. bracelet to prove he'd paid for the privilege of walking in their midst. Michael voiced his concern.
"Junior, you see all them people getting pelt out by the bouncers?"
"Yeah..."
"But Junior, you see de size ah them bouncers?"
"Yeah I see...but this is my band don't worry. After the $250.00 that I spend, them better damn well leh me in!" No sooner had Junior spoken those words than he was confronted face to chest with the biggest, toughest looking bouncer a civilian could ever have the misfortune to encounter. Junior's eyes travelled up the never-ending expanse of black t-shirt, melded to muscle like paint to steel. They travelled across bunching biceps and powerful triceps to a thick neck pulsing with barely-restrained energy, then to meet piercing eyes and a smile of recognition so

unexpected, that Junior almost peed himself with relief.
"Junior my man! What you saying?"
"T. Hey man!" They pounded fists.
"Wha' going on Junior man, I thought you was jumping wid we, who this fellah?"
"He wid me, he wid me. T, this is Michael." The young man looked at T sceptically, unsure whether he actually wanted to trust any part of his anatomy to him, he nodded in acknowledgement instead. Junior continued, now more confident. "Yeah man I was jumping, but things bad man, we had an accident at home and Michael and me here looking for a doctor name Owen Cummins, that supposed to be in the band. You know him?"
"Yeah, yeah, I know him." T. looked around distractedly. The men moved along with the rest of the band as it chipped towards Spring Garden. Another bouncer requiring assistance called out to T.

"Excuse me a minute Junior." Both Junior and Michael turned their heads away from the sight of three young civilians flying like chickens through the air, one of them hitting the sidewalk with a loud crack. The bouncer with T. dusted off his hands and headed towards Junior and Michael with dangerous intent. Ten muscular fingers gripped Michael's arm firmly. But fortunately T. came back just in time to stop him doing serious damage. "He wid we, he wid we, it cool it cool." The bouncer very reluctantly let go.

"Well T. If them wid you, you better give the two of them some tags or something, otherwise next time I see them, they out!"
"Yeah, I hear you man, we going take care of that right now."

Junior and Michael were issued florescent green bracelets and caps that read 'Generation Ex' Crew. This allowed them to walk through the band unharmed.
"T, Dr. Cummins, you got any idea where he is?"
"Not a clue, I see that man walk up and down here suh many times, I ain't even know if he still in de band. All I could tell you is he jumping bout wid a lot uh Trinnies and in the orange section...but since we ain't really got nuh sections any more, you would have to check the whole band."
"How old he is, how he look?"
"He 'bout forty, a bit lighter than you...he tall enough, got a good build like he's work out and ting, and he ain't bad looking neither...sporting a moustache, and he's wear glasses too.

"Alright I could work wid that. Michael how 'bout we separate, any man you see 'bout that age, ask if is Cummins, and leh we check back wid one another in...
" Junior checked his watch "lets say fifteen minutes at the music truck."
"Which one?"
"The one in front with the live band."

"Alright check yuh later." The men separated. Junior started from the front of the band, working his way back, while Michael was to focus on the peripheries checking amongst the A-wallers. It was not long before he was held onto by a very happy female for a quick wuk up session. He happily obliged. Then feeling guilty for enjoying himself when he was supposed to be helping his friend, he took the opportunity to ask her if she knew the doctor. When her answer was negative, Michael moved on.

Exactly fifteen minutes later they met at the music truck, then twice after that. Finding Owen Cummins was proving to be more difficult than they'd expected. Junior, determined not to give up, made his move through the band's ranks again. Two young ladies escorted by a big man, seeming to fit Cummins' description sandwiched Junior between them. The orange tassels around their waists swung hypnotically while they danced, safe in the knowledge that if things got out of control, their personal bodyguard would come to the rescue.

As luck would have it, their "bodyguard" turned out to be none other than the brother of Owen Cummins. He was obliging enough to escort Junior to where they had recently left his sibling and sister-in-law. Junior was led towards a group of five or more people a few yards away. They came chipping down the road, one lady still with her flagpole in hand. She apparently hadn't hit the wall; had bypassed it in fact, because her entire costume - headpiece, anklets, bracelets with orange voile wings were all completely intact! Every so often she would pass the flag between her legs and twirl it like a majorette. When she noticed the others approaching she waved, then stopped right in the middle of the road for a special demonstration of her skills. Shortly afterwards she was joined by a man, not as steady on his feet, who tried to follow her movements. He held on to her waist with one hand while keeping his drink steady in the other. Though his rhythm was questionable he somehow managed not to spill a drop of the cup's contents. The couple moved forward again smiling and waving at their approaching posse.

Junior took a better look at the couple realising as they got closer that he had finally found the man for whom he'd been searching the past two days - Doctor Owen Cummins. He was tall, fairly well-built, did indeed have a moustache and even wore glasses as T. had described...and his eyes were glazed over. Junior felt his elation deflate as acutely as a balloon must feel when emptied of air. It was evident that the likelihood of Cummins stringing two coherent words together was very, very slim. Junior groaned.

"LOUIS!" Cummins shouted at his brother who was right in front of him. "LOUIS! I thought you was going for more drinks man?"

Junior groaned again, thinking cynically to himself that the man was not only drunk but had gone deaf too. He had to admit however that he was impressed by Cummins ability to string more than two words together, even if with a heavy slur.

"Yeah Owen we going fuh dem now, but dis fellah was asking for you, so I bring him tuh yuh."

"Whish fellah?" he asked staring into his brother's mouth foolishly.

"This one." Louis turned his brother's head towards Junior.

"Oh!" He said abruptly. Cummins tilted forward and struggled momentarily with his balance. Then he looked at Junior. "Who you?"

Junior was feeling less hopeful by the second, but held out his hand to introduce himself to the doctor anyway. "I'm Junior, Sir."

Dr. Cummins slapped away the offending hand and chupsed, asking Junior what he felt he was doing trying to shake people hand 'pun Kadooment day. "You ain't know dis is de bacchanal time? Bacchanal, bacchanal, bacchanal, bacchanal time!" Cummins punctuated each word of Rudder's song with pelvis jerking forward and hands in the air. Finally he lost his cup. The black drink splattered on the ground all over his shoes. "Louis man, wha' happen wid de drinks man?" Cummins complained to his brother upset at his loss.

"I going now ah tell yuh, but talk to this man here." He said patting Junior on the back before turning

away to get the drinks with his two charges. Cummins looked at Junior puzzled and curious.
"Wha' you name?"
"Junior Sir."
"Wha', Junior man, wha' you doing in a band wearing jeans and T-shirt, you is a bounsa? But you look too skinny to be a bounsa."
"No Dr. Cummins, I'm not a bouncer, and I'm not jumping either."
"So then wha' you doing here?" Cummins obviously thought Junior rather stupid, as he would anyone who came to Kadooment but not to party. "...and wha' you calling me docta fuh? I ain nuh docta today. *I...am the centre of...the univeeerrrse, from which the light flows giving all...their much needed light glow...*" Cummins spread out his arms like wings completely caught up in the fantasy of his orange section. His face contorted in the most ridiculous of expressions. Junior was worried the man might actually believe all the bull-shit he was saying.

Cummins continued, turning toward the lady in orange who had remained by his side during the encounter. "... *and this is my beautiful stellar through which all forces are united, to bring together the worlds and peoples of the world... into the next...MILENIUM!"*

Junior could hear Chinese gongs and all kinds of cymbals going off with Cummins last words, and wondered if whatever the man was suffering from might be contagious. The beautiful stellar who was actually Cummins' wife, and whose name was Joan, held out her hand in introduction. She continued smiling and swaying from side to side and bouncing hips with her husband as though his behaviour were perfectly normal.

"Junior come to talk to me Joan." He said by way of explanation.

"Oh yes?" She said with a Trini accent. "What about?"

"I ain sure, but I know he cyan be looking fuh nuh doctor 'cause I ain wukking today." Cummins gave his wife a playful bump with his hips making Junior smile at the wonderful camaraderie that existed between the two. Joan noticed his disappointment.

"You need a doctor?" My husband really not too sober right now yuh know, he only standing because I'm holding him up."

"Yeah, I can see that." Junior mumbled.

"What happen that you need a doctor though?"

"Mrs. Cummins, I been trying to find your husband since yesterday...but yuh know is Crop Over and I guess he's a busy man. I even went looking for him at Cohoblopot last night."

"Oh, so you not looking for him because somebody sick in the band!"

Joan held onto Junior urging him to move forward with the rest of the band that was quickly leaving them behind. The bouncers holding the ends of the long ropes which separated them from the onlookers herded the stragglers together like mindless cattle. Junior got into step and chipped down the road next to Joan and her husband. He was going to have to try and make this work, find a way to convince Joan to sober her husband up, because Cummins caught up in his own world, had long stopped listening.

"No, ahmn we had an accident at home and my, my sister's daughter died...."

"Your sister's daughter died...and...?" Junior watched Joan's smiling face change as she repeated his words suddenly becoming aware of their import. She stopped then, causing her husband to trip. Junior helped steady them both.

"What you jus' say?!" Her mouth hung open in shock. "But how you could say that so calm? Owen you hear that!?" She turned shaking her husband hard by the shoulder. He looked over surprised to see Junior still with them.

"What! Boy you still here? I tell you, I didn't going nuh where! Docta off-duty today." With that Cummins started wukking up again. His wife held on to his waist firmly, trying to calm him down. But it wasn't easy.

"So what exactly you need Owen for?"

Junior explained what he knew of Pearl's death and all the police had told him about normal procedures in such matters and how unhelpful they had been and that after two day's search, her husband was his only hope.

Michael in tow, the others returned laden with drinks in time to hear Junior's woeful tale. It would have been difficult for even the hardest of party revellers to feel unmoved. And, since it was clear Cummins had it within his power to resolve the problem, his family appealed to his humanitarian nature. He must leave the band and help the two young men. This did not please Cummins in the least. It is not easy to defend yourself against the pleading looks of a wife, family, friends and two pitiful faces however, especially when your only reason for not helping is your desire to stay drunk and party all day. Cummins felt himself quickly caving in. And he protested like a little boy whose bedtime had arrived one hour early.
"But why me, we can't wait till it done? This is the first vacation I tek in a whole year!"
"Honey, have pity on the poor fellah nuh, he been looking for you so long..."
"Listen man, they got nuff other doctors in this band, why wunnuh don't go an trouble none a them? You cyan see I having fun!"
"Yes I know you having fun, but how you would feel if something bad were to happen to our little girl? Put yourself in his place. Wouldn't you want to know there was somebody out there willing to help? Is not like you can't jump again next year, and anyway, you forget we already book your flight to Trinidad Carnival

next year... and is not like you didn't get to jump at all. Look, we more than half-way there."

Well after that kind of reasoning who wouldn't break down? Junior felt sorry for the man and forever indebted to his wife. Not only was she pretty, but she could really make a man feel guilty. Now they only had one problem: how to sober him up?
"But you cyan see I drunk, I could barely stand up. How I supposed to drive my car and take care ah anybody?"
"Don't worry about that Mr. Cummins." Michael offered quickly. "I have my vehicle parked not too far from here, I could go get it and we would drive you."
"But I drunk, I cyan tell my left foot from my right and you want me to work? I would have to sober up first." The same man, who minutes before had been carrying on foolishly, was now all business.
"Don't worry darling I going help you with that" Joan said giving her husband a kiss. "Louis, do me a favour and get Owen some water from the drinks truck or even a coke or a sprite please." Junior smiled at the woman who was so willing to help a total stranger.
"Michael, you go get the truck, I going stay here with them and see if we could get him sober up and that way I could also make sure that we meet you at the truck without anybody getting lost. Mrs. Cummins, will you come with your husband?"
Dr. Cummins gave an indignant gasp. "Of course she coming wid me! You expecting me to go by myself? If

I got to stop jumping, she got to stop jumping too!"
Joan looked at her husband sharply, but understanding his frustration, chose to ignore his behaviour.
"Yes of course I'm coming."
"So Junior, where you figure we should meet?"
"I guess by the time you get back wid de truck we should be somewhere near Black Rock, so maybe by Grazette's round-about is good nuh"
After finalising their plans, Michael went off for the truck.

When the L200 pulled up at the round-about half an hour later Junior sighed with relief. With husband and wife securely strapped inside the vehicle he hopped in the back. Inhaling deeply, he rested his head against the back window and relaxed. For the first time in three days things had actually gone according to plan.

* PEARL *
16

As the bright red L200 turned into the narrow entrance that was Whit's End it made a screeching noise. Michael and Dr. Cummins had been engaged in such an interesting conversation about cars, that they had missed Junior's shouts to turn off. The truck braked suddenly then reversed. It would be the first of several more wrong turns, and the resulting noise from the driver's repeated revs that brought Sandra Murphy to her window.

She being the unofficial gatekeeper of Whit's End - no one entered or exited the neighbourhood without her knowledge - now rose to her full height of 5 feet 2 inches and leaned as far out the window as her excessive bosom would allow. Her mission: to determine the source of all that commotion. "Belinda who da is?"

Belinda quietly sitting outside with one short foot cocked up on the railing fanned herself from the heat. She turned a lazy head in her sister's direction and shrugged, unable or unwilling to put more effort into her reply. Sandra, who was still hanging half out

the window to see up the road, missed her sister's small gesture.
"Belinda! Ah ask you who da is?"
"Ah tell yuh ah ain noah!"
"Well look nuh!"
Her peaceful mood disrupted, Belinda chupsed, but leaned her body heavily over the railing to get a better look.
"Ah red truck coming down de road, some white fellah driving."
"Ah white fellah? Sandra up to this point had resisted going outside in the skimpy half-slip she wore pulled up above her breasts. However the arrival of a strange vehicle did away with the last vestiges of her modesty. She ran to the door, pushed it open and leaned over the railing next to Belinda. Her big breasts imprinted heavily against the thin black material of the slip.

"Hey *hey, is a white fellah fuh true!* Dem mussee loss, cause I neva see dis truck down hey before yet."
Perplexed, Sandra and Belinda watched as the truck kept coming down the road with a purposefulness that belied her statement. When it came parallel with their house the sisters recognised Junior perched in the back of the pick-up, but were unable to identify the man and woman wearing full Kadooment regalia sitting up front. Mouths agape, only their heads followed the truck's progress as it entered the village. The realisation that a miracle was about to

take place, slowly entered their minds. The Doctor had been found.

It was only after the truck had disappeared from sight that the sisters finally snapped out of their daze. They screamed at one another in excitement, jumping around the room in circles like a pair of maniacs. *"Jesuuuus chriiist!!!! De docta come de docta come!"*

As they grabbed hold of each other, the chair in which Belinda had been sitting was cast aside and now lay on the floor with a leg broken. Adrenaline pumping, they rushed back inside to ready themselves for the big event. "Belinda!" Sandra squealed "Whey my clothes? I gots ta put on some clothes, I ent wanta miss nuna dis!"
"Oh shite oh shite my hair, Sandra girl, I ain got nuh time to be worrying 'bout you clothes, you cyan see my hair! I gots ta tek out dese curlers, ah gots tuh mek muhself look good!" Belinda started tugging at her hair with both hands pulling out her curlers and dropping them on the floor. It didn't even seem to matter that she pulled out a few chunks of hair as well. Sandra, who finally had her jeans on, was looking round for a top and tossing every single item out of the wardrobe in her frenzy. "Hurry girl we gots ta tell Braddy, and if we don't tell Foxy, she ain goin' neva speak to we again!" "You guh long an get Jackie, I gots ta find my girl Fay, cause whenever she

get piece a news she does always share it wid me. Girl dis ting sweeeeet!"

By the time the sisters departed, the Murphy house looked as though it had been ravaged by a hurricane. They tore a fast path down the road, forgetting to shut their own front door. Hollering and screaming as they went, they knocked on people's doors shouting. *"HE COME!!!! HE COME!!!! DE DOCTA COME!!!!"*

Jeffrey who had also been sitting by his window and playing with the chipped paint on the ledge looked up in amazement at the sight of the two hippopotami galloping down the road. Belinda was still fighting with a stray curler, while Sandra struggled with the zip of her too-tight jeans. Like many others in the neighbourhood, Jeffrey had also seen the red truck pass but thought nothing of it. How could they know it was the doctor anyway? He felt his natural curiosity stirring but not enough to get up and follow those two mad women down the road. He just wanted this whole Pearl episode to be over. He wanted his life back to normal, and he wanted his friends back. Omar was behaving so strangely that he no longer knew what to say to him. Sometimes he felt that his friend silently blamed him and he didn't think that was fair since they had all been in it together. Right now he couldn't even remember whose idea it had been to begin with.

Omar was at that very moment staring broodingly at the television in Chicken's living room and sitting next to his friend on the couch. Various Kadooment bands passed before them in a jumble of images. The boys had hardly exchanged a word since Omar's arrival some hours earlier. Omar knew he wasn't being good company but he couldn't bring himself to behave any better, and he couldn't stand being at home. The house reeked of dead flesh and he seemed to be the only one able to smell it. The night before he'd spent the entire time completely covered with the sheets. He had even sprinkled some Shilling Oil on his pillow and rubbed himself down with a little more to disguise the suffocating smell coming from the room next door. He didn't know what was wrong with his mother but she was behaving so strangely that he also preferred to avoid her whenever possible. In addition to that he was still very shaken up by the nightmare he'd had the evening before. Nothing had ever felt so real. His tongue felt heavy and sore from the numerous bites he had subjected it to while reassuring himself it was still there.

The two boys were still sitting on Abuela's red crush-velvet sofa when Jeffrey walked through the door. They both jumped in surprise. Everyone was so tense they imagined ghosts all over the place. "Hey." Jeffrey said feeling a bit shy and uneasy.
"Hey." Chicken answered back.

Omar sat slouched on the sofa, his blue shorts bunched around his privates, an old grey shirt hung limply around his shoulders. Chicken sat in a similar position, his home clothes a pair of old khaki school shorts and a thin blue vest. It simply was too hot to be wearing more than that. He couldn't imagine how all those Bajans jumping around the stadium didn't die of heat stroke. Chicken scratched his head after swatting a fly that had settled there. At the back of his mind was the niggling memory of his grandmother rummaging through her doll case muttering to herself about 'la muñeca' gone missing. Seeing Jeffrey was a much needed distraction from the day's monotony.

"Yuh all hear that the doctor come?"

"What doctor?" asked Chicken absentmindedly.

Omar's head jerked up. "Junior come back with the doctor?"

"It seem so. I see Sandra and Belinda Murphy running down the road behind a red truck, shouting and hollering hard enough...like it was going to your house..."

"So wha' you feel we should do? If the doctor come, I really ain want to go out there."

"Me neither."

"But if we don't go, you feel somebody would suspect something?"

"Well..." Jeffrey thought long and hard, weary of making any more wrong decisions. "It seem to me that if Pearl is your sister, then, normally when somebody in a family... uhm ...you know, everybody's band together to give support. The only reason they wouldn't do that is if they had a quarrel with the person."

"We had a quarrel with Pearl?" Omar sounded like such a little boy even to his own ears. He hated how this entire experience made him feel. He felt so guilty about Pearl, and scared, of so many things. Maybe the best thing would be to just go straight home and see what the doctor was doing, instead of guessing at endless possibilities.

"We didn't have a problem with Pearl; things just went a little out of control. Maybe it isn't even our fault."

"NOT OUR FAULT JEFFREY!!!" Omar jumped out of his seat, shouting, indignantly. "Who you trying to fool? You was there, we was all there and if things go down, don't pretend that you ain know nothing 'bout it!

"But Omar you really believe that dah obeah work? We was just fooling 'round!"

"If it was just fooling 'round how come you and Chicken all of a sudden suh quiet? If you know it never was going work, how come we went to all that trouble to get chicken blood and full moon an all them other things?"

Both boys were in each other's faces shouting at the top of their lungs. Chicken tried to alert them to the fact that Abuela was sleeping and if they didn't want her to wake up they'd better calm down and lower their voices.

"We back at this again? I never expect it to work. I just thought we were doing it for fun! If it really had work all that woulda happen is she woulda be jumping round from the needles we stick in the doll. That is all!

"Well it work Jeffrey, cause she dead so I ain know wha' foolishness you talking 'bout now. It just work more than we expected it to." Omar sighed. For the past two days Jeffrey had been singing the same song and he was tired of it. He felt guilty and that was enough for him. "Listen I cyan stop 'round here doing nothing, so I may as well go home and see what my mother doing. You coming?"

"Yeah, I guess so."

"Good 'cause I ain really want to go by myself."

The three boys weren't the only people in the neighbourhood walking towards the Walcott home. In fact a mini pilgrimage was taking place. When they got there, it was to see that the entire neighbourhood had responded to Sandra's and Belinda's calls like rats to the Pied Piper.

A very subdued Loretta stood by her front window watching as the group descended from the vehicle. Though she wouldn't admit it, the ordeal with Pearl had taken its toll over the last two days. For the most part her feelings for her daughter were a jumble of confusion and hurt…the thought that her own flesh and blood could indeed be so spiteful...still deep down inside she hoped and prayed to God that the doctor would tell her something contrary.

Junior walked up the steps to the house with Dr. Cummins at his side. They had first made a stop at the Doctor's office to collect his medical bag and necessary documents. Now he stood, bag in hand, medical coat thrown over his costume waiting to be escorted in. When Loretta finally opened the door she forced a polite smile on her face shaking hands with the doctor as warmly as she could, then led them down the dim passageway to Pearl's room. A dusky scent permeated the house, a smell the doctor usually associated with his old grandmother, a smell of mildew and overripe vegetables. He watched the girl's mother pause, back rigid as she came to the end of the passageway and gently pushed open a door. Rightly assuming it was Pearl's room he hurried towards it. Loretta stood by the doorway allowing him to pass. The man literally reeled backwards when the putrid smell reached him. A supportive hand from Junior helped him regain his balance. Mrs. Cummins who had been right behind them instinctively made a U-turn to the living room. She did not need to be there.

The light in the room was dim. The drawn curtains made the mood even more sombre. Cummins held his breath and braced himself for entry into the girl's room. He strode towards the window and in one swift movement whipped the curtains open, pushed the shutters up and stuck his head out for a breath of untainted air. Cummins inhaled deeply. When he opened his eyes he found himself staring upon the curious gaze of a large and rotund woman.

"Hey" Sandra smiled sheepishly. "You de docta?"
Cummins blinked. Before he could properly respond she was joined by a fairer version of herself "I'm *A* doctor, and you are...."
"I's Pearlie friend."
"We's Pearlie friend" Belinda said in a husky voice bumping her sister "You cum ta tell we if she commit suicide or not?"
"I'm sorry Madam" he said looking at Belinda, "that's not a question I'm at liberty to answer. I'm simply here to certify this young lady's death. Is that good enough for you?" Cummins figured he'd had enough of the strange encounter with the two women and left them staring after him by the window.

From somewhere else in the house Annie could be heard chastising the two sisters, asking them if they weren't ashamed to be peeping through people's windows like common criminals. It was at precisely this moment that the three boys Omar, Chicken and Jeffrey arrived. Seeing so many people gathered at the scene did little to calm their frayed nerves. Fortunately some kinder, more compassionate person ordered the crowd to clear the path and let them pass.

Cummins returned to the job at hand. He'd fashioned a make-shift handkerchief out of one of his wrist bands and held it over his nose. With the other hand he very gently caressed Pearl's body following a similar path of so many before him. He ignored the women still peeping through the window even when one tried to speak with him again.
"Docta, you see de pill bottle in she hand?"
They seemed determined to help him do his job, pointing out the pill bottle in Pearl's hand and even suggesting he check her pulse. Had it not been for the overpowering smell, he would have long closed the window.

Cummins climbed onto the bed with Pearl, in an effort to get a closer look. He shone a small pin light in her eyes but the lids were so heavy and the body so stiff, it was obvious there was little expectation of the girl reviving after two days without breathing. Loretta let out a giggle at the sight of the silly looking man in a white doctor's coat, his shiny pink sequined butt in the air, hovering over her daughter like the tale of Sleeping Beauty gone slap-stick. When Annie and Davy looked at her strangely she felt she had to explain. "Well it don't look funny?" The two shrugged not knowing how else to respond.

Omar, Chicken and Jeffrey stood by the door, hands long like scarecrows. When Cummins breathed in, they breathed in. When he leaned forward, they leaned forward. When Cummins heaved Pearl's heavy body aside everyone froze. It took them a while to realise she had not moved on her own. Their mouths dropped open when he held up a tiny white pill between his fingertips. With the window right behind him, the light surrounded it like a halo. All three boys moved forward at once, each with his own set of questions. Where had he found it? Were there more? Was their deep dark secret about to be exposed? Cummins foraged beneath her on the sheets looking for something. When he eventually came up with a fistful of similar white pills, their world began to spin.

Jeffrey would never live down the moment when he peed his pants at age twelve plus. The fact that no one even seemed to notice or care was of little significance. He was a man, he had after all kissed a school woman, felt her breasts even. It just was not supposed to happen. He couldn't remember "it" ever having happened before. Yet when the doctor had held up that fistful of pills, he'd stood in a puddle of his own making. It hadn't trickled, but gushed down his legs and quickly spread across the wooden floor-boards, following the pattern of the grain. It puddled around Omar's and Chicken's bare feet uniting them as one. He remembered that Omar had looked down, but what had happened after, would forever be a mystery, because while up until that moment, time had seemed to virtually stand still. Everything afterwards had moved in fast forward. Years later he would hear Omar and Chicken dispute regularly over who had peed themselves that day, each believing it had been the other. The thought had never occurred to either of them that it might have been Jeffrey. And Jeffrey had never known how to confess.

"Well I guess we can rule out suicide" Cummins said shouting at the window.
"Yuh mean Pearlie ain kill sheself?"
"Well this bottle isn't very big, and it would take a lot of these to kill a person in one go...Ms. Walcott could you come over here a minute, I'd just like you to confirm something for me."

First to hear the doctor's diagnosis, Sandra and Belinda ran off to spread the word. With big whoops and shouts they bellowed the news to anyone who would listen. *"Wunnuh hear dat? PEARLIE-LIKESHE-AIN'KILLSHESELF AFTA ALL!!!"*

Meanwhile Omar, and Jeffrey, and Chicken, not close enough to hear the whispered conversation between mother and doctor prepared for the worst. They knew that their plot against Pearl had somehow been discovered. That now the police would be called and they would be sent to prison. The two adults continued

the conversation looking in their direction. Loretta pointed at the children signalling to Omar.
"Come here a minute." Omar moved forward like a zombie, the gentle touch of his mother's hand upon his brow coming as a shock. It felt so warm, almost a caress. "Omar you feel ok?"
"Huh?"
"No he don't have fever. Omar when you take these pills before you ever feel sick?"
"No Mummy..."
"Well you should let him get checked anyway."
Omar looked back at his friends, as perplexed as they were. Chicken had just become aware that he was standing in something wet. He sniffed the air and looked down at his pants checking for any telltale signs. Jeffrey had long since stepped away from the pair and the only one remaining in the puddle was Chicken.

It would be several tense hours before Omar's guilt would finally leave him, the remainder of the afternoon passing with unnatural calm. The children had been sent outside. All three boys sat in their usual positions, doing little more than staring into space while awaiting their fate. The only flurry of activity in the hours immediately following the removal of Pearl's body came from his mother. She'd rushed outside with a bundle of sheets and quickly set them alight.

From a rubbish bin at the front of the house, flames shot high, consuming the material in minutes. Aside from this, the adults had remained indoors talking in hushed tones for hours amongst themselves. Omar didn't quite know what to make of it; his one consolation that his friends had stayed beside him. By the time the red L200 had driven away, the street had become quiet again. The steady trail of onlookers had finally come to an end.

And then his mother called him in for supper. The anger that had been there in the morning was gone... replaced by something else...adults were so strange. They overreacted when you did little things, but then when you did something you knew you should really be punished for, they acted like this. Omar just wanted to get it over with. "Mummy you going punish me?"
"Punish you for what Omar?"
"For not telling you about Pearl."
"And how would your telling me about Pearl have made a difference Omar?"
"Well I..."
"Pearl died in the night...you were sleeping. I was sleeping."
"But I could have..."
"You couldn't have stopped an allergic reaction Omar. It happened too fast"
"I couldn't have stopped...an allergic reaction?"

"No. Is just like Doctor Cummins explained to me. Sometimes these things build up, wearing down your resistance over time and then one day you just..."

"Die...?"

"Yes...exactly...sometimes you just...die."

Omar looked around for his friends. *Were Jeffrey and Chicken hearing this?* Half in half out the door, they'd been bracing themselves to face their final judgement.

"All your sister took was two little headache pills and *whoosh...like a candle blown out.*"

Omar tried not to think about how close he'd come to getting a licking, or how silly he'd acted at the sight of a fly. But he'd sure learned his lesson and was certain his friends had too. It would be a cold day in hell before he ever tried to work obeah on anyone again.

There were few words to describe the impact Pearl's absence had on him. Suddenly he was an only child, with no one to nag him, no one to tease him, and no one to look out for him. He was glad he hadn't killed her...the doctor had said that without an autopsy it was still only a professional guess, but that the traces of a rash on her body pointed almost certainly to an allergic reaction, Penicillin the likely cause.

It had been such a long day.

* PEARL *
17

Pearl's funeral was held at the Holy Redeemer Pentecostal Church. A tiny single room structure - that is, if one didn't include the closet of a rector's room and its miniscule bathroom. It was a simple church, made of simple pine, its pews and altar also of pine. The only furniture crafted out of good old Barbadian mahogany was the pulpit; and that church would have been a dark and gloomy place had it not been for the beautiful stained glass window donated by an area representative some years before. A timely gift - elections being just around the corner - Pastor Williams accepted the gift in the spirit with which he knew it had been given; from the goodness of one's heart and absolutely nothing to do with government trying to garner votes! The stained glass, depicting an unusual tropical scene, permitted light entrance through its bright yellow sun, and white halos crowning the sacred family. A Nubian Mary and her boy Jesus, looked down upon the congregation to the backdrop of black-belly sheep and coconut trees.

Pastor Williams was quite proud of his church, as well he should be; always packed on Sundays, with the devoted coming on Wednesdays and Fridays, and of course, Easter, Harvest and Christmas were standing room only. Today, Pearl the young girl who'd died... Bless *her soul...* was doing justice to God's house. She had evidently lived a good life and spread the word to many, for his church was full, *so full* that many more remained outside, hoping to catch a glimpse of the proceedings. And this was no easy feat, for windows were few, and high off the ground. Yes, people had come from all over the countryside to pay their last respects. There were even some brothers and sisters from town. Pastor Williams bowed his head solemnly acknowledging a group of schoolgirls, undoubtedly classmates of Pearl's. It especially pleased him to see them so well turned out, their uniforms so neatly pressed. At his instruction they would bear the coffin in, while the grieving family would bear the coffin back out. Already seated in the second row were the good doctor and his wife. They'd been escorted to their seats by the girl's uncle.

The Pastor trembled under his robes in anticipation of so many well-respected members of society, Junior's employers and colleagues, *observing him in his moment of glory*. Among them was even a highly placed civil servant whom he'd heard worked with the Foreign Affairs Ministry. A congregation of this calibre, Pastor quite fancied himself on the front cover of the weekend paper. It was with great pride...*and of course...deep* regret, that he would conduct his sermon today. Pastor Williams glanced over at the front row of pews reserved for the bereaved. At that moment, the lone occupant was Loretta Walcott - mother of the dearly departed. Hardly strong enough to support herself, she would not be escorting the coffin. He watched her through the veil of her stylish black hat; a work of art, broad brimmed, made from finely woven threads of soft and supple straw. Tied around its break was a large burgundy silk ribbon, on which he followed a trail of delicate cross-stitches. So special was the hat, that he'd borne witness to its presence on only two other occasions; those being the burial of her beloved aunt five years prior and the burial of old lady Marshall - that passing similar in many ways to the passing of her young daughter. A devout member of his congregation, and a generous guilt-ridden donor, Lady Marshall had never missed a sermon, so he'd sent someone to find her. With a week between Sundays, and a house sealed tight - unusual for the summer, her corpse was first identified by a terrible unrelenting odour.

Like old lady Marshall, Loretta Walcott was one of his most cherished parishioners. And for that very reason Pastor Williams would never allow the slightest speculation regarding her character. Had the fathers of her children indeed been one and the same, and might he now stand somewhere cleverly hidden within the crowd? That she had never married; of this he was almost certain. That the children's father was happily married; he'd certainly heard the rumours. The truth, he might never know, because Loretta Walcott kept it close, moving into the neighbourhood, with her children already half- grown. In these days of inflation, it was a struggle he was sure, but she more than kept her head above water, giving whatever she had left to the Lord. She had hardly missed a Sunday and made sure her nearest and dearest were never far behind. Ironically the burgundy carpet which presently lined the aisle and which she had single-handedly laid some weekends before now bore the weight of her daughter's casket as it approached the altar.

The casket was a dignified oak, and girlish ribbons tumbled from a beautiful spray of white chrysanthemums and pink anthurium lilies arranged on top. One girl in uniform cried openly at its side. As the casket rolled forward it became evident that it supported her and not the other way around. He guessed this was Pearl's best friend Shelly. He'd seen her accompany the girl to church a few times, but their family had never been regulars. With the order of service leaflets handed out, Loretta's friends Annie and Davy took their seats beside her in the front row. Not quite family, but as good as. He cleared his throat as the last chords of the electric organ faded away. It was time to begin.

Loretta didn't really listen to the sermon. Pastor Williams had been known to go on quite a bit and frankly she wasn't in the mood. Instead she thought about the day. It had dawned like so many others. In fact there was nothing to distinguish it from the day before, or even the day before that. She however knew the difference. This was a never-to-be-repeated day, the day she would bury her daughter. If she hadn't known better, she would have said that Omar was excited. He looked sharp in his church pants and jacket; wearing the crisp new shirt Junior had bought him with the tie he'd proudly knotted himself. Whatever the reason, she guessed she should be happy he was no longer walking around her house like a zombie.

The funeral ended quickly. Pearl was buried quickly. Hers was a Friday morning funeral, the air light and fresh, the flowers bright and colourful. Even the birds, not long awoken - their songs were bright and fresh too. At least a quarter of the congregation followed the family back home. People filled Loretta's small living room and kitchen, some trickling onto the veranda through the rarely-open front door. Both halves lay open against the house's outer walls - an occurrence which usually heralded the start of the Christmas season and the thorough cleaning which came with it. The crowd mingled and chatted over food. Even so, there would be lots more to eat and drink for days to come. Loretta wasn't sure where it had all come from, whether from generous neighbours, Annie, or courtesy of the funeral home. All she knew was that there were people in her house, and she wanted all of them gone. There were those who knew Pearl, reminiscing over old times, and those who felt some neighbourly or work-related obligation, standing uncomfortably to one side. Loretta ignored them all. She wandered from room to room. Looking for what? She wasn't quite sure. Still it was only a matter of time before she found herself in Pearl's room going through her things. She walked around the narrow space, from corner to corner passing her hand over random objects, stopping when something in particular caught her eye. Pearl had liked to keep 'things'. There were perfume bottles and nail polish bottles, powder puffs and blush brushes, hair clips and earrings everywhere; objects and trinkets abounded in every shape, size and colour imaginable. Scraps of cloth were flung carelessly over the back of a Morris chair in the corner. In contrast, about twenty of her favourite cassettes were stacked neatly on top of the second hand tape deck by her bedstead. It was a teenager's room by anyone's standards.

Loretta continued over to the lace-curtained window carrying a stark white envelope in her hand; an acceptance letter from the Polytechnic. Why did children have to be so difficult? Why did they have to be so secretive? Why had Pearl felt she couldn't share this news with her mother? Loretta supposed she would have just seen her one day, preparing for classes...or hadn't she planned to go? Happy voices filtered through the window interrupting her musings; on the other side, crouched Omar, he and his forever sidekicks at play. The ever-present dog, Commando, jumped around excitedly. Oblivious, they continued their game of marbles in the usual bantering way. Having already discarded his jacket, Omar watched as Chicken lay prostrate on the dirty ground, angling for the perfect shot. Meanwhile, Jeffrey along with another young boy, very meticulously measured the distance between the two points. The fact that they were soiling their good church clothes was of little importance to them. Target hit, Chicken jumped up in elation exchanging hi-fives with Omar. Moments later, their celebrations were cut short when someone called Omar into the house.

"Omar!"
The little boy looked around pausing mid high-five. "Yes Annie?"
"Come here a minute please."
"Coming back there now fellahs, don't do nothing without me." Jeffrey and Chicken sent indignant looks after him. How could he even think for a moment they would cheat in his absence? Omar bounded up the stairs two at a time. "Yes Annie?"

"Omar come here. Look in this fridge. They got more food than we have space. Help me throw out some of this stale food in here."
"But I outside playing with Chicken and Jeffrey."
"This won't take two minutes, so come help me." Annie grabbed him by the shoulders none too gently and turned him towards the open fridge. "This bowl of macaroni here, your mother want this?"
"No."
"What 'bout this lettuce down in the bottom?"
"It look old and shrivel up to me. Annie, Mummy ain going get vex even if you throw 'way the whole fridge so don't bother so much. Throw 'way whatever you want."
"That is easy for you to say Omar, but you going have to start caring and paying lil more attention to people now..."
For several moments they stared each other down. Omar impatiently rifled through the fridge while Annie continued to berate him. ..."You got to take things more seriously..."
"Here, give Mummy this," he said, holding up a bag of pealed cane. "Give her this and she going be happy. Anything else you could throw away."

Annie stared at the spot where Omar had stood long after he'd bailed out on her. She was angry and had half a mind to haul him right back inside to explain his rude behaviour. The other half of her mind said it wasn't her problem. He would either grow up to be a man a woman could respect, or he would become part of a bigger Barbadian problem.

"Annie?"

Annie pushed on the door lightly. "Loretta you in here?" she peeped into the room not sure whether to disturb her friend or not. "I was looking for you all over the place"
"Yes?"
"Omar tell me to give you this, say it would make you happy. That little boy so strange sometimes, but anyway, I figure I shouldn't let good cane go to waste, *so ah bring it to you just in case you feel like you could do wid a little sugar rush."* Annie jiggled the bag temptingly before Loretta, hoping to see a smile light her face. Tears rolling down cheeks were not quite the response she'd expected.
"Omar tell you to give me this?"
Annie nodded, coming in halfway. She watched as Loretta's shoulders started to shudder, a low moaning coming from deep in her throat. She hugged her belly. No one could have been more surprised than Annie when those tears turned to laughter. "That boy, he ain half bad you know."
"Loretta you alright?"
"Come bring that cane here leh me get a good suck man!"

Not quite sure whether to be concerned or pleased, Annie opened the bag and helped Loretta to a piece of cane. Loretta sucked cane, cried and laughed simultaneously. "I alright Annie, is alright go 'long, I going just stay in here a little while longer...this bringing back memories... good memories..."

A Mother's Memories

There was a ripple among the cane fields, an unnatural movement, bending not only the fronds, but the entire cane as well. It was quite unusual to those hot summer days, had anyone taken the time to notice.

Omar, Chicken, Jeffrey, the dog Commando trailing by his side, and two other boys - distant relatives of someone in the neighbourhood - ran through the field of cane, disturbing the stillness of the day. Their slight figures single-filed down tracks of their own making, trampling the dead trash. Each carried deftly-broken sticks of sugar cane in their hands and now made quick escape. Crop time was officially over and good sweet cane was hard to find. The fact that they were on someone else's property only made their acquisition all the more precious.

Nowadays they say that Barbados is over populated, but back then, were one to have flown over the island, one would have noticed how little space is occupied by housing in comparison with how much more is still dedicated to the planting of cane. During the final months of the year when the wind is strong and the rains have fallen, one easily becomes hypnotised by the never-ending-sea of green which flows beneath soft feathery arrows... becoming nostalgic of boyhood days, of shooting lizards and scaring little girls without care, on a dare. One dreams of long forgotten barefoot walks and bicycle rides through the countryside with only walls of green taller than inquiring eyes can see for company. And one remembers, harvest; when all that remains of a field that was there yesterday, is a few scattered egrets alerting observers to recently-exposed worms, homeless mice and mongooses. On those days, from above, Barbados looks like dried toast, yet drifting upwards from its core is the smell of fresh soil, and sweet, heady bagasse piled high at a nearby factory. From the road, the unevenness of clumped mud and rocks in tangled roots that make uneven beds seems like perfect representations of perspective and symmetry. The odd tractor-harvester in the background gives depth and harmony, breaking monotony. On those days, just after the last harvest, nary a palm tree sways, nor a cloud blows by. Till for one moment, that stillness is changed.

One by one the boys emerge from the tall grass; first watching for potential danger, they scurry across the road like mice to safety. A car zooms past, making Omar dodge back into the field for cover. Commando on the other side wags his tail expectantly. They had come a fairly long way by their standards. Still, there was nothing but bush and grass between the field and home.

Loretta stands at the top of the stairs with a kitchen towel in her hand. She's wearing her usual denim skirt and garden boots. She surveys Omar as he lumbers home with his share of the loot and shakes her head. "Omar, where you get that cane from? I didn't know Mr. Marshall still had cane to give you some. I hope you didn't steal it." Omar shakes his head. "No Mummy. Me and de fellahs was walking down the road and spot these like they fall off a truck..." Loretta harrumphs, not convinced by his tale, since the canes had obviously been broken and not cut. Omar rests his cane in a corner of the kitchen and takes one stick with him to eat immediately. His mother hands him a slop bucket as he yanks away the first pieces of hard fibre with his teeth. "Do not dirty up my house Omar Walcott. Any mess you make, clean it up."
"Yes Mummy." Omar slurps.
Pearl comes out of her bedroom at the sound of peeling cane. She's just about to take up her own stick when Omar stops her. "Them is my cane girl! You don't know how to ask before you take up people things?"

Pearl laughs, cocking an eyebrow at him. "Omar, you can't talk. When I bring cane home I don't hear anybody asking my permission...and I could tell you that my cane don't be tief like how I sure you tief this one. MUMMY! Why you don't tell your son to stop tiefing?" Loretta harrumphs again. "Omar tell me it fall off a truck, I would have to believe him. Right Omar"? Omar ducks his head, avoiding his mother's stern gaze. Pearl sucks her teeth. She stands by the sink examining the cane before washing it. The water turns black with loosened dirt. "Who ever see harvest cane brek? I thought the people used to be called cane cutters because them does cut cane, not brek um." Then she looks at her brother with disdain. "Omar you ain frighten you break your teeth on that hard grass. Now that they invent knives, people don't need to be peeling cane with their teeth anymore."

Omar slurps cane juice noisily as some trickles down his chin. He chooses to ignore his sister, too happy with his treat to bother with an answer. Pearl turns to Loretta, holding out her cane. "Mummy, peel my cane for me nuh? I can't get it cut as good as you." Loretta says nothing, but after directing a long look at her daughter, takes the knife and cane away. She peels the long strips away in swift skilled movements, revealing the crisp white fibres underneath. Pearl sits down at the table opposite her mother, giving her puppy eyes.

Loretta shakes her head with wonder. Her two children either took her for a fool or simply couldn't help being children. As quickly as she cuts the cane into neat little quarters, Pearl helps herself to more. Figuring she deserves them, Loretta takes a handful and puts them away in a tiny transparent plastic bag for later, and sits down for one relatively peaceful afternoon next to the two banes of her existence.

THE END

GLOSSARY

Barbadian Dialect:

(N.B. *Words that begin with TH or have TH within them are replaced by the letter D, while many vowels, particularly the O vowel are often replaced by U or UH.)*

- **Ah/uh** I *or* of *or* a
- **Ain** am not/is not

- **Bajan** from the island of Barbados. Barbadian - Buhbajan - Bajan
- **Brek** to break

- **'Cause/Causin** because
- **Cyan** cannot or can't

- **De** the
- **Dem** them
- **Dey** they/there
- **Din** is not/was not/did not

- **Ketch** to catch

- **Leh** to let

- **Muh** me or my
- **Mussee** must be

- **Nuh** will you? Isn't it so *or* please

- **Obeah** voodoo or black magic (pronounced Oh-bee-yah)

- **'Pon** on/upon

- **Suh** so/ to say

- **Tek** to take
- **Tief** a thief/to steal
- **T'ing** a person or thing whose name is temporarily forgotten or substituted

- **Wid** with
- **Wuk** to work
- **Wuk-up** to dance or grind/work up (often on a person) in a suggestive manner through movement of hips and waist.
- **Wun** would not
- **Wunnuh** you plural/all of you: from the African word unno/unnuh of same meaning.

- **Yuh** you

Expressions, Exclamations & Commands:

- **Aye** expression of pain/Ouch

- **Boah!** an explosive exclamation used to add emphasis to a statement

- **Chupse** to kiss or suck teeth. A noise made from the pursing together of lips to attain a sound of annoyance or disgust.
- **C'dear** an expression of sorrow, pity, or appreciation: similar to "oh dear" and possibly from the French 'Que dire?' meaning 'What to say?' A variation of this is "Good dear".
- **Comma** a command for someone to "come here"

- **Hear** used as both exclamation and as a question "do you hear me?" Often ending a sentence to imply threat, or used to ensure listener acknowledges comprehension.

- **Tha' Fuh Lick Yuh!** An expression of admonishment, meaning "serves you right".

- **Wuh Laaws!** an exclamation used in a moment of high drama or intense pain.

Flora & Fauna:

- **Clammy Cherry Tree:** *Cordia obliqua* - native tree with clusters of pale pink, sticky berries (known as poor man's glue) often used by children to stick kites.

- **Dunks Tree** thorny native tree with miniature apple-like fruit, the size of a cherry, & with one solitary seed. They are sour when eaten green, and are sweet red and soft when ripe.

- **Paling Cock** a territorial rooster that spends its time on a high perch (usually a paling/tall zinc fence) to guard his territory.

Culture:

- **Cou-Cou** a favourite Barbadian dish often eaten with Flying Fish, replaces rice in a meal, and is a soft yellow mass of corn meal cooked with finely chopped/sliced okra.

- **Crop Over** a period of cultural celebration in Barbados, lasting approximately two months. The Festival is at its height during the month of July and is associated with the end of the sugar cane season – when the crop is over.

- **Kadooment Day** this final jump-up day, (always the first Monday in August), culminates with carnival-like festivities in which thousands of Barbadians wear themed costumes and party to local calypso music with their respective bands.

- **Pudding & Souse** a favourite Barbadian dish often eaten on Saturdays, consists mostly of the less desired, less expensive parts of the pig (tail, ears, snout, and feet). Pickled with cucumber, lime & hot pepper it is served with a side dish of boiled/roasted breadfruit and seasoned sweet potato stuffed in pig intestine. The dish is eaten cold.

ABOUT THE AUTHOR

Inspired by the cultural diversity of the Caribbean, Melanie Springer started writing *"Pearl – A Caribbean Story"* while at film school in Cuba. As an experienced filmmaker, fine Artist, and educator, Melanie has worked for years in the fields of Brand communications and Multi-media production.

When she's not producing television commercials and documentaries, Melanie shares her knowledge of the creative world as a tertiary level educator, and consultant of matters pertaining to the performing arts. Her multi-national background and love of travel has played a pivotal role in shaping the author she is today. *"Pearl – A Caribbean Story"* is her first novel.

Printed in the United States
by Baker & Taylor Publisher Services